Death
by
Injection

Mary Lee Tiernan

Death by Injection

First Paperback Edition
July 2023

ISBN: 978-0-9830672-9-0

This book is a work of fiction. Names, characters, places other than geographic locations, and incidents or events are the product of the author's imagination or are used fictitiously. Any similarity to actual events or persons, past or present, is coincidental.

Cover: Background photo of Sabino Canyon in Tucson, Arizona, by Nsirlin; image of hypodermic needle from Can Stock Photo Inc./vectomart

Table of Contents

Chapter 1   Leila's Blackout

Leila's eyes battled with her brain. Her head told her to open them; her eye lids acted as if they were screwed closed like a tight lid on a jar. A sudden weight dropping on her lap decided the issue, and her eyes fluttered open. Her cat Hobie meowed plaintively. As she automatically began to pet and soothe him, she glanced around. Where was she?

Obviously, she was sitting on the Euro-style recliner in her 24 ft. motorhome. She'd fallen asleep in the comfortable chair before; the question was why now? Since the slide-out was in, she knew she wasn't camped somewhere. She let her foggy brain wander back in time. That's right. She'd been driving to Alamo Lake State Park in a remote part of the Arizona desert to camp for a week or two, depending on how much she liked it.

She swiveled the chair slowly to glance out the front, side, and back windows. A variety of cacti, ocotillo, Palo Verde trees, and an abundance of creosote bushes stretched for miles around her. Not a building or another vehicle in sight. Only the isolated road indicated a sign of civilization.

The RV was parked on a gravel turnout on the side of the road. More details filtered through her foggy brain. After driving for hours, she'd stopped for a potty break, to let the blood circulate to her numb buttocks, and to quench her thirst: all advantages of traveling in an RV. If she could find a place to park, which was rarely difficult in a small RV, she had all the benefits of home with her. She'd hoped to arrive at the park by 1:00. A 15-minute break wouldn't have jeopardized her timeline.

When she glanced at the clock, she jerked, prompting Hobie to jump off her lap and mew his disapproval at her sudden movement. 3:25. How could it be 3:25?

Leila didn't remember being tired, just stiff from sitting in the same position for too long. Fortunately, intermittent overcast skies made the long drive through the desert easier since she didn't have to fight eye fatigue from staring into the unrelenting desert sun. Even in autumn, the temperatures often soared into the high 80s. A break had been welcomed, yet she'd fallen asleep for hours?

She stood up to check the time on her phone, hoping the clock was wrong. As she did, she noticed dirt on her clothes. Hobie had followed her outside, and he loved to roll in the dirt. She assumed he'd transferred the dirt on his coat to her by brushing against her while she slept and when he jumped into her lap. She wiped the dirt off with her hand.

Her iPhone verified the clock's time. 3:28 now. Leila leaned against the kitchen counter. What time had she stopped? Hmm. A little after noon? That's about right. She'd figured a break wouldn't affect her projected arrival time: 15 minutes one way or the other didn't make a difference. But three hours? She'd lost over three hours?

Think, Leila told herself. What had you done when you stopped? She pictured herself climbing out of the driver's seat, grabbing a Sprite from the fridge, and going out the side door to walk around and stretch her legs. And then … And then what?

Blank. A total blank. Her mind whirled. What happened outside? How had she ended up back inside on the recliner in a deep sleep?

Leila retraced her steps, including grabbing a drink from the fridge, but this time a bottle of water not only to appease her thirst but to hydrate: always a necessity in the desert. She opened the side door, and stairs automatically unfolded for her descent.

Hobie usually tailed her to the door. After checking for danger, if none existed, he followed her outside. Not now. As soon as she opened the door, Hobie raced to his hidey-hole, a niche under the end of the built-in bed. Weird.

3

She immediately noticed a mini can of Sprite lying on the gravel. Her can. When she picked it up, she heard sloshing and poured out the remaining soda. As an avid recycler, Leila couldn't imagine carelessly dropping the can on the ground: with soda still in it, no less.

She walked around the perimeter of the RV, but nothing else seemed out of place, nor did anything generate a memory. But she did feel vulnerable outside after the time loss and her mysterious nap. Leaving was the best option. She still had a drive ahead of her, albeit a short one, probably less than an hour. She wanted to be safe on a campsite surrounded by other people.

Chapter 2   RV Park

Since her GPS would warn Leila of any upcoming turns before she reached the state park, she allowed her thoughts to drift to the black hole in her memory, or more specifically, to possible causes of the blackout.

A head injury might have caused a concussion which triggered memory loss, but Leila didn't recall striking her head or falling or bumping into a hard object. Her head felt fine: no headache or pain. Surely, a whack on the head strong enough to knock her out would leave a tell-tale sign. She steered with her left hand and slowly raked the fingers on her right hand across her entire scalp but didn't find any tender spots or bumps. She decided that pretty much eliminated a head injury as a possible cause.

She'd heard of sleepwalking, of course, and that could explain the blank spots, but surely, she'd remember going back into the RV and sitting down on the recliner before she fell asleep. She concentrated her thoughts on leaving the RV. Yes, she remembered going outside and walking around. But one didn't fall asleep while walking around. She dismissed sleepwalking as an explanation.

The last option Leila thought of was rather farfetched: dissociative identity disorder (DID), commonly referred to as multiple personality disorder or split personality. When different personalities took over, the host personality experienced blackouts or time loss. DID was usually caused by severe trauma during early childhood from extreme, repetitive physical, sexual, or emotional abuse. This did not apply to her at all. She'd experienced a happy childhood with loving parents and never had blackouts before.

However, she'd read recently that DID could also be triggered by physical problems within the brain such as temporal lobe epilepsy, strokes, Alzheimer's, sleep or sensory deprivation, and encephalitis. Leila couldn't evaluate if a personality change had occurred, but the blackout certainly had. Skip the personality change for now.

What if the blackout had been caused by one of the other disorders she'd read about? She didn't believe she suffered from any of them, but the idea that she might scared her to the core, especially the possibility of dementia or Alzheimer's. At age 62, the possibility was all too real. What if her recent experience was the first sign of a problem within her brain? "Hold on," she warned herself. "You need to consult with a doctor before assuming the worst."

The GPS began talking to her, warning of an upcoming turn. Leila switched her full attention back to driving. A few more twists in the road and she arrived at the park gate. After checking in, she followed the park map to her campsite, backed up into the site, and breathed a sigh of relief.

The site was exactly what she'd hoped for; it was perched on a hill with an unobstructed view of the lake. It was marred somewhat by the thickening overcast skies. Leila wasted no time setting up the RV: hooking up to electricity and water, setting the stabilizers, and extending the slide-out. She always liked to arrive at a campsite early because she hated setting up in the dark and tripping over cords and hoses. Except for the time loss, she would have had time to arrange her outdoor table and chairs and enjoy a leisurely cup of coffee while savoring the view. Not tonight. Besides the late hour, gray skies had turned black, threatening a downpour. Then there was Hobie.

Leila found it odd that Hobie had not left his hidey-hole and attempted to look outside. Hobie didn't like traveling; he wanted out, to get his feet on *terra firma*. Usually, he scurried down the stairs and underneath the RV. From there, he surveyed his new surroundings for danger and satisfied his feline curiosity. If he was outside by himself, he generally stayed underneath the RV where he felt protected. When she was outside, he joined her by lying next to her chair or exploring his new environment. Staying in his hidey-hole was strange behavior, and Leila wanted to comfort and reassure him.

Sitting down on the recliner, this time knowingly, Leila called to him. He loved to sit on her lap and be petted. He didn't budge. She continued to talk to him in soothing tones. No response. She leaned back in the recliner and stared out the screen door at the gloom. The door! He'd retreated to his hidey-hole when she'd opened the door after waking up. Something outside had scared him. Something that happened during her blackout.

"Okay, Hobie, I'm going to close the door." She walked to the door and slammed it shut. "See, baby, it's safe now." Two golden orbs peered at her from underneath the bed. Progress. He'd stuck his head out. The outline of his body was barely visible as his black fur blended into the growing darkness inside the RV.

Leila turned on lights as she walked to the bed and sat down on the floor in front of him. "You're okay. I promise. I wouldn't let anything get you," she said as she reached out to stroke his head. She knew he had begun to relax when he turned his head, so her fingers rubbed the side of his face and underneath his chin, a favorite. "What do you say? Are you hungry?" Hobie stretched out his front legs and spread his paws wide, a prelude to getting up. "Okay, then, let's get you some food."

For Leila, getting down was easy, getting up, not so much. She braced herself with her left hand against the wall while the lower part of her right arm pushed down on the bed. She struggled to her feet. Hobie stretched his body, then gracefully rose. "Show off," Leila said.

As she watched the cat eat, Leila wondered what had frightened Hobie so badly. "If only you could talk," Leila said to him, "I'd know what happened during that missing time."

Hobie ignored her and continued crunching his dry food.

Chapter 3   Changes Begin

The rain began to fall as Leila prepared dinner. Bursts of lightning flashed across the sky. Normally, Leila enjoyed watching the lightning displays because they varied from horizontal to vertical to pops of light like a flashbulb. Not tonight. After one burst, her hand shook, and she dropped a knife. A few minutes later, her arm twitched causing her to drop a plate. She decided she was more upset than she realized and scrapped making dinner to settle for a nutrition bar and fruit. Her body continued to twitch as she ate.

Thunderstorms didn't normally bother Hobie. A crack of thunder directly overhead only caused him to lift his head momentarily. That's the only reaction she'd ever witnessed. Tonight, however, he cried with every burst of light. Finally, he jumped on the bed and buried himself under the pillows.

The storm escalated quickly. Claps of thunder increased in volume, lightning strikes came close enough to light up the inside of the RV, and rain began to pelt on the roof. Leila pulled down all the shades on the windows to block out the lightning. She was now glad she hadn't had time to set up her outdoor furniture.

She'd planned to read after dinner but the long drive, the blackout, and now this annoying twitching caused her to change her mind. What she needed was rest. Wanting, too, to calm Hobie, she decided to climb into bed so he could curl up next to her and feel safe. First though, the nightly routine: change into her pajamas, wash her face, brush her teeth, and turn out the living room lights. When she finished washing up, she put her Kindle and glasses on the bedside shelf, climbed into bed, switched off the bedroom light, and snuggled down under the covers. Hobie immediately curled up next to her.

Thunderstorms don't last long in the desert. As the storm moved off, the thunder quieted from a roar to a grumble, and the rain changed to a tapping as it hit the roof. Leila closed her eyes and fell asleep to the rhythmic patter of the rain.

She awoke suddenly. The digital clock showed 11:32. The storm had ended: no rain, no thunder. No other sound, either inside or outside the RV. Hobie slept peacefully stretched out along her side. She lifted the shade and peeked out at the darkness, thinking about the day's odd events: the blackout, the odd reaction to lightning, and now this twitching. Another unexplainable anomaly. What was happening to her? Leila was a logical person not given to flights of fancy. She wanted reasonable explanations. There weren't any. She'd fallen asleep to the sounds of the rain; perhaps the

11

cessation of sound had awakened her. At least that explained why she woke up. As for the other questions, she fell back asleep without any answers.

2:36. Leila awoke again with a fading image from a dream. She'd been standing outside her RV when a sudden flash of light made her feel drowsy. That was all she remembered. This small slice of a dream gave no hint as to what had occurred before the light. She didn't feel drowsy now. A lingering unease from the dream and the continuing twitching of her body kept her awake. Instead of trying to fall back asleep, she turned on the overhead light and picked up the Kindle and glasses next to the bed, hoping that immersing herself in a story would distract her.

5:45. The overhead light shining in her eyes roused Leila. Her Kindle had fallen to her side; her glasses lay nearby. They must have fallen off while she slept. Thank goodness she hadn't broken them. Occasionally, the TV had lulled her to sleep, and she'd woken up to a different program. Never before had she fallen asleep while reading. If she felt drowsy, she put the book and glasses aside before closing her eyes. Leila was weary of one more odd incident.

Leila sat up and tugged on a self-winding window shade. The dark of night turned the window into a mirror; all she saw was her own reflection. She pulled the shade back down and reached for the robe at the end of the bed. Darkness or not, she'd had enough of trying to sleep. Morning promised a new beginning, maybe even a glorious sunrise.

As she climbed out of bed, Hobie opened his eyes but quickly shut them again. At least he was relaxed enough to enjoy his slumber.

Leila turned on lights and flicked on the heater to dispel the chill. As she reached for the coffee pot, she changed her mind and decided to substitute lavender tea, a recognized natural stress reliever. After filling the teapot with water and setting it on the stovetop to boil, she rolled up the shade part way on the small kitchen window, enough for her to catch dawn's first light, not enough to invade her privacy. While she waited for the water to boil, she headed to the bathroom.

A glance in the mirror became a stare. Deep wrinkles on her face and neck had become finer lines; fine lines had transformed into smooth skin. Most of the gray hair mixed into her curly hair had disappeared. While she'd always been pleased that most of her hair had retained its original light auburn color, she couldn't deny the continuing appearance of gray hair. Now, the gray looked blonde. She looked years younger. Impossible, just plain impossible. Wishful thinking? That's it, wishful thinking. Her shock after the time loss and the uneasiness caused by the lightning had her imagination running overtime.

The persistent whistling of the teapot tore her attention away from the mirror. Dazed, Leila returned to the kitchen and prepared a cup of tea, functioning on autopilot. She then turned toward the recliner, forgetting the tea and leaving it on the kitchen counter. She sank into the chair and stared into nothingness.

Chapter 4   Last of the Changes

Light inching through the kitchen window snapped Leila out of her zombie state. Hobie sat patiently on the floor in front of her staring directly at her. His meow translated into "Breakfast time, Mom." Attentive cat owners know the meaning of a cat's simple meow depends on its tone and the situation. A cat might be saying it's hungry or hurting or wants attention or simply conversing.

Their interaction sparked an idea. She fed Hobie, of course, but while she did, she devised a plan. She'd never understand her strange experiences if she zoned out as she had just done. What she needed to do was search for confirmation. If she had developed a brain disorder that caused her blackout, she needed a doctor and medical tests to confirm that. Could that brain disorder, if she had one, also explain why she imagined that she looked younger or hadn't been able to sleep for more than a few hours at a time? Or why she reacted aversively to lightning when she never had before? If a medical doctor didn't find a physical cause, a consultation with a psychiatrist or a psychologist came next.

Both would ask numerous questions. Not wanting to rely on a faulty memory, Leila booted up her laptop to create a record of her experiences and her questions. Keeping a journal in and of itself was a positive step. It gave her an outlet for the troubles haunting her. She must remember, too, Hobie's strange behavior. Was he reacting to her or were his reactions a confirmation of her own experiences?

By the time Leila caught her journal up to date, bright morning sun streamed through the window. She turned off the lights and opened all the shades. She'd keep to a normal routine as much as possible: make the bed, take a shower, eat breakfast. She cautiously approached the bathroom. There was no way to go into the small room and avoid seeing herself in the mirror. She breathed deeply, stood tall, and opened the door. Once again, the mirror reflected a younger Leila.

She disrobed and stepped into the shower. As she washed her body, she noticed the crepey skin on her arms and legs looked smoother, too. Sure, why not? If she imagined smoother, firmer skin on her face and neck, why not on the rest of her body, too? She made a mental note to add her newest discovery to her journal and then try to let it go.

Once dressed and fed, Leila opened the side door letting in a cool morning breeze. Cool for now, but she bet the day would warm up quickly. The lake sparkling in the morning sun invited her to sit outside and enjoy the view. Or maybe go for a short walk before the sun threatened her Irish skin and she hid from it in the shade under her awning? Leila opted for a walk; she had all day to sit.

Dog walkers shared the road with her. Most said, "Good morning," as she passed. When a dog drifted in her direction to add his own greeting, Leila stopped to pet the dog and exchange a few words with the owner. Those brief conversations gave her an idea. What if she could ask one of those strangers how old they thought she looked? No, that won't do. Too weird, unless she could come up with a conversation starter that led to such a question.

When Leila returned to the RV, she extended the awning and set out her lawn chairs and side table. Her activity interested Hobie who appeared at the screen door and meowed. "Hey, baby, are you ready to come out?" Leila opened the door, and Hobie predictably scurried down the stairs and disappeared under the RV. Good. Normal was good. He, at least, had left behind his anxiety and relaxed. If only she could do the same.

For three days, Leila's getaway settled into the R&R routine she'd come to the park for. Almost. Each morning, she noticed fewer and fewer wrinkles and smoother skin all over her body, although the change was not as drastic as the first time she'd noticed it. The gray hair had become blonde highlights. She noted in her journal her ability to continue her delusion about regressing in age. In all, she estimated she looked 30 years younger. She also slept better despite the nightly howling of the coyotes and braying of the wild burros. Most of the twitching had also stopped, allowing her body to relax.

Chapter 5   Drone Fails

Harvey glanced up briefly as the door to the lab clicked open. Will walked in, locking the hall door securely behind him.

"Hey, Harv, how's our subject doing?"

"Alive and functioning. That's about all I can tell."

Will walked around Harvey's desk to look over his shoulder at the screen. "Can't you zoom in?"

"That is zoomed in."

The shot showed the bottom half of a woman sitting on a chair under an RV awning, her legs covered by pants.

"She stays under that awning and has it angled down against the sun. Haven't seen her face at all."

"Can you bring the drone down lower on its next flyover?"

"To get a clean shot under that awning, we'd have to bring the drone down very low. Orders are to stay high. They don't want anyone to spot the drone."

Will waved his hand at the screen. "Well, they're not going to be happy with that."

"Tell me something I don't know."

"She's got to move away from the RV at some time

19

or other. Maybe we should change the schedule for the flyovers."

"I'm not breaking protocol without a direct order."

"We need eyes on the ground."

"I keep telling them that, too."

Chapter 6   Leila Meets Jeff

On the morning of her fourth full day at the park, Leila sat outside while Hobie roamed about investigating the campsite. Suddenly, he came charging back, heading for the door. Leila knew immediately that he felt threatened and quickly rose to open the door. He never stopped to let her unhook his leash. A few seconds later, a springer spaniel raced around the corner of the RV, his leash trailing behind him. Upon seeing her, the dog skidded to a halt.

"Hey, boy," she said. "Are you looking for Hobie?"

The dog sat and cocked his ears. A streak of white fur bisected his predominately brown face. It ran down his forehead, widened around his nose and mouth, and ended in a white chest.

"I bet you broke loose, didn't you?"

"He sure did," a voice panted. A man rounded the same corner of the RV as the dog had. He'd been running but switched to taking large steps to slow down. "I'm sorry if he upset you."

"He didn't," Leila said, "but I can't say the same for my cat."

"Cat. That explains it."

21

Leila sat down in her chair and held out her hand toward the dog. "Come here, boy."

"Jethro. His name is Jethro."

"Come say hello, Jethro."

The dog walked over, wagging his tail. Leila picked up Jethro's leash to prevent him from running off again, or worse, in case he decided to look for Hobie.

"You should sit for a minute, too, and catch your breath."

"Thanks. Jethro runs fast. Hard to keep up with him." The man sank into the other chair. "My name's Jeff, by the way."

"Leila. Jeff and Jethro, huh?"

"Makes it easier for people to remember his name."

Leila laughed. "What if people think you're Jethro and he's Jeff?"

"It's happened." Jeff shrugged. "No big deal."

While they talked, Leila stroked the dog who leaned his head on her knee. Thirty years ago, Jeff would have appealed to her: handsome in a rugged way, brown hair with eyes to match, and a tanned, slim, yet well-toned body. She also liked his easygoing manner.

"You here by yourself?"

"Don't forget Hobie."

"Hobie?"

"The cat."

Jeff grinned. "I'm here by myself, too, but I've gotten to know some of my neighbors. We're going fishing as soon as I get back, and tonight we're having a fish fest to enjoy the fruits of our labor. Would you like to come?"

"If it's a joint effort, does that mean everyone is bringing a dish?"

"Oh, don't worry about that. There'll be more than enough food. I'm making a big salad. We'll just say it's our contribution."

Leila picked out the words "we" and "our." Was Jeff inviting her on a date?

Jeff noticed her hesitation. "Please say 'yes.' It'll be fun."

Leila figured it would be easy enough to excuse herself if needed. "I'd like to go, Jeff. Where do I go and what time?"

"I'll come here and pick you up, so to speak, about 5:30. That okay?"

"Sounds good."

Jeff stood up. "I'll get Jethro back now and make sure he's tied securely or he's likely to come visit you again. He likes all the attention you're giving him."

"Will he be there tonight?"

"Yeah. My friends' dogs, too. Not a good place for a cat."

Leila laughed. "Hobie would agree with you." She handed Jethro's leash to Jeff. "Later," he said and left.

Leila went inside to check on Hobie and detach his leash. Undisturbed by his recent escapade, he lay on the bed giving himself a bath. She unhooked the leash and kissed the top of his head.

On purpose this time, Leila went to stare at herself in the mirror. Jeff was young enough to be her grandson. There was no reason for him to invite The Old Leila to join him and his friends for an evening. Unless he hadn't seen The Old Leila. Unless he had seen the Leila reflected in the mirror, the now thirty-ish Leila. If so, she had confirmation that she wasn't delusional. That her age regression was real. That didn't explain how and why it happened, but relief overshadowed those concerns for the moment. Not delusional. She smiled at herself in the mirror. In general, she looked forward to socializing at the evening gathering; in particular, she hoped his friends accepted her as a peer, a definite confirmation.

Chapter 7   Fear of Going Home

The next morning, Leila and Hobie lounged on the patio. Hobie warmed himself in the sun while Leila gazed at the lake drinking her coffee and reviewing the previous evening. She'd enjoyed the camaraderie, especially because Jeff's friends had accepted her as a peer. A few tricky questions had popped up in the getting-to-know-you process, such as what she did for a living. "Retired" didn't work at all, so she answered as truthfully as possible with details from her life some thirty-odd years ago.

"A teacher," she'd replied.

"But isn't school in session now?"

Time to fudge a little. "Right now, I'm substituting so I told them I was unavailable for a couple of weeks."

"Wish I could do that with my job," someone said.

Problem averted. The conversation had drifted to other subjects. Jeff's holding her hand when he walked her back to her RV confirmed without a doubt that others saw the Leila reflected in her mirror. When she returned home ...

Her hand jerked, threatening to spill coffee over the lip of the cup. She steadied her hand and put the cup down on the side table. Now that she knew her younger appearance was a fact and not a delusion, returning home brought a slew of problems she hadn't considered before. Strangers accepted her as is; people who already knew her wouldn't. They'd ask a lot of questions, questions for which she had no answers. Strangers too. Imagine being asked for ID and showing them her driver's license with her photo and date of birth.

Leila stood up and paced back and forth across the patio mulling over potential answers. She stopped dead in her tracks when she acknowledged she had none. Not one. Until she did, going home was out of the question.

Chapter 8   Changing ID

"Incoming dog."

Leila recognized Jeff's voice. "Jethro's safe. Hobie's inside."

"Jethro's safe?"

"You haven't seen my monster cat."

Leila closed her Kindle as Jeff and Jethro appeared, Jeff grinning and Jethro straining at the leash to get to her. Jeff dropped the leash, and the dog rushed over.

"Hello to you, too," Leila said as she bent over to hug the dog. Jethro responded with a volley of licks.

"Okay, okay, that's enough, Jethro. Sit."

Jethro followed his master's command to sit but leaned forward, attempting to reach Leila and continue his shower of "kisses." Leila circumvented him by standing up. She froze momentarily as it registered that she'd regained her feet easily and gracefully. Note for journal: muscle strength was returning, changes were internal as well as external. She hadn't noticed any more changes in her appearance that morning, and that was a good thing. The idea of reversing chronology until she ended up back in the cradle as Brad Pitt had in the movie *The Curious Case of Benjamin Button* scared her.

Leila waved toward a chair. "Have a seat."

"Thanks, but I need to continue Jethro's walk and let him burn off some energy. How about joining us?"

"Sounds good. Let me grab my key and lock up."

Leila picked up her Kindle to put it inside. Her Kindle. Books. Movies. ID. "Have a question for you."

"Which is?"

"Let me lock up and we'll talk while we walk."

"So, what's the question?" Jeff asked as they strolled down the road.

"In a book I'm reading, the character needs to change his identity, so he goes to some guy who forges new ID for him. Happens often enough in books or movies. Thing is, they rarely explain how the character finds the forger. The question is how does a person do that?"

"Thinking of changing your identity?"

"You caught me. I want to become an international art thief, so I need an alias."

Jeff laughed. "You know a lot about art?"

"No. I'd have to learn about that, too."

Jeff laughed again. "You have an active imagination; I'll give you that. Seriously though, why do you want to know?"

"Just curiosity. When I read about or see that kind of scenario, I wonder how realistic it is. They make it seem as though it's no big deal to find a forger."

"Never thought about that, but you're right.

Someone always knows someone who knows someone, etc. We should ask Walter. Do you remember him from last night?"

"Uh-huh."

"He's a cop. He might know."

At the end of the long Loop B, they turned around and walked back, stopping by Walter's RV on the way. Walter was cleaning the interior of the boat from yesterday's outing. "What's up?" he asked as he swept the decking.

After Jeff summarized their conversation, Walter paused and said, "Forgers aren't uncommon, only the good ones are. Mostly, you'll find them in cities where they'll get the most business and it's easy for them to hide."

"Is it usually criminals who want to hide their real identity?" Leila asked.

"All sorts of people do for one reason or another. Hey, Jeff, will you hand me that bucket of water?"

While Jeff handed the bucket up, Leila asked, "Are forgers easy to find?"

"Not as easy as looking through newspaper ads or the yellow pages, but word gets around. It's no different than finding a drug dealer if you travel in circles that engage in crime or vice. Underworld figures learn who to ask about anything illegal." Walter pulled a sponge out of the bucket and began wiping down the seat cushions.

"What if the character isn't a criminal, like the character in my book? What's if it's a woman, for example, who wants to hide from an abusive husband?"

"Those women often have help from some underground railroad organization. It's the organization that provides them with a new identity. Witness protection is another example. Only in that case, it's the government, of course, who provides the new identity."

Walter held out two cushions toward Jeff. "Will you take these cushions as I wipe them off and stand them against the picnic table to dry?"

"What if the person wanting the new identity isn't part of an organization?"

"You're back to someone who knows someone, or the person is good with a computer and can forge his own. Some runaways simply stay off the grid and don't use official ID."

"If they 'stay off the grid,' does that mean they have to sever any connection to their old life like friends or family?"

Walter handed Jeff two more cushions. "Yes, if they really want to disappear. A good investigator can trick a friend or family member into divulging information about the person's location. A crook will use force."

"How about all the peripheral stuff in our lives like banking accounts or medical or insurance policies?"

"They'd have to establish new accounts under their new name. For that, they'd need new ID. A person truly living off the grid operates on a cash-only basis."

"Sounds like a rough life."

Walter handed Jeff the last of the cushions.

"It is. If they're honest, they can only get menial jobs at minimum wage where the employer doesn't care about their background. If they're criminal, they'll restart whatever they were involved in in a new location."

Walter's wife, Cynthia, appeared at the screen door. "Ah," she said. "Now I know why Milo's been whimpering at the door."

"Let him out."

Milo lunged out at the same time Jethro pulled against the leash. Jeff dropped the leash. Both dogs ran to each other and began their excited circle dance of leaping and chasing each other.

"You're not going to get away until they calm down," Walter said, "so we might as well sit down." He turned toward the RV. "You coming out?" he asked Cynthia.

"Sure. Should I bring some beers with me?"

"Please."

By the time the dogs quieted down, the four adults sat comfortably in lounge chairs conversing about this and that. Leila avoided asking any more questions, other than one pertinent to their general conversation. She didn't want to raise any flags.

Chapter 9   Man-on-the-Ground

"Hey, Will, look. I just got pictures in from our man-on-the-ground."

Will wound his way around the equipment in their cubicle to Harvey's desk. The screen showed snapshots of Leila from roughly 20 feet away walking down the street in the park.

"We know it's supposed to be the Petterson woman, but she looks different. Can you zoom in on the face?"

"Yup."

Harvey manipulated the keyboard to isolate Leila's face. A grainy photo emerged.

"Let me clean that up."

With additional keystrokes, the picture slowly clarified.

"Holy shit! Look at that!" Will exclaimed. "Can you bring up a photo of the old broad for comparison?"

Harvey didn't answer, just did what Will requested. He split the screen and within seconds, the old Leila appeared side by side with the younger Leila.

"I can't believe it! They look alike and all that, but ... but wow! How old do you think she looks now?"

"Early thirties. Half her age, anyway."

"Call the boss and tell him, no, ask him, to get down here on the double. He'll want to see this."

Harvey swiveled his chair around and the two techs stared at each other.

"Maybe they found a look-alike," said Will.

"How? The drone's been keeping track of her the whole time. Don't forget we have a man-on-the-ground now, too."

"What if it is the same person? What are they doing in that lab anyway?"

Harvey slapped Will on his shoulder. "No questions, remember?"

"If it is, I wish I knew what they did to change her age."

"I'll forget I heard that. Don't get curious and ask questions. You know the penalty."

"Yeah, but I can think about it." Will waved at the screen. "If those two are the same person, she gets to live her life all over again. I wouldn't mind living my life a second time. How about you?" Will asked.

Harvey rubbed his right hand on his chin. "Nah. What kind of life is she going to live? She can't live the life she had. Who's going to believe she's the same person? If she goes around telling people she went from old to young in a couple of days, they'll lock her up in a looney bin."

"Planning, Harv, planning. Of course, we don't know if she knew this was going to happen to her, but we would. You get a new life planned before you make the change."

"I feel a bit sorry for her." Harvey stared at the screen. "If she got thrown into a new life, without warning or preparation, can you imagine the problems she's going to have?"

"Bah. Who cares? She's young again. Look at her. Does she look depressed or unhappy?"

"No. But she's not grinning from ear to ear either."

Chapter 10   Deciding to Go Home

After adding the day's pertinent activities to her journal, Leila scrolled back to reread what she had already written and to check her to-do list. With only two nights and one full day left of her two-week reservation, the most important question was what to do first. Since she'd eliminated going home right away, she prioritized finding another place to camp. She hated staying in the 'sardine parks' in cities where you could practically reach your hand out the window and touch the RV next to you. Larger cities, however, offered more anonymity and public transportation erased the problem of driving and finding adequate parking in town for an RV.

Going to a medical doctor headed her list. It seemed obvious now that whatever had happened to her during her blackout had caused the time regression. She wasn't delusional about that. And if the cause was external, rather than internal, there was no brain disorder and no need to be tested for one.

It occurred to her that walking into an unknown doctor's office required filling out paperwork and handing over ID to be photocopied. Just what she wanted to avoid. One look at the ID compared to the person standing in front of them, and they'd think she was an imposter and refuse her service, or mentally ill, or worse, and call authorities to report identity theft.

After speaking with Walter, Leila realized changing her identity wasn't the best idea; it was too complicated and beyond her resources. What she needed was ID in her real name showing an updated birthdate and picture. She'd use that ID when a situation required personal verification such as paying for purchases by check or credit card. Leila Petterson wasn't about to disappear and forfeit a lifetime of savings that she'd planned to live on during her retirement years. She handled most of her banking, bill paying, insurance policies, and the like through the mail or over the Internet. None of that had to change.

On second thought, she might have made a mistake with the decision not to go home. Surely, she could convince her family doctor that she was the same Leila Petterson who'd been his patient for years. She wanted advice more than anything else, but a checkup and a few basic blood tests would reveal any changes in her metabolism. She'd ask the doctor, too, to hazard a guess at her current physical age. All accomplished confidentially.

Thinking of confidentially, Leila added visiting the attorney who'd written her will to her list. He didn't know her well, but she had some connection to him. If there was a legal way of changing her ID or resolving the issue of the old and new Leila, he'd know.

Dealing with a doctor and an attorney who knew her were the best options because it avoided the hassles of establishing who she was. Because she couldn't prove who she was. Because her problem became apparent when she walked in the door. They might not believe her at first, but she'd be able to provide personal information that only she and they knew.

Going home needn't be a disaster, not if she went to a local RV park rather than to her house, thus avoiding most friends or acquaintances. During needed trips around town such as to the grocery store or ATM, she'd camouflage her appearance as much as possible. She'd buy a hat, which the old Leila never wore, and pick up a couple of trendy outfits appropriate for someone in their early 30s that showed a lot of skin: smooth, un-creased skin. If she bumped into someone she knew, hopefully, they'd dismiss her as a look-alike. If she didn't talk to them. If they didn't recognize her voice.

Chapter 11   Last Day with Jeff

The next morning, Leila called for appointments as soon as the doctor's and attorney's offices opened. With those arranged, she called the Oasis RV Park to reserve a campsite. Whether it was from having a definite plan or from her younger body, Leila hopped up to tackle the day with more energy than her older body had allowed.

The energy prompted her to go outside for some physical activity. Jeff hadn't stopped by yet on Jethro's morning walk, so she walked down the road toward his RV. Jethro spotted her RV away and barked an enthusiastic welcome.

Jeff opened his RV door. "Quiet, Jethro. What are you barking at?" He looked up and spied Leila. "Hey, good morning."

Leila turned into his site. "Good morning to you, too." She bent down to pet Jethro. "And you, too." Jethro wiggled with pleasure, his tail whipping back and forth. "Thought I'd meet you at the start of your walk."

"Oh, sorry. We already walked. I figured you'd be busy this morning. This is your last day, isn't it?"

"Last full day. I won't be doing any packing up until tomorrow. Today is for leisure only."

Jeff grinned. "Does leisure include Jethro and me?"

"Definitely, unless you have other plans."

"That's a definite no."

Leila already knew the downside of the day was going to be saying goodbye to Jeff. His companionship had brought a whole new pleasurable dimension to her R&R, not only for the normal socialization she hadn't expected but for his confirming she wasn't delusional. Of course, he didn't know that. His friendship had calmed her, at least in the short term. Given the right circumstances, she'd discovered that she was capable of functioning normally despite her secret.

They spent the entire day together: walking Jethro, playing cornhole with his friends, relaxing on the patio, and making dinner together. The walk back to her RV that night was bittersweet. Before they parted, they exchanged phone numbers. As Leila added him to her contacts list, she realized she didn't know his last name. Such details didn't matter when one's purpose is "to get away from it all" and relax. They both laughed when she'd asked him; he didn't know her last name either. She added "Gordon" to her contact details; he added "Petterson" to his.

Leila didn't have high hopes of staying in touch. She'd learned during her RVing days that long-distance relationships formed during a few days on a vacation seldom lasted. Add to that her odd circumstances. She imagined his horror if he ever discovered her real age.

She'd never want him to experience that.

Chapter 12   Leila Becomes Anna

Two men sat in spacious brown leather armchairs in a sound-proofed library: one a wealthy business tycoon, the other a scientist. Normally, the armchairs were angled toward the French doors leading to a stone-paved patio and the sweeping green lawns of the businessman's Bel Air estate. For the day's conference, Miles Grayson had automated the system which slid hidden pocket doors shut and locked, sealing off both sound and visibility from the outside and all light to the inside. He replaced the natural light by turning on several lamps to illuminate the seating area. Shadows partially hid his huge desk and computer systems in the back of the library. The other entrance to the room, the thick hallway door, contained soundproofing between its layers of mahogany. Once inside the library, the men were safe from prying eyes or eavesdropping.

Miles raised his Waterford crystal glass of Dom Perignon to salute the scientist. He smiled and said, "To success."

Henry Hoover grinned, not only because he agreed with the sentiment but because he seldom saw Miles display any emotion, not even a smile or a frown. One deduced Miles's approval or disapproval by his words and tone of voice, not by his facial expressions or body language. Henry raised his glass in acknowledgment, "And more to come."

Conversation ceased momentarily as the men savored the taste of the vintage champagne.

Miles stretched out his long legs in front of him and broke the silence. "Congratulations. Your 20-year compound worked."

"On her," Henry said. "On Anna. Almost too well."

Miles raised an eyebrow in question. "Anna?"

"I've decided to give our new subjects a code name, as they do for storms, to avoid confusion from using the generic word 'subject' and a number. From now on, it will be Anna, Betty, Claire, etc. The names will obscure their real identity but give us an easy reference to a particular subject."

Miles nodded his approval. "Now clarify what you meant when you specified the compound worked 'almost too well' on Anna."

"It was well worth the time to vet a good candidate. She was physically healthy for a 62-year-old, but more importantly, had a functioning brain without any indication of disease or disintegration. Our other test subjects had mental deficiencies."

"A shame. They were so docile and gullible. You did gather some data from them, didn't you?"

"Some. The most obvious was that the compound

doesn't work on subjects suffering from dementia."

The tycoon nodded. "I know you suspected that from the beginning. I argued because of the ease of acquiring such subjects. The vetting process requires more time, research, and money."

"But worth it in the end. I hope you are vetting more candidates."

"Yes, my team is working on it. We have one man I already approved. Like Anna, he's a loner with no family. We'll inject him with the same dosage we gave Anna. It will be interesting to compare the results to Anna's. Once we know the compound works on him, too, we can shorten the time considerably if we abduct and test several subjects at the same time. The team is looking, but I fear not all those subjects live as socially isolated as we'd like."

"Let's call the man you already approved Adam," Henry said.

"Adam, it is. I will, however, wait a week or two before injecting him. I want to keep track of Anna. I'm curious to know how she will handle the change and want to make sure she does nothing to jeopardize our project. If she does, I'll make dealing with her a priority. The change in age might be enough to keep her quiet. Who would believe her if she told people all she did was wake up one morning and was 30-something years younger?" Miles laughed.

"Isn't it going to be suspicious if numerous healthy

people disappear at the same time?" Henry asked.

"I thought of that. Tucson worked well because it already had a history of people wandering off and dying in the desert. We'll add other locations to spread the abductions in different jurisdictions to avoid the police connecting them. Our labs in Tucson can handle all the work. We'll only need a few mobile units with secure high-tech computers to dispatch to the location of a vetted subject and drones for surveillance to identify the perfect time to capture and inject the person. I suggest we take them to the safe house in Tucson. We can watch the physical reactions the subjects have as the potion takes effect."

"I like the idea of bringing them to the safe house," Henry said. "We don't have any idea how long it took for the compound to take effect on Anna or how her body reacted during the transition."

"Do you have a supply of the compound already made?"

"Yes. I'd like new subjects to be injected with the same compound we used on Anna but in varying amounts. I'll use the results we collect to refine my formula. I'd like to find one formula that works well for all our potential clients, regardless of their sex or size. Since during the vetting process you were able to collect photographs from the school yearbooks when Anna taught school, in addition to the computer software, it's safe to say Anna regressed some 30 years, which I might add, surprised me. I attribute that partially to her low body mass. I might have given her too much of the formula for her size. Most of our clients will not want to reverse back that far. I want the regression age to depend on the dosage amount and not use different formulas for different outcomes."

"Adam is a healthy male both mentally and physically: he's 65, 6'1", weighing 170 pounds. His age change will give you an immediate clue as to whether or not size is a factor."

"Yes, it will," Henry agreed, "and I'm most anxious to see those results."

"I'll have the surveillance team inform you immediately after he's been injected and start sending photos."

"Thank you. But, of course, I can't base the final formula on only two cases. My goal now is to ascertain how much or little of the compound is needed per body type for the number of desired years of regression, the same way medical doctors adjust dosages on prescription drugs depending on an individual patient's needs."

"That would be best." The tycoon refilled their champagne glasses.

"We don't need a drastic change in age to determine if the compound is working," Henry said. "For the new test subjects, I'll start with lower dosages. Once I have a baseline number of years regressed for the dosage administered, I'll increase the dosage on other test subjects and be able to create a reliable ratio of dosage vs. the number of years regressed. It will never be a perfect ratio, however. You'll need to warn the clients about that."

"I don't see that as a problem," Miles said. "We'll quote a range of a few years. I am concerned, however, about the amount of time your experiments are taking."

"Miles, you can't rush science, not if you want reliable results. How are you tracking Anna? Drones?"

"While she was at the state park, our man-on-the-ground hid a tracking device under her RV."

Chapter 13   Visit to Dr. Carter

After the six-and-a-half-hour drive home yesterday, Leila wanted to release her pent-up energy and decided to walk to Dr. Carter's office at the other end of town for her appointment. She judged the distance to be two to three miles for the journey back and forth, or forth and back as the case may be: not too much of a challenge for a young body. Besides, she had a day's wait until the appointment with Mr. Bradshaw, her attorney. If she tired herself out, so much the better. She had nothing to do but hide in her RV for the day.

As Leila dressed, she noticed how loosely her clothes fit. They made her look frumpy. Adding sunglasses and a wide-brimmed sun hat that shaded her face hid her facial features. Most of the businesses on Main Street were set back from the road with parking lots in front: the distance from the road further concealing her. Drivers whizzing by had no time to look closely.

After checking in at the doctor's office, an assistant led her to the back to weigh her, check her height, and give her a cursory eye exam. The scale confirmed what her clothes had already told her: a weight loss of over 10 pounds. She'd added unwanted pounds since menopause, 20 or so, forcing her into a size 12. That was pudgy for someone 5'4". As she walked down the hallway to the exam room, Leila smiled at the idea of chucking her size 12s and buying new size 10s. Then she told herself not to be hasty. If she lost more weight, she might soon be chucking the 10s for 8s. She liked the idea of reaching her dream size; prudence suggested she not waste money on a new wardrobe of 10s. On the other hand, she hated the way the pants hung on her shrinking frame; she didn't even have to unzip them to get out of them. Soon, they'd slip off her hips. She'd satisfy herself with a compromise. She'd buy a couple of cheap outfits at the local Walmart and have no guilt getting rid of them if she did lose more weight.

Dr. Carter's professional demeanor slipped when he walked into the exam room. Usually, he greeted a patient and walked over to a small desk in the corner to lay down the patient's file. He stopped short when he saw Leila.

"Leila?" he asked.

"Yes, it's me."

He recovered his composure and closed the door but never went to the desk. File in hand, he opened it and flipped through a couple of pages. "Let's review your medical history." He began asking questions about past ailments, operations, and medications. Satisfied with her answers, he closed the file and stepped straight to the exam table to put the file down behind Leila who sat on the front edge. He placed his hand on her chin and turned her head from side to side.

"Have you had plastic surgery?"

"No. Since I'm sure you'll ask a lot of questions to which I'll answer 'no,' let me explain first."

As Leila related her tale, Dr. Carter pulled over a stool, sat in front of her, and listened attentively. When she finished, he said, "You're saying you have no idea what caused these changes?"

"None. Not a clue. At first, I thought I had a brain disorder. I blamed the blackout on that and thought I was imagining the age regression, that I was delusional."

"What changed your mind?"

"I met a guy named Jeff and his friends at the park. They all treated me as though I was a peer. They were in their late twenties or early thirties. Do I look about that age?"

"Yes. I'd say that fits. Are you still regressing in age?"

"I don't think so unless the changes are inside. My outside changes stopped after a few days before I met Jeff and his friends."

"What is it you want me to do?"

"I'd like to know that's nothing biologically wrong with me and if I'm as young inside as I am outside. I hoped you'd run some blood tests," she shrugged, "or whatever tests you suggest. Wouldn't that tell you my inside age?"

"To some degree, yes. We expect results to fall within certain parameters depending on the sex and age of a person. I couldn't give you an exact age."

"An estimate works."

"Let's give you a physical exam, then I'll send in a phlebotomist to draw blood. Depending on the results, I may ask you to come in for other tests."

"Okay. Maybe, just maybe, you'll find a biological reason for my age regression?"

The usually serious doctor laughed. "I'd be rich if I discovered a way to make a person young again. I'll order the usual panel of blood tests. Once I have those results, I can determine if further tests are needed or would be of help. Until I get those results, is there anything else I can do for you today?"

"Yes, but I don't know how to ask. The reaction you had when you came into the room? That's going to happen every time I see someone I know. They're either going to flat-out accuse me of lying or they're going to ask a million questions I can't answer. How do I handle that? And what about when I must show my ID? It says I'm 62. Who's going to look at me and believe that? Any advice?"

"I think you are looking at two different issues. Unfortunately, neither fall within my area of expertise. As to the identity issue, that's a legal problem. You might want to consult an attorney. Do you know one?"

"Yes, and I've already made an appointment."

"Good. The second issue is behavioral, learning how to cope. I suggest you talk to a psychiatrist. A psychiatrist, not a psychologist, since a psychiatrist is also a medical doctor. He'll help you explore your options and might be able to help you break through to your blocked memories. Do you know a psychiatrist?"

"No."

"I can help you with that. Would you like a referral?"

"Yes. Please."

"Wait here."

When Dr. Carter returned, he held a list of four names and phone numbers.

"I would highly recommend Dr. Schwartz, the first name on the list," he said. "He's retired now but occasionally accepts cases he finds interesting. There's no doubt he will find your case very, very interesting. If you like, I will call him and summarize your situation. I think that will sway him more than a cold call from you."

"I'd very much appreciate that. If I called him out of the blue, I'll bet he'd say 'no' because my story is so unbelievable."

"Give me a day or two to make sure I connect with him. I'll call you after I speak with him."

Chapter 14   Visit to Attorney

When the attorney's receptionist escorted her to Mr. Bradshaw's office, he stood up behind his desk, waved toward the guest chair on the other side of the desk, and invited Leila to sit. She noted her file on his desk and a quizzical look on his face. After inquiring about the reason for her visit, Leila opened her purse and pulled out her wallet before answering.

"I want to show you something." She opened the wallet and extracted her driver's license which she handed to him. "Please note my date of birth."

He looked at the license and back up at her. Tapping the license on the desktop, he said, "This is impossible. Are you Leila's granddaughter?"

"No. I'm Leila." She waved at the file on his desk. "That's my file, isn't it?"

"That's Leila Petterson's file."

"The information in that file is confidential, is it not?"

"Yes."

"Why don't you quiz me about the information in the file, especially the information that only Leila would know? That might convince you I'm Leila."

"Why did you come here today?"

"Because I have a big problem, the one we're having right now. No one is going to look at me and believe I'm 62 years old. I hoped you'd be able to tell me if there was some legal way to obtain ID with an updated photo and date of birth."

The attorney continued asking questions: when and how would she use new the ID; did she plan on changing all her legal documents and records; how had the physical change happened; how many people knew about the change? To Leila, the questioning felt more like an interrogation.

Finally, Mr. Bradshaw opened her file and sat back in his leather chair, holding the file up to block her view of the contents. More questions. Lots more questions. After she'd answered them all, he closed the file. Her correct responses swayed him to believe her, although his eyes said she was lying. Her perfect responses raised suspicion. A person's memory is faulty; an imposter memorizes details. He decided, however, to give her the benefit of the doubt.

"I still have difficulty believing you. It's possible someone saw your copies of the documents in the file and familiarized themselves with the contents."

Leila felt close to tears. "I don't know how else to convince you, and I need help."

"You said you've already visited your physician?"

"Yes. He, too, quizzed me about my history and was

satisfied with my answers, but he knows me a lot better than you do."

"Would you mind if I speak to your doctor?"

"Not at all." Leila supplied him with Dr. Carter's name and phone number.

"I know him. I'd like you to contact him and give him permission to answer my questions and share any information I might need."

"I'll do that. Does this mean you'll help me? Do you have some ideas about how to obtain new ID?"

"I might have, but I'd also like to consult other attorneys before discussing options with you. Do you have any objection to my sharing your case? Just the details of the case. Your name would not be disclosed."

"No objection."

Mr. Bradshaw reopened her file and read her address and phone number out loud. "Are they still accurate?"

Leila confirmed the phone number and explained why she was temporarily staying in an RV park. The attorney nodded and stood up, signaling the end of the meeting, and promised to call her.

With a heavy heart, Leila returned to the Oasis. The specter of failure loomed over her. If Mr. Bradshaw didn't help, she didn't know where else to turn. She was glad, at least, that she'd contacted both a doctor and an attorney who knew her. She'd had enough trouble convincing them, especially Mr. Bradshaw. Her chances with a stranger amounted to zero. With nothing to do now except wait, Leila stopped at the RV park office to pay for her site for another few days.

Chapter 15 Checking Anna's Movements

The business tycoon, Miles Grayson, sat in his library studying a report on his computer. His man-on-the-ground had hidden a tracking device underneath Anna's RV while she was at the state park. Drones weren't always practical, especially after Anna left the isolated park and returned to a populated area. Miles wanted to know how Anna reacted to her physical changes: where she would go and what she would do. He acted not only out of curiosity but primarily to ensure the safety of his project.

Anyone who jeopardized his plans was terminated. A couple of his employees with loose lips had met with fatal accidents. He had paid them enough for their silence, double the salary they might expect to earn elsewhere. If that wasn't enough to ensure their loyalty, then they suffered the consequences of betrayal. Having to replace them annoyed him. It took time to find suitable replacements which interfered with the smooth flow of the operation. He'd divided the operation into sections so only he knew the full extent of the organization. Henry, of course, had a good idea of the scope but not the details, nor did he care. If he received the data he needed from a test subject, he didn't concern himself with how the individual was captured or dealt with afterward.

The tracking device on the RV only told Miles where Anna went, what time of day she traveled, and how long she stayed, but he'd deduce from that what she was doing. The results so far were rather intriguing.

From the state park, she'd driven straight home to Benson but not to her residence. She'd checked into an RV park. He concluded the age change had intimidated her. She wasn't announcing to the world her miraculous transformation. She remained stationary for two days keeping out of sight.

When she went out again, she drove to a strip mall. The address showed that she'd parked in front of a hair salon. A hair salon? Miles thought it incongruous that she didn't want to be seen but was concerned about her appearance. It struck Miles, too, that she hadn't gone to a doctor, the first place he'd have guessed she might go.

He picked up the phone and called his surveillance team. He didn't need to identify himself because that phone in the computer lab was solely for his use. "Subject: Anna. I want to know every business in that strip mall she visited," he barked.

"Yes, Sir."

Chapter 16   Taking Chances

Leila paced up and down in her RV which now felt like a cage. She missed the freedom of the state park. Snowbirds or winter visitors, or whatever one wanted to call them, flocked to the warmer climes of southern Arizona to escape the cold and snow of northern states. Since most stayed for three to six months, they tended to be friendlier than short-stay campers because they sought companions for the season. Most were retirees. They'd naturally be curious why she wasn't working if they saw her around the park all day or invite her to join them for coffee in the clubhouse in the mornings. For her, that was another problem. She didn't want to get friendly and exchange background information or makeup lies which often backfired. If she rebuffed friendly gestures, she'd earn a reputation as odd or unfriendly and, thus, bring attention to herself. Hence, she confined herself to the indoors.

Wait, wait, wait. Wait for the results of the blood test, wait to see the psychiatrist Dr. Schwartz who Dr. Carter had contacted for her, and wait to hear back from the attorney. She had things to do. The laundry basket overflowed as her closet emptied; sheets and towels also needed washing. The park had a laundry room, but hanging around it during the hours it took to do several loads placed her in a confined public space where women tended to converse as the washers spun and the dryers tumbled.

Hobie's conversational meows stopped her. She imagined him asking why she paced or what was wrong.

"You're right, baby. This pacing around is silly." She sat down on the recliner and grabbed the TV remote. "Come sit with me, and we'll watch TV."

Hobie immediately accepted her invitation.

After two episodes of House Hunters, a rerun of CSI, and a mystery movie on the Hallmark channel, a moonless night pressed at the windows. When she got up to pull down the shades, she realized the park was dark. Retirees went to bed early. Muted window lights here and there suggested only a few people were still awake behind their shades. It was a perfect time to do laundry, except the park closed the laundry room at 8:30.

Leila lived only a couple of miles from the park. The laundry room in her house never closed. While her neighbors stayed up later than retirees, within an hour or two, they'd be fast asleep, too. A clandestine trip home not only allowed her to do the laundry, but to fill the closet with more clothes to supplement the few she'd originally packed for her trip to the state park.

She hated the idea of 'closing up' the RV by

disconnecting in the dark but decided the effort was worth it. After stripping the bed and gathering the towels, she began a list of other staples needed to restock the RV. Next came the RV itself. She stowed away any loose items that might fall during travel and retracted the stabilizers, awning, and slide-out. Lastly, she went outside and disconnected the electrical cord and water hose from the RV but left them connected to the post. There was no need to take the time and effort to stow them when she'd be back in a few hours to reconnect them.

On the way home, a police car pulled behind her. He didn't turn on his flashing lights, so she kept going, driving as carefully as possible. But, oh, how nervous he made her. If he stopped her to check her registration and driver's license, she'd be in trouble. The cop stayed behind her through several turns. No question he was following her. Finally, she turned down her street and pulled into her driveway. The cop stopped on the street in front of her house. She picked up the laundry basket and exited the RV. After all, who brings something into a house if they planned to rob it? She walked to the front door, keys in hand, put down the laundry basket, and opened the door. Before she entered, she waved to the cop as though thanking him for escorting her home safely. As he pulled away, she picked up the laundry basket and stepped inside. Leila closed the door, leaned her back against it, and slid to the floor.

Once the shaking stopped, she filled the washing machine and turned it on. Laundry ate up the most amount of time. Everything else she aimed to accomplish, she'd do between loading and unloading the washer and dryer. The hours passed. She finished as the dark of night faded, heralding the impending arrival of dawn. Once back at the Oasis, she reversed her former actions in record time. She was so tired that she didn't bother to make the bed. She simply threw a sheet over the mattress and fell onto it fully clothed.

Chapter 17   Medical Test Results

Leila awoke to the chimes of her phone. Dr. Carter wanted to see her in his office at 5:00. She agreed, of course, hoping that meant he had some answers. In the interim, she made the bed, hung up the towels, and began putting away the laundry and other clothes and staples she'd brought from home. She didn't have quite enough room inside. She piled up the leftover items to store in an outside bin.

Her neighbor, a senior citizen like most of the long-termers in the park, sat on his patio. "I heard you go out late last night," he said.

"Oh. Sorry if I woke you." She smiled, knowing he was waiting for her to tell him why. She didn't explain. After she stuffed the leftovers into a bin, she turned off the water.

"Going out again?"

Leila weighed the question. Where did common civility end and disclosure begin? "Doctor's appointment." Leila figured that wasn't giving much away, and it was the truth.

He nodded, assuming he now knew the reason for her departure last night: trip to emergency. So that's why she kept to herself; she was sick.

"Would you like me to drive you instead of having to pack up the RV again?"

Tempting. Oh, so tempting. Too tempting. "I don't want to cause you any trouble."

"You aren't. Old guy like me doesn't have much to do. Driving a pretty girl around would be a pleasure."

"I'd appreciate it."

"When do you want to leave?"

"Since I don't have to close up, half an hour or so?"

While she waited, Leila thought about her own car, only a few miles away. She could tow it, if she found a way to get to it without running into neighbors. She shuddered at the thought of another midnight trip and the police following her. She bet she'd raise suspicion if they saw her taking a car from the garage. If they questioned her? She's back to the same old problem of not having believable ID. Besides, hooking up a tow car, something she'd never attempted before, and in the dark, seemed like an insurmountable feat.

When the neighbor joined her, he held out his hand. "Name's Ted."

Leila shook the proffered hand. "Leila."

During the short drive to the doctor's, she and Ted chatted about inconsequential subjects. She was relieved that he didn't ask any personal questions. When he pulled up in front of the office door, she thanked him for the ride and went inside.

An assistant escorted Leila to Dr. Carter's office instead of an exam room.

"Let's start with the good news," he said after they'd settled into chairs. "Your test results all fall into the normal range for a female adult age 25 to 35."

"Meaning my body has gotten younger?"

"Seems so."

"Will it stay young or will I wake up one morning and be 62 again?"

"Since I don't know what caused the regression, I can't answer that. You already told me you don't recall eating or drinking anything unusual, but somehow a foreign substance entered your system, most likely a drug. I assume you'll age as you did the first time, but if I had to hazard a guess, barring any serious illnesses, I'd guess it will be a normal progression."

"And the blood test? It didn't show anything unusual?"

"No. That surprised me a little. I was hoping we'd find some clue in your blood. This regression happened several weeks ago, didn't it?"

"Yes."

"I think the drug did its magic and then dissipated. Again, I'm guessing, but I think the twitching you experienced was the drug working."

"When I stopped twitching, the drug was gone from my system?"

"That's my guess. Dr. Schwartz, the psychiatrist I

recommended, has requested a copy of your files. I assume you contacted him."

"Yes. Thank you again for calling him for me."

"I'm glad I could help. When is your appointment?"

"On Wednesday."

"I'll get the files to him immediately."

"Thank you."

"Leila, I hope you realize I'm extremely interested in what happens to you. I've never had, and doubt I ever will have, another patient with such an extraordinary history. You are a walking miracle. Naturally, I'm concerned about your welfare and sorry I couldn't do more to help but admit to also being curious. Will you keep me apprised of how you're doing and the progress you make in solving the mystery of the reverse chronology?"

"Oh, but you've helped a great deal. You were the first person who believed me; I'll never forget that. You also gave me a direction to go. Because of you, I've connected with Dr. Schwartz and ... I assume Mr. Bradshaw called you?"

Dr. Carter nodded.

"I'm not sure he believed me. Confirmation from you that I am who I say I am means he will help me, too. I'll be more than glad to keep you informed."

The doctor handed her a business card with a phone number handwritten on the back of it. "That's my personal cell phone number. Our exchanges will be completely private."

On the way out of the office, Leila realized she hadn't thought about the trip back to the Oasis. She mentally shrugged. No big deal. It was a long walk back to the park, but she'd already done that on the first visit without a problem. She certainly needed some exercise after hiding out in the RV.

When she exited the building, Ted's car was one of the few left in the parking lot. He must have been watching for her because he opened the car door and waved. "Over here, Leila."

"Oh, Ted, I'm sorry. I didn't mean for you to wait all that time."

"Nonsense. How else were you going to get home? It wasn't that long anyway."

Ted's kindness had done more than save her from the dreaded routine of preparing the RV for travel for the second time in less than 24 hours. He'd also made her realize that opening up to others, at least on a surface level, needn't be so bad, especially if they weren't nosey. Of course, she'd opened up to Jeff, but that was different. The circumstances were different; they hadn't connected during an everyday life situation. If she'd asked Jeff to drive her to the doctor's, he'd have been concerned and asked all kinds of questions. Still, she missed him; she missed the companionship. Love him as she did, Hobie wasn't enough to satisfy her social needs. Perhaps it was time to reach out and call a trusted friend, a friend not prone to gossip. That narrowed down the possibilities.

Chapter 18 Wendy

Leila scrolled through the contacts list on her phone looking for a trusted friend to call. Since retirement, her contacts with old friends had dwindled to Christmas greetings for most of them. It was true, she decided, that proximity and shared experiences such as work defined most friendships. Take away what they had shared or distance yourself by moving, and a friendship faded. Toward the end of the contacts list, Wendy's name popped up. Wendy. Of course. Leila chided herself for not thinking of Wendy immediately. They lived over an hour apart now but had still managed to keep close with a Girls' Day Out several times a year. Leila tapped Wendy's name, then the 'call' icon.

"What's up?" Wendy answered in her usual cheerful voice.

"I'm in trouble; I need your help."

"Oh, no, what happened?"

"I can't explain on the phone. Will you drive over?"

"Yes. Of course. When?"

"As soon as you can."

"I don't have any plans this afternoon. Is that soon enough?"

"Thank you. Yes. This afternoon is fine. Just one thing. I'm not at home. I'm staying at the Oasis RV Park on the edge of town. Site 24."

Wendy paused before answering. "You're camping? What's wrong with going home? Did the house burn down or something?"

"No. Nothing like that. Please just come. I'll answer all your questions when you get here."

"Well, okay. But I'll die of curiosity in the meantime. Should be there around 2:00."

"Thanks, Wendy. You have no idea how much this means to me."

When Wendy arrived several hours later, Leila watched her as she parked and walked to the door. She looked about the same as always. Tall, about 5'7" if Leila recalled correctly, dark hair streaked with gray, or perhaps at this point, gray hair streaked with dark highlights. She'd put on more weight, too, as older women tended to do. Leila loved that she was now losing weight instead of gaining it. However, she realized that simply losing weight may not be enough. To firm and shape her body back to the dream one she'd had at age 30, the size 8 body, with the weight distributed in the right places, required a regimented exercise program.

Leila didn't go to the door to open it. Unsure of what Wendy's reaction might be, Leila wanted Wendy to be inside the RV for the revelation. When Wendy knocked and called out "I'm here," Leila replied, "Come on in."

"My knees sure don't like these steep steps," Wendy said. She focused her attention on the two interior steps as she climbed up. "Made it," she said when she reached the top of the stairs and looked up at Leila. "What the hell?"

"Hi, Wendy."

"What is this? Some sort of scam? You're not Leila. No wonder you didn't want me to go to the house."

"I am Leila. Honest. Let me explain."

"Forget it. I'm not interested. You may look like her, but you're a little young, don't you think? Leila's my age in case you didn't know."

"I do know. You're 66."

"Like hell. You're an imposter." Wendy stepped backward and down one step. "And that's what I'm going to tell the police. I want to know what you did to my friend."

"But I phoned you. You recognized my voice."

"Bah. You stole her phone. Yes, your voice is similar, but so what." Wendy backed down another stair.

Leila took a step forward. "Please, Wendy."

Wendy held up her hand. "Stop. Don't come any closer to me before I start screaming bloody hell."

"Do you remember when I sat by your side at the hospital all night after Jed's accident? Or, how about when I picked you up at the airport at 1:00 in the morning because your car wouldn't start? Those are memories. They aren't written down anywhere. How would a stranger know?"

"Scammers can find out stuff like that. Maybe you tortured Leila."

"Ask me a question about you. Something I wouldn't even think about if someone was forcing me or tricking me into disclosing memories."

Wendy stared at her for a moment in silence. "Sure, why not? It'll prove you're lying. When I first met Leila, what was the name of my dog?"

Leila paused.

"Don't know, do you?" Wendy backed down to the exterior step. One more and she'd be on the ground.

"Satan. That's it, Satan. You said he was a devil because of all the trouble he got into. But you were broken-hearted when he escaped from the yard and was hit by a car."

Wendy gaped at the response. "Okay, I'll give you that one, but I'm sorry. This is too weird for me. I'm leaving."

"It's a lot weirder for me. I understand if you want to leave, but please don't call the police. If you don't believe me, what will they think? You'll get me into all kinds of trouble."

"Maybe you should be."

"Please, Wendy. Please. In the name of our friendship."

Wendy grunted. "What friendship? I don't know who you are."

"Can you give me the benefit of the doubt? Like you did with your student? I forget her name, but the one you thought had stolen money from your wallet. She swore she didn't do it, and you had no proof so you didn't report her."

"How did you know about that?" Wendy air-eased her question by waving her hands in front of her. "Never mind. I won't go to the police but don't call me again or I will."

Wendy turned around and stepped on the ground.

"And Wendy, please don't tell anybody what you saw today."

Wendy turned her head back. "That's for sure. If I did, they'd think I had dementia and stick me in a nursing home."

Wendy walked away. No wave, no goodbye, no other farewell.

Chapter 19   Tracking Anna's Phone

Miles reread the second report from his tracking team. The only place Anna had driven since the strip mall was to her residence late at night. The second part of the report included a list of businesses in the strip mall that Anna had visited. Two businesses stood out: a chiropractor and a law office. While the chiropractor was a possibility, Miles leaned toward believing the law office had been her destination. He wondered what she had hoped to accomplish there. He closed his eyes and relaxed back into his chair to let his mind wander. It didn't take him long to decide on an answer when he combined that information with the first part of the report.

Leila had driven to her residence in the middle of the night to remain undetected while retrieving personal information or documents, likely at the behest of her lawyer. She was 62 going on 30-something. None of her existing documents, especially her identification, were valid. It amused him to think of her explaining the discrepancy to a cop. He wondered how she'd convinced the lawyer. She must have, somehow, elicited his help in changing or forging documents. If she was worried about exposing her secret, he was no longer worried about her exposing his. The date for any residue left in her system from the injection had long since passed. He'd keep track of her though; he might pick up a few pointers to pass on to his clients when he introduced the "fountain of youth" to them.

Miles picked up the phone and called the surveillance team.

"Your report states that Anna has only gone out once since her trip to the strip mall. I find that highly unusual. Are you sure the tracker on the RV is working?"

"Yes, Sir. The signal is constant."

"It's a small town. She might be walking or getting rides or taking a bus. Are you tracking her phone?"

"No, Sir. We weren't told to do so."

Miles was on the verge of lambasting the tech for not being able to think for himself but stopped. It was on his order that techs were only allowed to do what he directed them to do. He permitted some latitude, but not much, not after a problem arose with a former tech who took it upon himself to start combining bits of information and asking questions about the larger picture. The tech wouldn't be asking any more questions from anyone.

"Hack into the GPS on her phone as a backup."

"We'll try, Sir."

"I don't pay you to try. I pay you for results."

"Yes, Sir. We'll get right on it."

Chapter 20   Setting Up a Trust

Walking had become Leila's favorite mode of transportation because it got her outdoors and was a healthy form of exercise. She only needed to calculate her timing. She didn't want to turn up too early for an appointment and wait where others had time to assess her, but she didn't want to be late either. She used Google maps to figure out the distance to Mr. Bradshaw's office. Driving time was useless information. If she noted the time on her phone before leaving and when arriving, she'd be able to calculate a basic walking time.

"The consensus among my colleagues is that you can't get legal ID showing just a new photo and change of date of birth," Mr. Bradshaw began once they'd been seated in his office. "Since 9-11, rules have tightened considerably. You need two accepted forms of ID to get a third. You have none."

Leila slumped in her chair. "What am I going to do? I won't even be able to get a job. Isn't there any ID that's easy to get?"

"There is, of course, fake or forged ID. The easiest to fake is a birth certificate."

Leila sat up straighter in her chair. "Won't a new birth certificate help me get a legitimate ID?"

"Birth certificates are not considered valid ID anymore, except perhaps for a child with an accompanying parent. Every state has its own form and design for a birth certificate. There is no standard for the document, which is what makes it easy to fake. If you could get one, it won't do you much good. Remember I said you need two IDs."

"What if I had a birth certificate and a social security card? Those are easy to get."

Mr. Bradshaw shook his head. "Not anymore. Not for an adult. A new social security card requires two other IDs just like everything else."

"So, either I'm screwed, or I'm forced to get forged documents? I don't even know how to find a forger."

"Hold on. I said you couldn't get legal ID with just a different photo and birth date. You can get legal ID if you recreate yourself, starting with a new name."

"I did some research. I saw several sites where one can do that."

"And end up with documents that look as fake as they are. I'm talking legal. I spoke to a judge I know who can create a new identity for someone, a legal identity. He was very interested in your story."

"If I have a whole new identity, doesn't that mean I have to give up everything I have now?"

"Since you are 30 or so again, you'll have to give up

Social Security income and Medicare or any other senior benefits you receive. As you age again, when you reach 62 again – and likely long before that – the government is going to wonder why they're paying benefits to someone who is 124. They'll investigate, of course, and you'll be exposed as a fraud. Defrauding the government has serious consequences. You mentioned not being able to get a job. With new identity, you will, and you'll have all the benefits that go with a job, such as an income and medical insurance. Losing your government benefits isn't catastrophic."

"What about my investments or bank accounts or physical property like my house and RV?"

"Investments and bank accounts will be rolled into your estate. As to the physical property, the beneficiary can opt to keep them or sell them. I'll draw up a new will for you. In reviewing the will in place now, I noted that your beneficiaries are educational foundations. We'll change the beneficiary to the new you."

"I'll inherit my own money and my house and RV?"

"Exactly."

"That's not so bad, then. Oh, wait. To inherit, I'll have to die first."

"Yes, you will. But let's not dwell on that now. I also want to be named executor. It's a level of protection for you. If anyone comes snooping, I can claim attorney-client confidentiality and stop most of the inquiries."

"Most of them?"

"A will is probated by the court, and I will have to answer any questions by the court. However, there's also a way around that if the will is included in a trust. A trust is not probated, hence, no questions. I will charge you to set up the trust, but in the long run, it will save you money because I won't have to spend the time researching for the information you will provide for the trust such as property you own, banking accounts and investments, credit cards, etc. I will name myself as trustee for the same reasons I asked to be named executor of the will. Are you agreeable to setting up a trust?"

"Yes."

"I'll draw up the trust today. You can pay my fees for setting up the trust and changing the will when the trust settles. Speaking of money, I suggest you stockpile some cash. There'll be a hiatus between the time you disappear and the time the trust settles. You'll need cash to live on during that period."

"Can't I cash in an investment now to get a large sum of money all at once?"

"I don't suggest it. We don't want to raise any red flags by showing you might have been preparing to disappear. Periodically take money out of your banking account a little at a time so it appears to be cash for everyday living."

Mr. Bradshaw swiveled his chair around to pick up a thick pack from the credenza behind him and put it on the desk in front of Leila. "I will warn you that it takes quite a bit of time to fill out the paperwork even if your files are well organized."

The thickness of the pack intimidated Leila. 'A bit of time' was an understatement. Her files were organized, and she had the time, but her personal papers were in her house. She almost missed hearing Mr. Bradshaw's next words worrying about how to get to those files.

"One caveat to making these plans work. The judge wants more than my word that you are Leila Petterson. Proof, in other words."

Leila threw up her arms and sank back into her chair. "Here we go, back to the beginning. A Catch-22, isn't it? I need ID to prove who I am, but I can't get ID unless I prove who I am."

"I realize you're frustrated but stay with me. Have you ever been fingerprinted?"

Leila sat up. "Yes. For my teaching credential. That was years and years ago."

"I assumed since you were a teacher, you had been. Fingerprints don't change." Mr. Bradshaw reached into his desk drawer and pulled out a white, legal-sized envelope which he extended toward her. "This contains an order signed by Judge Hersey to have a lab he trusts fingerprint you. They will compare the results to those on file with the State. The name, address, and phone number of the lab are included in the envelope. The lab will send the results to Judge Hersey. If they match, the judge will help you."

Leila reached out her hand to take the envelope, but Mr. Bradshaw didn't release his end. "One last thing, Leila. A warning. I'm an officer of the court. If the fingerprints don't match, I will turn you over to the court."

"They will match."

Mr. Bradshaw released the envelope. "The sooner you have the fingerprinting done; the sooner we can get the new identity process started. In the meantime, decide on a new name and date of birth and give some thought to creating a new background. The name, date of birth, and a new photo, I'll need next time we meet. The background can wait but start thinking of your options."

And start thinking about how and when I'm going to die, Leila thought to herself.

Chapter 21   Sneaking Home

On the walk home, carrying the heavy bundle of forms Mr. Bradshaw had given her, Leila's thoughts focused on how she'd be able to fill them out. Not only did she need the records in her house but the time there to go through them.

If she drove the RV home pretending to have returned from her trip, she'd need to stay there before pretending to take off on another trip. The longer she stayed, the higher the chance of neighbors seeing her, especially Mrs. Beckenour next door. She loved to drop by after one of Leila's trips to catch Leila up on the neighborhood gossip. If Mrs. Beckenour saw her, the whole neighborhood would learn about the young Leila within hours. She also didn't recall a time when she'd taken back-to-back trips, and that, too, might raise a red flag.

The easiest solution was to lock up the RV for a couple of days and walk to her house. Since she stayed inside the RV ninety percent of the time, people in the park wouldn't even know she was gone. Except for Hobie. She could leave enough food and water in his bowls for a couple of days, but he'd be upset.

Cats are social creatures. If he felt abandoned, he might begin crying or howling. She didn't want to put him through that, nor did she want to draw attention to the RV. There was no way to carry him. While he liked to sit on her lap and snuggle up in bed, he hated to be picked up and fought her when she did. A fight with a 17-pound cat on the long walk to her house while also carrying the heavy bundle of legal forms was out of the question.

By the time Leila arrived at the Oasis, she still hadn't formed a plan. Ted was outside fiddling with a broken lawn chair as she passed his RV.

"Hey, Missy, I haven't seen you. How are you feeling?"

Leila stopped, wondering why he added "feeling" to the traditional "How are you?" Then she recalled that the last time she'd seen him, he had driven her to her appointment with Dr. Carter. He must think she's sick. The now-too-large clothes hanging on her body helped that impression. "Been better, but okay, I guess. How about you?"

"Doin' good for an old fart."

Leila stepped toward him. "Ted, I'm in a bind. Could I ask you to help me?"

Ted stopped tinkering with the broken chair. "Well, sure, honey. What can I do for you?"

"I have to go away for a couple of days, and I need someone to feed my cat while I'm gone. Is it too much to ask you to do that?"

"Hell, no. I'll be glad to help. When you goin'?"

"Sometime tonight. It's kind of sudden. I need you to feed him tomorrow and the next day."

"You just show me what I need to do."

Ted followed Leila into her RV where she introduced Ted to Hobie. Hobie hissed when Ted walked toward him.

"He don't like me much."

Leila laughed. "He'll love you tomorrow when you feed him. Let him come to you. Cats like to decide when it's time to make friends."

Leila pulled the cat food out of the cupboard, stacked it on the countertop, explained the proportions to give him, and said to fill up the water bowl.

"You need me to drive you someplace tonight?"

"Thank you for the offer, but no. Someone's coming to pick me up."

The only remaining business was for Leila to give Ted a key. Instead of giving him the entire spare set, she detached a key for the side door. She planned to stow her laptop in an outside bin. Without the key to the outside bins, he didn't have access. She didn't believe he'd go through her things, but her journal was on the laptop, and she didn't want anyone reading that.

When Ted left, Leila tried to balance her exuberance for having found a solution with her guilt for letting Ted think he was helping a sick neighbor.

At about 10:00 p.m., Leila headed out carrying a large tote with a purse, phone, and trust papers inside. She already had whatever else she might need at home. The weight of the tote slowed the pace of her walking. After turning onto her street, she kept to the shadows and silently slipped up her driveway without being noticed. Her hand automatically reached for the light switch, but she caught herself in time. No lights. She'd sleep during the night and work in natural daylight. No one knew she was home, and she wanted to keep it that way. At least she thought no one knew that she was home.

Chapter 22   Meeting Dr. Schwartz

The day of Leila's appointment with the psychiatrist, Dr. Schwartz, arrived. After dropping the trust papers off at Mr. Bradshaw's office, Leila continued to Tucson. The first stop in Tucson was the fingerprinting company. She wrinkled her nose remembering her first experience with fingerprinting all those years ago: the mess with ink on her fingers and then the solvent to get it off. She was glad to learn they had perfected a scanning technique: no ink involved.

That chore done, Leila navigated the RV through the twists and turns of the hilly roads in North Tucson into a well-established neighborhood of large homes. Expensive homes. The doctor's adobe-style house sat back from the road. A curving flagstone walkway to the front door and the minimalistic landscape of rust-colored crushed stone and Palo Verde trees set his house apart from his neighbors' houses.

Leila half expected a maid to answer the door, but the doctor himself did. His short stature accentuated the extra weight he carried, a testimony to living well. He wore his thick silver hair combed back and rimless glasses over gray eyes. After greeting her warmly, he showed her to his study to the right of the foyer and gestured toward a pair of armchairs.

Since the moment he opened the door, he hadn't taken his eyes off her. Leila began to feel uncomfortable under his continuous stare. She squirmed in her chair and looked down at the carpet. The doctor read the signs.

"Please excuse me for staring, Lelia. I don't mean to upset you. Dr. Carter explained your situation to me when he called, of course, but I'm completely fascinated, nevertheless. We are of the same decade, but you could easily pass for my granddaughter."

"And that essentially is my problem. How do I lead a normal life when I look in my early 30s and my ID says I'm 62? I'm scared I'll get into trouble."

"Have you looked into remedying the ID problem?"

"Yes. I went to an attorney." Leila summarized the plans to create a completely new identity. "We've just started the process. I stopped on my way here to be fingerprinted. Once the judge is convinced I'm Leila, he'll do whatever he needs to do. I'm not sure how long the process takes."

"The important thing is that you've begun the process. That must be a relief."

"Sort of. I'm still nervous about the interim and what it's going to feel like to have a new name."

"That's where I will be of help. Tell me what you've done since your return to Benson."

Leila explained her alarming midnight trip home to do laundry, her second trip to fill out the trust papers which worked out well, and her disastrous decision to call Wendy and the consequences. As an afterthought, she mentioned her neighbor Ted who drove her to see Dr. Carter as one example of spending time with a stranger. "He didn't pry so it worked out okay," she concluded. "He also fed my cat for me while I hid out at home filling in the trust papers."

"And you've been home for how long now?"

"Almost three weeks."

"The activities you've described only account for a small portion of that time."

"Mostly I stay in the RV: reading, watching television, or on the computer. I'm afraid of situations where I must deal with someone I know. For example, I can't go to the bank where the tellers all know me and withdraw money. They'd call the police. Fortunately, ATMs work for that. I'm afraid of being asked for ID, and I'm afraid of conversations with people I don't know. I don't want to expose myself by answering a lot of questions. I feel like I'm in hiding."

"You are hiding. Perhaps the first thing we should consider is getting you out of Benson. You might have to take a trip back to see the attorney, but I think you'll be traveling back and forth to Tucson much more frequently to see me. When you register to stay in an RV park, what kind of information do they ask?"

"Name, address, phone number; year, make and model of the RV; and the license plate number."

"No driver's license or other form of personal identification?"

"No."

"When you registered in Benson, did they question you staying at the park when you lived in town?"

"I told them my house was being renovated and I couldn't stand the mess and noise."

Dr. Schwartz smiled. "Then you are quite capable of sidetracking an issue when needed."

"I guess so."

"Since showing ID at an RV park isn't a problem, I'd like you to consider moving to one here in Tucson because it will give you more freedom. You'll be dealing with new people, so there's little chance of an identity conflict and you can be out and about as much as you want. We have a public transit system, so you won't need to drive too often and risk running into the police again. Perhaps best of all from my point of view, you will slowly meet new people. Instead of us theorizing what to do and say, we can analyze what works and what doesn't from real situations."

"That's a good idea. I should have thought of moving."

"Don't chastise yourself. You are in an overwhelming situation. I'm very impressed with how well you have thought through options and functioned."

Leila turned her head to stare out of the window.

"Leila, what are you thinking?"

"I should tell you about Jeff."

Dr. Schwartz waited without replying.

"I met Jeff at the state park. We had a wonderful time together. I had no problem developing a relationship with him, yet he was a stranger when we met." Leila turned back to face the doctor. "I wasn't paranoid at all like I am now."

"I take it this was after your age regression."

"Yes."

"What was Jeff's last name?"

"Gordon."

"Can you think of any reason why you were at ease then and not now?"

Leila closed her eyes and leaned back to rest her head against the armchair. Again, the doctor waited to give her time to think. Silence filled the room for several minutes.

When Leila reopened her eyes, she smiled. "It's the RVing. When you go RVing, you leave your normal life behind. There's no schedule, no appointments, no business to tend to, no to-do list, no 'must haves' or 'shoulds.' You can go to bed early or stay up all night reading. You can go on hikes or sit in a lounge chair all day staring at the view. You do what you feel like doing without any restraints. People take you at face value. They don't delve into your life with a lot of questions. If you say you're 30, then you're 30. Occasionally, a question may pop up, like someone asked me what I did for a living. I responded truthfully according to my life when I was 30." Leila grinned. "And you were right. I can sidetrack an issue. When that person asked me how I could camp when school was in session, I simply said I was a substitute teacher and made myself unavailable for the week. That was accepted. Relationships on the road are transient, so most are surface level. Now I'm back in the real world. But I don't have a normal life anymore so I'm at odds with myself."

"Did you leave Jeff behind, too?"

"Not quite. We've texted back and forth a couple of times." She smiled recalling his first text. "Jeff had a dog named Jethro who always greeted me enthusiastically. I joined them on their walks around the park. Jeff sent a picture of Jethro after I left. He was lying on the ground in the middle of my site with his head resting on his paws. Jeff explained that when they first got to the site, Jethro walked around it whining, then plopped down and refused to move. He was waiting for me to return."

"Did that photo and message make you happy or sad?"

"Both. I was fond of Jeff and Jethro. I enjoyed their company especially after what I'd been through. I felt accepted. Now I feel like I'm lying to Jeff because I'm not the person he thinks I am. I'd feel horrible if he found out the truth. I can't imagine what it might do to him."

"Leila, you are still the same person you always were. Younger, yes, but your personality, the inner essence that makes you unique, hasn't changed."

"Still."

"I'd like to know more about your relationship with Jeff."

"It's in the journal." Leila pointed toward the envelope on the table.

"Is that the printout of your journal I asked you to bring?"

"Yes." Leila handed over the envelope.

"And you haven't made any changes to the original writing of the entries."

"No."

"Good. It means more if I read your initial impressions rather than modifications made in hindsight. I think this is a good point to break. I'd like time to read that journal before we proceed any further. Because of your unique situation and the immediacy of your needs, I'd like to see you as often as possible. Is that acceptable to you?"

"Yes."

"How about two days from now at 10:00?"

Of course, Leila agreed.

Chapter 23   Tracking Anna

Miles smiled after reading the latest report from his surveillance team. Once again, he'd been right. Of course, he always was. His meticulous planning and ruthlessness in business had earned him millions, most of which were safely tucked away in protected accounts in Zurich and the Cayman Islands. His goal now was to turn those millions into billions, an easily attainable goal once Henry Hoover perfected his formula. Other tycoons would gladly pay a small fortune to be young again. He would take the compound and live another lifetime, or lifetimes if he took the compound more than once, to enjoy the lavish lifestyle he deserved.

Miles scanned the report on the computer screen once again. Tracking the GPS on her phone confirmed Anna had been walking. She had visited the attorney again and had returned to her residence under the cover of darkness for two days. Miles grudgingly gave her credit for operating in her hometown without being exposed. She showed more ingenuity than he'd expected from an old maid schoolteacher.

After her clandestine visit to her residence, she drove the RV to Tucson, stopping briefly at the lawyer's office. Her next stop at a fingerprinting company confirmed his conjecture that the attorney was helping her to change her identity; she was planning to disappear. He knew from research that to change an identity legally, she had to prove she was Leila Petterson. Fingerprints would do that.

Miles didn't mind her disappearing. Let her enjoy her restored youth if it wasn't connected to him. She was as expendable as the others but might have been useful as an example when approaching prospective clients. Although he had the before and after pictures, they were not as convincing as a live person. He'd use the promise of anonymity to dispel their objections.

According to the next item in the report, Anna had driven to a private residence in Tucson where she stayed for well over an hour. His team identified the address as belonging to Dr. Irving Schwartz, a retired psychiatrist. That was a bit unsettling because he wasn't sure why she went there. Schwartz could be an old acquaintance; the attorney might have required the visit; or she may be seeking advice in adjusting to a new life. No matter the reason, Anna was protected again by confidentially. He'd wait for the next report to see if she returned a second time.

After she left Schwartz, she drove around Tucson, stopping at several RV parks. At the last park, she parked briefly in one spot, then moved to a different location in the same park. Miles concluded correctly that she planned to stay in Tucson and not return to Benson. He assessed the benefits of doing so and decided she'd made a smart move.

If disappearing was her goal, Miles decided to help, albeit more for his protection than hers. He wrote a memo to his IT Department ordering them to double-check all records mentioning Anna, erase any reference to the name Leila Petterson, and delete his memo. As Miles was about to delete the memo from his computer, the telephone rang. The conversation absorbed his attention, and he unconsciously saved the document instead of hitting the delete button.

Chapter 24   The "How"

"I did it," Leila announced as soon as Dr. Schwartz opened the door. "I moved to Tucson."

"I take it you're happy with your decision."

"That was rude of me. I should have said hello first."

"We don't stand on formality here. Your exuberance is a fine welcome by itself." He waved toward the office. "Tell me."

Leila described her search for an RV park after their last meeting, finding one, and checking in. "I never returned to Benson. I feel so much freer. I even took the bus here today."

"I assume you had a bit of a hike coming up the hill. As I recall, the bus stop is a mile or so away."

"True, but I've been walking a lot, so it wasn't too bad. Much better than being stopped by the police for some reason."

After Dr. Schwartz closed the door to his study behind them, he said, "Your journal was intriguing. You included enough detail that I had a clear picture of what happened to you after the injection."

Leila sat down. "Injection?"

"We know you didn't voluntarily swallow a pill or

95

drink some concoction without knowing what was in it. I surmise the drug or drugs had to be administered by injection."

"But when, how, was I injected?"

"I have a house guest who may be able to help us answer that because of his extensive military training. I have known and worked with Zack Taylor for numerous years and trust him implicitly. I took the liberty of creating a scenario to the point of your waking up and asked him how an injection may have been administered."

Leila squirmed in her seat. "You told him?"

"As I said, I created an imaginary scenario. Rest assured that I did not mention you or disclose any personal information. I would like to ask him to join us because his insights may answer the when and the how. However, doctor-patient confidentiality comes first. I will respect your decision if you do not want him involved."

"But you think he can help?"

"Yes."

"And he won't talk about me afterward?"

"I can guarantee that."

"Then yes. If he can provide some answers, yes."

Dr. Schwartz picked up a house phone and asked Zack to join them. Leila expected an older man, close to the doctor's age, so she was surprised when a younger man in his late thirties entered. He was dressed casually in jeans and a black tee that fit snuggly around a muscular body. He was neither good-looking nor unattractive; his was a non-descript face that blended into a crowd. His medium height of 5'10" and short sandy brown hair wasn't likely to attract attention either. Nothing about him stood out until he smiled and she saw his penetrating blue eyes up close.

After introductions and the three of them had sat down, Dr. Schwartz said, "Zack, the scenario we talked about happened to Leila. We are most interested in your opinions."

Zack turned to Leila. "Let's start by reviewing that scenario with a few questions thrown in. Begin with the road you were on. Describe it."

"It was a narrow two-lane road that led to the state park where I planned to stay."

"Paved?"

"Yes."

"Only to the park? No intersections or towns or buildings along the way?"

"None. It was 38 miles of desert."

"And you saw nobody or any other vehicles?"

"Not unless you count the wild burros crossing the road. I stopped to let them cross." Leila smiled. "Two of them were young and so cute. They completely ignored me and walked at their leisure. The adults, however, eyed me suspiciously. One stepped back from the road to let me pass."

"Ah," Dr. Schwartz said. "With age comes wisdom."

"But you did stop another time," Zack said.

"Yes. There were a couple of turnouts along the way. I pulled over at one."

"Because?"

Leila blushed. "Because I desperately needed to go to the bathroom. While I was stopped, I decided to grab a soda and go outside to stretch my legs."

"How far along the road were you when you stopped?"

"I didn't pay attention to that. I'd guess a third to halfway because the rest of the drive seemed longer."

"So roughly 12 to 19 miles."

Leila shrugged. "I guess so. Is it important?"

"I'm trying to gauge how long it would take a car to catch up with you. You remember getting the soda and going outside?"

"Yes. Then there was a flash of light. I don't remember anything else until I woke up back in the RV."

"And you thought the flash of light was lightning?"

"I thought that after I woke up simply because I had no other explanation. It didn't make a lot of sense though. The skies were overcast, but not stormy."

"When you woke up, besides being back in the RV, what did you notice that was different?"

"My clothes were dirty, dusty really. Before I took off, I walked around the RV for any clues about what had happened. I found the mini can of Sprite I'd been drinking on the ground. It still had some soda in it. I'm a recycler; I can't imagine dropping the can and leaving it like that."

"You were out for how long?"

"A little over three hours."

"Plenty of time."

"Plenty of time for what?"

"Here's what I think happened. For one, you were being followed."

"But I didn't see another car."

"You didn't need to. You were being tracked by a drone. When you stopped in an isolated place, you offered the perfect opportunity to whoever was tracking you. The light you saw was likely the drone emitting gas directly on you. The gas rendered you unconscious, and you fell to the ground, hence, the dirty clothes. Meanwhile, the people following you were already driving toward you. It wouldn't take long to drive 12 to 19 miles. When they reached you, they picked you up and carried you inside the RV. If another vehicle passed, they wouldn't want anyone to see an unconscious body on the side of the road. Once inside, they injected you and left. They were messy, though. They should have brushed off your clothes and picked up the soda can."

"You mean this all happened because I stopped?"

"If not then, later. As you said, the road only went one place: to the state park. They knew where you were going. And you're sure you didn't find anything else when you woke up?"

"Nothing unus..." Leila stopped herself. "Wait. Nothing unusual, but I didn't consider the commonplace. My upper left arm started itching. Scratching it didn't help much, so I looked closer at it. It was turning red. I figured I'd been bitten by a bug."

"The injection site," Dr. Schwartz said. "Mind if I take a close look at your arm?"

"Not at all."

Leila rolled up the loose three-quarters sleeve on her blouse and held out her arm to the doctor as he stood and stepped close to her. He turned her arm slightly right and left.

"Nothing there now, but I bet your 'bug bite' was right about here." He rested his finger on her arm.

"Yes, that's about right."

"Typical injection site."

"Typical?"

"Think about flu shots or other vaccines you've had. That's where the needle is generally inserted. How long did it itch?" the doctor asked as he sat back down.

"I put some Cortisone cream on it, and the itching stopped. It began again later that night so I put more cream on it. It didn't bother me after that."

"I'm curious what they injected you with," Zack said.

Leila looked to Dr. Schwartz. "You didn't tell him?"

"No. As I said earlier, I only created a scenario to the point of your waking up for his insights into the when and how. Any more you want to tell him is your choice."

Zack turned his full attention to Leila. "Please," he said. "I figured out the when and how for you. Don't you think I deserve to hear the rest?"

Leila looked into his eyes. "Like a thank you?"

"Something like that."

Leila took a deep breath. "I'm 62 years old."

Zack's normal placid countenance changed to one of utter surprise. He leaned forward in his chair. "Excuse me? 62?"

"Yes, 62."

Dr. Schwartz intervened and succinctly explained the changes Leila experienced after the injection.

"Amazing. Astonishing. I don't know what I expected, but never that." Zack sat back in this chair and shook his head. "I'm having trouble absorbing the idea that age regression is possible."

"I would have dismissed the idea as pure science fiction," Leila said, "until it happened to me. Now I want to know why. Why was I injected? Why me? I'm a retired nobody."

Zack's eyes widened. "Maybe that's why. Because you're a retired nobody."

"Thanks a lot."

Zack laughed. "You said it, not me." He stood up abruptly. "I have some research to do. Nice meeting you, Leila. Doc, mind if I hang around for a few more days?"

"Stay as long as you like, Zack."

In a few long strides, Zack reached the door, exited, and pulled the door close behind him.

"Well, that was a quick departure," Leila said.

Dr. Schwartz said, "True, but I expected it when I saw his eyes widen. It's a tell-tale sign he had a breakthrough idea. Once that happens, Zack's all business. Let's hope the research he mentioned may lead to the answer of why."

Chapter 25 Wendy

As usual, Wendy turned on the 10:00 p.m. local news report on Channel 13 and settled back into her armchair to watch. One of the stories covered the disappearance of another senior, a Benson woman this time. Too many of them, Wendy thought. Poor souls. They usually had some form of dementia and wandered off. Their bodies were often found in the desert, days, weeks, or even years later. The police were asking for tips from the public from anyone who had seen the missing woman. A photo appeared on the screen as the news anchor described the woman.

Wendy bolted upright in her chair. The news anchor's words were lost as Wendy stared at the screen. She was staring at a picture of Leila. Wendy asked herself why she was so surprised after the run-in with that lookalike. She'd known then that something wasn't kosher. Why, why, why hadn't she reported the incident to the police? Because she'd been covering her butt, that's why. Because she didn't think the police or anyone else would believe her story. Because there had been a hint of truth in what that young woman had told her. She'd known too much about private moments that

Leila and she had shared. A tear rolled down Wendy's cheek. She'd put herself first, instead of thinking about her good friend. The weirdness, the confusion, had driven her to inaction. Ignore it, and it will go away? Was that what she'd been thinking? And now Leila was officially gone.

Wendy tuned in again to the news story when a picture of an RV like Leila's replaced the personal photo. According to the neighbor who had reported her missing, she'd been leaving on a short trip in her RV when the neighbor last saw her. The neighbor didn't know to where or exactly how long she'd be gone but had gotten suspicious that something was wrong when time stretched into weeks and called the police. The news anchor verbalized the license plate number as it appeared on the screen and asked anyone who'd seen the RV to call the police.

A neighbor? Wendy wrung her hands. A neighbor who hardly knew Leila had been worried enough to call the police and she hadn't? Sorry excuse for a friend she'd turned out to be. Not anymore. She picked up the phone and dialed the police station.

Detectives Morales and Forbes knocked on Wendy's door the next morning. They stood in the living room as Wendy began her story. The more she talked, the more distraught she became, and the detectives feared for her well-being. They guided her to a chair, then sat down on the couch opposite her to remain at the same eye level.

"I know you don't believe me when I say she looked 30 years younger. I mean, who would?" Wendy dissolved into tears.

"We do," Detective Morales said.

Wendy wiped at the tears on her face. "You do?"

"We believe you saw a younger woman. We just don't think the woman was Leila Petterson."

"But she looked like Leila. Well, like Leila looked years ago."

"We're sure she did," Detective Forbes said. "A good imposter will. They say we all have doppelgangers. Plastic surgery works, too."

"But if she's trying to replace Leila, why make herself so young?"

"That's a major wrinkle in our case. We don't know right now," Detective Morales admitted. "We also got a call from a neighbor at that same RV park in Benson where you saw her. He never questioned her age. He recognized the RV, not her picture."

"You might have been a test case," Detective Forbes added, "to see how someone who knew Leila reacted to her youthful appearance."

"That didn't work too well," Wendy said. "I wouldn't even listen to an explanation."

"But she did convince you to keep quiet, didn't she?"

Wendy hung her head. "Yes. It was those personal touches about things other people wouldn't know."

"It could also mean the imposter did extensive

research into her life," Detective Morales said.

"You knew her well, didn't you?" asked Detective Forbes.

"Very well." Wendy's voice caught in her throat. "We've been friends for years."

"Tell us about her."

"She was a very caring person. She loved teaching and her students. I think she was married once when she was very young, before I met her. She didn't talk about it; it was just an impression I had. I say that because she didn't date much. I always thought the marriage had soured her desire for another relationship. She let her friends fill her social life."

"Family?"

"None. Her parents died many years ago. She was an only child, so no other immediate family."

"Extended family?"

"She had an aunt back East who she mentioned occasionally, but that was way back when. I doubt the woman is alive now. After retirement, she became somewhat of a loner. She moved to Benson because she liked the small-town feel, but I don't think she developed any close friendships, although we stayed close. But she loved that RV of hers. She'd pack up and travel about. She said she was catching up on all the places she'd missed seeing."

"Long trips or short ones?"

"A mixture. She bought her RV before she retired

and took off for the summer. She loved it. When she first retired, she continued to take longer trips. A couple of months at a time. Mainly, she stayed in the West because she liked the open spaces and all the natural wonders like the Grand Canyon or Yosemite. Recently, the trips were shorter. More like a week or two at a time." Wendy laughed. "Everything gets harder as we get older. It amazed me that she still had the energy and ambition to travel. Me, I like staying home."

Wendy caught a look between the detectives. "What?" she asked. "What aren't you telling me?"

"Might as well tell her," Morales said. "It'll be on the news tonight anyway."

Forbes nodded in agreement.

"We found her RV this morning," Morales continued. "At an RV park here in Tucson."

"In Tucson? And you caught the imposter?"

"No. The RV was empty when we found it this morning. We arrived early, hoping to catch the younger woman before she had a chance to start the day. We think she's gone. Her phone was all that was obviously missing, unless she had a computer?"

"Yes. She used a laptop when she traveled."

"Everything else was in place: purse, clothes, toiletries, food. Even her cat was there."

"That settles it," Wendy said. "The woman was an imposter. Leila would never leave her cat behind. Never. What's going to happen to Hobie?"

"The animal shelter picked him up."

"I'd like to give Hobie a home. It's the least I can do now for my friend. Can that be arranged?"

Morales pulled out his cell. "I'll do it right now."

Chapter 26   Leila Escapes

The same morning the detectives interviewed Wendy, much earlier in the day, knocking on her door woke Leila. She peeked under the shade at the gray light that marked the transition between night and day. The knocking continued. Leila rolled out of bed and put on her robe.

"Who's there?" Leila asked.

The knocking stopped. "Zack. Open the door."

As soon as she did, Zack forced his way into the RV. "We're leaving." He glanced around and spied her computer. "Do you have any other information somewhere in here about your situation except what's on the computer?"

"No."

"Get your phone and let's go."

"What's this all about? Why are you here at this hour?" Despite her protest, Leila picked up her phone as Zack disconnected the laptop and headed back to the door. "Zack, stop. Where do you think I'm going in my pajamas and robe?"

"I don't have time to explain." Zack took hold of her upper right arm and pulled her down the stairs. "You're in danger. I'll explain later." When they reached the ground, Zack let go of her arm and pushed the door shut. "Get in the car." Figuring she'd obey him, Zack stepped toward the car, but Leila remained standing where she was.

"What about Hobie? I can't leave him here by himself."

"Dammit." Zack took a step back, grabbed Leila's arm again, and pulled her forward. "We'll get him later." When they reached the car, Zack opened the passenger door and shoved Leila in. "Close the door and lock it and turn off your phone."

In the time it took Leila to close and lock the door, Zack had run around the black Honda Accord and jumped into the driver's seat.

"When are we coming back for Hobie?"

Zack ignored her and started the engine. His instincts told him to step hard on the gas, but he restrained himself because he didn't want to attract attention racing through the park. Although early, he'd noticed lights on in several of the RVs. When he turned out of the park onto the road, he breathed a sigh of relief at its emptiness. A hundred yards down the road, however, three police cars passed them going in the opposite direction. He watched in the rearview mirror as they turned into the park.

"You see those cop cars?" Zack asked.

"Of course, I did."

"They just turned into the park. They're on their way to arrest you."

"WHAT?" Leila turned around in her seat, but the squad cars had already passed out of sight. "Arrest me for what?"

"For being an imposter who murdered Leila Petterson."

"What? No. What are you talking about?"

"Did you see the news last night?"

"No."

"You were one of their lead stories." Zack summarized the news report.

"But why? Why did the news think I was missing?"

"One of your neighbors was concerned because you'd been gone so long and called the police. That started a search for you."

"How did they find me?"

"You give your license plate number when you register at an RV park, right?"

"That simple?"

"That simple. The picture of an RV like yours didn't hurt. Either the parks checked their registration forms after the news and called in or the police called the local parks. Either way, it didn't take long to find you."

"Why come so early in the morning?"

"It's the ideal time to catch a suspect at home. You wake them up and they're sleepy. Many suspects slip and say something they wouldn't say if they were clear-headed."

"How did you know they were coming for me?"

"Suffice it to say I have my sources. Do you understand now why I was in such a hurry? Another few minutes and you'd have been history."

"Yes. Thanks." Leila looked down at her robe. "Aren't I going to be a little conspicuous running around in my robe?"

"There'll be clothes for you at the motel."

"What motel? Don't you ever give information without my prying it out of you?"

"Mr. and Mrs. John Walker are going to check-in to a motel on the other side of town. When we do, there's no need for you to accompany me to the office. I'll spirit you into the room so no one will see you. Later, a colleague will bring clothes and a wig to disguise you."

"Isn't it a little early to check into a motel?"

"We've been driving all night. We need to get a couple of hours of rest and to freshen up before our meeting this afternoon."

"Here we go again. What meeting?"

"Whatever meeting you want to go to, Mrs. Walker."

Leila sighed. "Okay, so I'm not used to this cloak-and-dagger stuff."

Leila's phone chimed.

"I told you to shut that thing off."

"I was going to and then you got into the car and distracted me. Can I ..."

Before she completed the sentence, Zack grabbed the phone and threw it out the window. Leila heard it smash on the road.

"What the hell did you do that for?"

"You're a slow learner. You just missed being arrested. You would have been if I hadn't forced you to move. When I say to do something, you do it immediately. Ask questions later."

Leila folded her arms across her chest. "So, if you tell me to jump, I ask how high?"

"No, that's a question. You jump first, then ask how high."

"That makes a lot of sense."

"If you were hiking in the desert with a friend and the friend told you to freeze, you'd continue walking and ask why. The friend wouldn't have to answer because by then, the rattlesnake would have already bitten you."

Leila ignored his jibe. "What's so important about turning off the damn phone anyway?"

"Because it has a GPS locator. They can hack into your phone and know exactly where you are. There's no point in my trying to hide you if you're going to lead them straight to the door."

"Whose 'they'?"

"Whoever wants to find you. The cops. The people who injected you. Take your pick."

"Then why tell me to bring my phone?"

"Your phone has a wealth of information on it: your

contacts, the call history, access to your email and social accounts, to name a few. A hacker may already have retrieved that info, but there was no sense leaving it behind in case they hadn't."

"And what about the contact information I've lost?"

"What good is it to you now? How many people on the contacts list did you plan on calling again?"

Leila didn't respond immediately. She wasn't thinking her best. Of course, she wouldn't need the information stored on the phone. It belonged to the old Leila. Except for Jeff. She'd never had any real hope of continuing their relationship, but their time together at the park had been the one normal interlude in her life since this nightmare had begun. Now that was gone. Losing contact with Jeff chipped away at hopes for an ordinary life if that were even possible.

"I still need my doctor's and lawyer's numbers," Leila said peevishly.

"Look them up in a phone book or on the Internet."

Leila let it go. It was her surly attitude that bothered her now. She was acting childishly. She didn't need to bother Zack with questions she was perfectly capable of figuring out the answer to. If she'd felt at odds with herself before, as she'd told Dr. Schwartz, the abrupt morning wakeup and the flight hadn't improved her disposition.

They reached downtown Tucson as dawn broke on the horizon. Despite the early hour, the city was coming to life with businesses preparing to open, deliveries being made, and workers who wanted to get a jump start on their day. Zack pulled into a three-story high-rise parking structure.

"Before you ask," he said, "we're here to change cars. We don't want anyone recognizing this Honda as the same vehicle we'll use at the motel."

"How would anyone be able to do that? The only cars we saw near the park were the police cars."

"Remember the drone? Switching cars is one of those better-safe-than-sorry measures."

Zack drove up to the second level of the parking structure and parked next to an older model Ford Focus. Leila cringed at the faded tan color and the dents on the side of the car and rear bumper.

"Is that thing safe? It's in awful shape."

Zack laughed. "Only on the outside. It's meant to look like a clunker. Under the hood is a high-performance engine in perfect condition."

When Zack opened his door, Leila opened hers. "No," he said. "Close the door and stay in the car until I tell you to come." Leila didn't argue this time.

Zack walked over to the Ford, opened the driver's door, and started the engine. He got out again and went to the passenger side to open the door. As he did, a car squealed around the corner. Zack waited until the car passed. The driver never looked in his direction as it drove by. Zack hastily opened the passenger door.

"Come quickly," he called to Leila.

Once Leila was in the Ford, Zack locked the Honda with the remote and backed out of the parking space. "Was that car looking for us?"

"I don't think so. Guy was dressed in a business suit, not the usual dress for thugs."

As they drove to the motel, Leila said, "Dr. Schwartz told me you had military training, but you're not any regular soldier or sailor. Were you in one of those special groups like the Seals?"

"You ask too many questions."

"You're sidestepping the question. Does that mean you're not going to answer me?"

"That's what it means."

Chapter 27 Henry Hoover

Henry Hoover, the scientist who had created the age-regressing compound, turned on the morning news while he ate breakfast. He was specifically watching for any report of another missing person. Since Miles hadn't wanted to inject another test subject too soon after Anna, Henry didn't expect to see one, but he liked to stay informed.

The news of Anna's disappearance on the news so startled Henry that he dropped his coffee and the cup shattered on the floor. The disappearance itself was bad enough; that the police had found her "abandoned" RV upset him even more.

Apparently, there had been a news report last night about her disappearance, asking viewers to call the police if they had seen Anna, or Leila as they referred to her, or her RV. Henry cursed himself for missing the news; one of the few occasions when he'd gone home, exhausted from the day's intensive work, and fallen asleep early.

The update he was watching reported that police had found the RV right here in Tucson but not Anna. The newscast left him hungry for more answers. What was she doing in Tucson? Why did the police think her RV had been abandoned? Where was Anna? Was he in danger of being exposed?

In a panic, he pushed the rest of his breakfast aside and called Miles.

Chapter 28 Grayson Loses Anna

The workday started early for Miles. He was still on the patio outside his library enjoying the eggs benedict his chef had prepared when the phone rang on his private line. He threw his napkin on the table in disgust. As he walked across the room to his desk, he said to the unknown caller, "This better be urgent or you're fired."

"Uh, Sir, this is Harv, I mean Harvey, from the surveillance team. I know it's very early, and uh, and it's not protocol to call you, but um, there's a development I thought you'd want to know about right away."

Miles rolled his eyes at Harvey's nervousness. "What is it?"

"I think we've lost track of her, Sir."

"Lost track of whom?"

"Anna, Sir, I think we lost track of Anna."

"How the hell did you manage that?"

Confidence returned when the topic changed to the specifics of his job. "The tracker on the RV is still working. It's the phone I'm concerned about. It showed her on the move at 6:07 this morning. That's daybreak in Tucson. The indicator moved quickly, too quickly for her to be walking, so I assume she was in a car. Then it suddenly stopped."

"Where?"

"That's the odd part. It stopped in front of undeveloped space. After that, we lost all contact. She may have turned the phone off, which she's never done before, or something happened to the phone itself and it's no longer working. We left the channel open on our end, but there hasn't been any further activity."

"Continue to keep the channel open. As to your breaking protocol ..."

Harvey's muscles tightened, afraid he was about to hear he was fired.

"... you made the right choice by calling me. I want you to call me immediately if the phone turns on again."

Harvey punched his right arm into the air after the call disconnected. If the boss thought him capable of making the right choices, maybe he'd see a pay raise or a promotion in his future.

The loss of the ability to track Anna via her phone bothered Miles. So much of his intel had come from that phone. The news worsened when his phone rang a second time.

It took Miles over half an hour to calm Henry. Of paramount concern to Henry was his personal safety and safeguarding his formula. Henry had been a prominent research scientist at Yale when he pushed the envelope with unauthorized experiments on the brain. Henry believed he was on the verge of discovering how to stop aging or at least impede the process. He'd injected two patients with an unapproved drug. Both had died. Although he avoided legal prosecution, the university fired him. As word spread about his rogue behavior, it became impossible to find work in either the public or private sectors. That's when Miles stepped in.

Miles had offered him an astronomical salary, a state-of-the-art lab, and freedom to run his experiments without consequence. The two conditions Miles imposed were that Henry keep his work secret and work not only on stopping aging but on regressing it. Henry had jumped at the opportunity.

Miles assured Henry that the surveillance team kept him posted on Anna's movement and explained Anna's intent to disappear. What he didn't mention was that he thought it was way too soon for her disappearance. He assumed the lawyer had found a legal avenue to change her identity. It was possible that all the forms had been filled out, and the lawyer was waiting for fingerprint confirmation on her real identity before moving forward. She'd been fingerprinted less than a week ago; bureaucracy operated slowly.

Not wanting to rely on Henry's babbling, Miles called a research assistant. "There were reports last night and this morning on Tucson news, Channel 13. I want everything you can find about a missing woman named Leila Petterson and I want it in the next 15 minutes."

"Yes, Sir."

While he waited for the report, Miles drummed his fingers on the desktop. Henry's question about why the news had labeled the RV as an abandoned vehicle also bothered him. If Anna had implemented her disappearance act, fine, but he had reservations about the timing, not to mention the mystery of what happened to her phone. Of course, she may simply have ditched it as part of the disappearance, but he was meticulous and didn't like guesswork. He picked up his phone again and called a source inside the Tucson police department. Using more diplomatic tones, Miles asked the source to find out why the police considered the RV abandoned and to call back as soon as possible.

His research assistant called back in ten minutes. The information he'd found confirmed Henry's, although the assistant presented the information in a logical format without Henry's emotional reactions. Soon after, his police source called. The police suspected the vehicle had been abandoned for two reasons. One, inside her RV, they found Leila's purse with her wallet which still contained her driver's license and credit cards. It was not something a woman left behind, unless that woman wanted to cut off the possibility of being tracked, such as by usage of a credit card. The police believed an imposter kept up the pretense of being Leila until the news broke the story about Leila's disappearance.

The other factor, the informant continued, was the hungry cat they found inside. During an interview with a friend of Leila's, the woman said Leila would never leave her cat, and the police reasoned that an imposter had no such qualms. The informant also mentioned that the police planned to impound the RV the next day for the CSI team to comb through it.

Miles thanked his source for the information and for the quick response. "As usual, you'll find a cash donation for your services mailed to your residence."

Miles picked up a glass paperweight from his desk and threw it against the wall where it shattered into pieces. First, the team lost contact with her phone; now Anna herself had disappeared. Miles fumed. He'd rather enjoyed his cat-and-mouse game with her. No more. A schoolteacher had outwitted him? Intolerable. He'd have his surveillance team focus on finding Anna again. It was time to terminate her.

Chapter 29   Hiding in a Motel

While Miles fielded early morning phone calls, Zack and Leila pulled into a Motel 6 parking lot. After Zack registered, he drove to a room toward the rear of the motel. As soon as they were safely in the room, Leila sank into a chair.

"Zack, I know I upset you. I'm sorry."

Zack turned to face her and crossed his arms across his chest. "I recognize you are in a difficult situation. You are caught in a game where you don't know the rules. I am used to working with professionals who are capable of thinking on their feet, not someone who can't figure out they can look up a doctor's telephone number in a phone book." Leila cringed. "I also am not used to having to explain or answer questions about everything I do, especially in an urgent situation. If I am to continue to help you personally, we are going to play by my rules. Rule #1 is that when I tell you to do something, you do it. Period. Rule #2 is that you don't ask personal questions. This is not a social 'getting to know you' situation. If I want you to know something, I'll share the information voluntarily." Zack lowered his arms. "I'm going out now to get us some breakfast. While I'm gone, you need to decide if you'll agree to play by my rules, those just stated and any others that may follow. Do not answer the door or the phone or peek out the window. And don't ask why not. Figure it out for yourself."

When Zack closed the door, the tears that had been collecting in Leila's eyes spilled over. She wiped them away impatiently. The tears had formed not from Zack's reprimand per se, but from the image she saw of herself mirrored in his words. She should have known from the minute Zack said the police had come to arrest her that she was in way over her head. She should have recognized before that, from Zack's urgency and the force he used to get her away from the RV, that she was no longer in control. Yet she'd hampered his efforts from the beginning by stalling, like asking questions about Hobie, instead of getting into the car.

Then instead of being grateful for his rescuing her, she'd badgered him with questions like an annoying child wanting attention. She could deduce the answers herself to many of the questions she'd asked if she'd taken a moment to think before letting the words dribble out of her mouth. She knew, for example, that her phone had GPS because she used it while traveling, watching the indicator on the map move as she did; she also knew smartphones could be hacked. Instead of putting two and two together herself, she challenged him with questions because she hadn't turned the phone off when he told her to. The worst was whining about losing the doctor's and lawyer's numbers.

In the past weeks, as she'd been capable of doing, she'd perceived problems and analyzed potential solutions. Up until this morning, that is. Before she simply tried to avoid the police; now they were actively chasing her and she had no idea how to evade them. Zack did. He had a wealth of resources at his fingertips. Questioning Zack, challenging him, had been little more than a vain attempt to make her feel part of the resolution. Pride kept her from relinquishing control. Looking at herself through his eyes, she didn't blame him one bit for being annoyed with her. On the contrary, she admired his patience.

Leila decided to shower and let the hot water wash away some of the stress. It wasn't until she stepped out of the shower and water from her hair dripped on her shoulders that she realized she had neither comb nor brush, nor skin lotion, nor a toothbrush. No transportation, no credit cards, no money, no clothes. Her whole world consisted of a pair of pajamas, a robe, and the flip-flops she'd stuffed her feet into at the last minute.

Hearing a knock on the door, she quickly put on her robe. Zack was back. Another knock and a muffled "Food." What if he needed help getting the door open while carrying two breakfasts and Styrofoam cups filled with hot coffee? She should open the door. No. She should peek out the window first to make sure it was him. No. There she was again trying to take control, doing what she thought best in defiance of what he'd told her. She sat down on the edge of the bed and waited.

Leila heard the door key turn. Zack opened the door, holding a cardboard carrier with two large cups of coffee in one hand while pulling the key out with the other. He threw the keys on the bed and bent down to pick up a paper bag before entering, then kicked the door shut with his foot.

"You passed the first test," he said as he put the food on the table.

After breakfast, Zack went outside while Leila cleaned up the mess on the table. She wanted to ask him why he needed to go outside, she wanted to peek out the window to see what he was doing, she wanted to ask him about getting the clothes he'd mentioned a colleague would bring, she wanted to ask him about her future. Hard as it was, she did none of those things. She plopped down on one of the double beds and turned on the TV.

After consulting the program guide, which listed only a few interesting choices at this time of day, she settled on a rerun of the old Matlock series. She liked mysteries. The show had barely introduced Matlock's case for the episode when commercials interrupted it. She ignored them and looked around the room. The room was standard for a middling-priced motel: two double beds with a built-in side table between them, a small table and two chairs, a bureau with a TV on one end and a large mirror attached to the wall on the other, white walls, blue printed bedspreads, and what passed as art on the walls. In short, boring. She thought longingly of her homey RV which, of course, made her think of Hobie and how much she missed him. She had to ask Zack about him; she had to. Surely, she was allowed one question.

Zack came in and handed his phone to her. "It's Sandra. She has some questions for you." He lay down on the other bed and changed the TV channel.

"Hello?"

"Hi, Leila. I'm going clothes shopping for you, but I need your sizes. Pants?"

"Size 10."

"A generous size 10 or a lean size 10?"

"Lean."

"Tops?"

"Medium, or large if necessary. I don't like them tight."

On they went through a list of basic clothes.

"As to style, do you like cutesy, frilly, sexy, plain, in vogue?"

"That's a tough one. Not cutesy or frilly. Does plain, in vogue make sense?"

"Yup. I also understand you need basic toiletries: a toothbrush and that kind of stuff. What about hair products? Zack says your hair looks like you stuck your finger in a wall socket."

Leila laughed so hard she struggled to catch her breath. "Thanks for that. I don't think I've laughed in weeks. He's right. I have curly hair which frizzes up without a good conditioner. A comb does wonders to help it, too."

"A comb, not a brush?"

"A wide-toothed comb works best. A brush tends to frizz it."

"It likely won't matter too much since the wig is going to flatten it."

"Oh. Didn't think about a wig."

"I'll bring a bunch of them, and you can pick. Zack said he thinks a dark color is best because it's a contrast to your natural color."

"Dark is fine, as in brunette, but not black. Black is too harsh and will look unnatural with my coloring."

"Got 'ca. See you in a while."

After Leila hung up, she leaned over to hand the phone back to Zack.

"What had you laughing so hard?"

"I understand you think my hair looks like I stuck my finger in a wall socket."

"It does."

"I agree. It's just that you said it. Joking is a side of you I'm not familiar with. Zack, may I ask you one question that's important to me?"

"Shoot."

"Hobie. What's happened to him?"

"I'm still tracking down the answer to that. I'll let you know as soon as I hear something, okay?"

"Thank you."

Zack stood up and stretched. "Here's the general plan for the day. I'm leaving now to tend to business. Sandra will call me when she's ready to bring the clothes over, and I'll come back because ..." He pointed at me to finish the sentence.

"Because I am not to answer the door or answer the phone or peek out the window."

Zack nodded. "I'll leave again while you try on clothes and wigs and such. The rest of the schedule depends on the time of day all that is finished."

"Okay."

"You'll be safe."

"Okay."

"No questions?"

"I have a million of them, but I'm not going to aggravate you with them."

Zack grinned. On his way out, he hung a Do Not Disturb sign on the doorknob.

Chapter 30   Zack's Involvement

Zack drove to Dr. Schwartz's residence and let himself in with a key. Dr. Schwartz looked up from his desk in the study.

"Good morning, Zack."

"Mornin', Doc."

"Want to join me for a cup of coffee?"

"I would, but I'd like to shower and change first. You'd better make that a pot of coffee. We have a lot to discuss if you have the time."

"I assume you're going to let me in on the full situation with Leila."

"Yes."

"Go shower. I'll meet you in the living room when you're ready."

After a leisurely shower, Zack and Dr. Schwartz sat comfortably in armchairs in the living room with a pot of coffee and a plate of pastries on the table between them.

"Because of the situation with the police and your security clearance," Zack said, "my CO has permitted me to bring you in on the case I'm working on. We believe Leila is key to the case and needs protection. Here's the background. Tucson has a long history of people who go missing in the desert. Some are hikers who get lost, some are injured, some aren't prepared for the desert sun and heat, like not bringing enough water with them to stay hydrated, and some are caught in flash floods. Criminals also use the desert to hide bodies. The category we're most interested in is the impaired individuals, usually seniors, who wander into the desert and can't find their way home."

Dr. Schwartz nodded. "The news issues a Silver Alert when they go missing but seldom discloses any follow-up information."

"That's the advantage of using the desert to hide nefarious activity. In the past year, the number of missing seniors has escalated significantly. They're the 'retired nobodies' as Leila called herself."

"Ah. I remember your reaction to her saying that."

Zack leaned over to pour more coffee. "This is so much better than the crap I drank this morning." He lifted the pot toward the doctor. "Want another cup?"

"I've had enough for the moment. I'm much more interested in your story. Please continue."

"I'm here to investigate why so many more seniors are going missing. I'd been researching their individual lives looking for common threads. Leila gave me my first insightful clue when she called herself a 'nobody.' They were all nobodies; that was the common link. After retirement, they didn't belong to any organizations or groups, so they had no social affiliations aside from a few friends or family if they had one. No one raised a public fuss about their disappearances. The authorities shrugged off the incidents as unfortunate individual accidents and their deaths attributed to dementia. The group became an ideal target; they were expendable without drawing public attention. I, we, believe many of them are victims."

"Victims?"

"My CO's uncle retired to Tucson because of its warmer climate. He didn't have dementia, but he was a docile man with an IQ in the low range of normal. When he first arrived, during a nature walk in the desert, he fell into a prickly pear cactus. As you know, their pads are full of needles which can be painful if inserted into human skin. The man was taken to the emergency room to have all the needles removed."

"A rather unpleasant experience."

"After that, he refused to walk anywhere near the desert. Six months ago, his body was found in an isolated area a mile or two into the desert. The police listed his death as an accident; my CO suspected foul play. He contacted the police with his suspicions, but they ignored him. He decided to look into senior deaths in the desert himself."

"And found too many of them so he dispatched you to look into it."

"Exactly. When Leila referred to herself as a 'retired

nobody,' I realized that's what all the victims had in common; they were easy marks. I'm sure some of the missing seniors met with accidents, but they all shared common traits: age, mental incapacity, loners. Even if they lived with family, they were left on their own most of the day."

"Leila doesn't exactly fit your profile."

"Yes and no. Her age and single status fit, but not the mental incapacity. When I learned her story, I began to wonder if they'd upped their game. She'd been injected with an unknown compound. What if the others had been, too, and the missing seniors were experiments? A flaw in their protocol was using subjects with diminished mental capacity."

"And you have no idea who 'they' is?"

"Not yet."

Dr. Schwartz rested his bent arms across his chest, folded his hands together with his index fingers pointed upward, and tapped the index fingers against his chin. Zack took advantage of the lull to help himself to a pastry.

After a few minutes, the doctor said, "Very interesting idea. As the mastermind of the body, age regression must involve the brain. I agree with you that a normal healthy brain would respond better. Does your theory include why a test subject was chosen from Benson rather than Tucson?"

"I believe they started vetting potential candidates.

They needn't have limited themselves to Tucson. Leila was smart; she kept herself as much as possible off the grid after the injection, but believe me, they're tracking her."

"Do you think she was the first in their revised protocol?"

"That I don't know, but she is the only one I've found. The CO likes my theory which is why he authorized funds and resources to keep her safe."

"Does Leila know any of that?"

"No, although she asked me if I was in Special Forces."

"Did you tell her?"

"No. I told her not to ask me personal questions."

Dr. Schwartz raised an eyebrow.

"She was driving me crazy during the extraction. She didn't follow orders and questioned everything I did. When we got to the motel, I gave her an ultimatum. Either she shape up or I was gone."

"You do realize how difficult this must be for her."

"I do, but I can't work with an albatross around my neck. Surprising, she responded well."

"That doesn't surprise me. She perceives you as her lifeline."

Zack's phone rang. He glanced at the display before answering with a "Yeah?" He listened, then said, "Meet you there in 30 minutes. I have a stop to make on the way. Would you mind stopping at McDonald's or whatever fast-food place you like and buy us all some lunch?" After a "Thanks," he stood up as he disconnected the call. "Got to run, Doc. That was Sandra. She's ready to bring Leila some clothes."

"And Leila can't answer the door herself?"

"She's under strict orders not to."

Dr. Schwartz stood to walk Zack to the door. "You know you can't leave Leila in that motel by herself for too long."

"She's safe."

"And bored and scared. She's living in a cage. Think about it."

Chapter 31   A New Look

Sandra was waiting for Zack when he pulled into a space in front of the motel room. He helped her unload the car. Leila eyed the shopping bags as they brought them in and deposited them on the bed and eagerly opened one.

"We eat first," Zack said.

"I bought Mc's combo meals, a McDouble for you, Zack," Sandra said as she distributed the food. She and Leila sat down on the two available chairs; Zack sat on the edge of the bed. Conversation was limited as they dug into their food.

Leila broke the silence. "I'm surprised I'm so hungry. I haven't done anything but watch TV."

"I always get hungry when I'm not doing anything. It's like my body's saying, 'Do something.' Isn't that why most people snack while they're watching TV?"

"And that's why those extra pounds start accumulating," Zack said as he rolled up his food wrappers and tossed them into a wastebasket. "I'll take my Coke with me. Before I leave, Leila, I have a present for you." Zack reached into his pocket and pulled out a phone.

Leila clapped her hands in delight.

"It's a burner phone, so you don't have to worry about anyone tracking it. I bought it using my name so it can't be traced back to you that way either."

Leila hugged the phone to her chest. "Thank you, Zack. I don't feel so alone now. I know I don't have many people I can call, but I do need to contact my attorney, or I can call for help if I need it."

"I already programmed my number and the Doc's into it. I entered your number into my phone, too, and will give the number to Doc. I'm off again to let you girls do the clothes thing. Call me, Sandra, when you're done."

The afternoon surpassed Leila's expectations. She had envisioned Sandra as another Zack: close-mouthed and serious. She was the opposite. They laughed, exclaimed over clothes that looked good on her, and made silly faces over the ones that didn't. Their camaraderie revived Leila's spirits.

"Don't worry about the clothes you don't like," Sandra said. "I can return them."

"You did a great job picking them out. I like almost everything. Those pants that were too loose and the top that was too tight are definite no's. I especially like these jeans." Leila twisted to see the back of them in the mirror. "I love the pockets."

"A tasteful bit of bling never hurts. Now to the wigs. They were harder to pick. Never having seen you, I didn't know the style or color to pick. On top of that was guessing size. They need to be snug, so they don't fall off, but not too tight or you'll get a headache."

They rejected some as soon as Leila put them on her head. Others they separated into a "possible" pile. Toward the end, Leila tried on a wig a few shades darker than her natural color minus the auburn red.

"I love it!" Sandra exclaimed. "First of all, the color is right for your complexion, and it contrasts your natural look: straight hair, instead of curly; short instead of shoulder length. The cut is cute, too. What do you think?"

"I like it, too. I look so different."

"That's the point, isn't it? How does it feel?"

"Comfortable. Snug, but not too tight."

Sandra walked around Leila to see how she looked on all sides. "Yup. That's the one."

Leila turned her head from side to side. "I wish I could see it from the back."

"I've got a small compact mirror in my purse," Sandra said as she walked to the table and took out the compact. "Not the best, but better than nothing."

She handed Leila the compact who held it up and turned from side to side catching glimpses of herself in the large mirror over the bureau.

"Go to the bathroom. You'll be closer to the mirror and the light's better."

"What do you think?" Sandra asked when Leila emerged from the bathroom.

Leila spread her arms wide apart and held them up. "Meet the new me."

"Good. I think it's by far the best one you tried on. Let's get all the rejects together and pack them up."

"Sandra, do you know who's paying for all these?"

Sandra stopped her packing. "Sorry. I don't know anything about your situation except that you're here. Zack is a needs-to-know man. He tells me to go shopping, I go shopping. I will be turning the receipts over to him if that helps."

Leila waved her hand to pretend the question wasn't important, even though it was to her. When they finished packing, Leila hugged Sandra.

"Thanks for everything you did today. I haven't had such a pleasant afternoon in weeks."

"I had fun, too. I'm supposed to call Zack before I go. Are you going to be all right by yourself?"

"Sure. I'll cut the tags off my new clothes and hang ... Now how am I going to do that?"

"I thought of that." She rummaged around her purse. "Here they are." She pulled out a small pair of scissors. "I figured anyone who didn't have a toothbrush wasn't going to have a pair of scissors. They're cheap but should work."

"You're very efficient."

Sandra smiled but focused her attention on calling Zack. "I'm leaving now," she told him. The rest of her part of conservation consisted of "uh-huh." She looked askance at the phone and hung up. "That man. He never says goodbye; just hangs up when he's done. Anyway, he said he'd be by later and you're supposed to watch the Channel 13 news."

Leila turned on the TV to Channel 13 and began cutting tags off her new clothes, starting with the ones she was wearing. She redressed in those, including the wig. As she did, she wondered who was paying not only for the clothes, but for the motel room, the food, and the phone as well. She'd been tempted to ask Sandra more questions but hadn't when Sandra said she didn't know anything about Leila's situation because Zack was a needs-to-know man. Yes, he was that, too much so. She wished he was a little more sympathetic to her plight. Maybe now that she wasn't pestering him, he'd loosen up a bit.

The news continued: two car crashes, a shooting, a city council meeting about some issue or other, the weather forecast. Leila generally watched the news, but she wondered why Zack specifically wanted her to see it. Then it came.

The news anchor said, "Police have not released any new information on the disappearance of Leila Petterson, but we have a heartwarming note this evening. We take you to our reporter on the scene. Felipa?"

The picture switched to a closeup of the reporter and Wendy. Wendy? Leila moved to the end of the bed to be closer to the TV.

"I'm standing here with Leila's good friend, Wendy Nelson. Wendy, do you have a comment you'd like to share?"

"I wish more than anything in the world that I could see my old friend again, but I worry ..." The words caught in Wendy's throat. "I worry I won't after the police found her cat abandoned in the RV. Leila would never do that."

The camera pulled back to reveal they were standing in front of the animal shelter. Wendy cradled Hobie in her arms. He seemed content to be with someone he knew after the strange hands and places he'd passed through during the day.

"The police arranged for me to take Hobie home with me," Wendy continued. "I'll take care of him for her. It's the least I can do for my friend."

The rest of the reporter's words were lost as the picture of Hobie mesmerized Leila.

"Oh, baby, you're okay. I wish you were here with me, but Wendy will take good care of you. Wendy, thank you, thank you, thank you. You did come through for me."

Leila dissolved into tears and stared blankly at the TV long after the news had moved on to another story. When Leila heard the door lock click open, she brushed away the tears and took a deep breath to calm herself. Zack stepped in and locked the door behind him. He didn't move for several seconds. Finally, he walked over to Leila.

"You've been crying."

"I saw the news blurb about Wendy taking Hobie home with her." Leila looked up at Zack and smiled. "I miss him terribly, but now I know he's okay. Wendy will take good care of him. How did you know ..." She hand-erased her words. "No. No questions. You said you'd track down what happened to him, and you did. You told me you'd let me know when you found him, and you did. What's most important is that I know he's safe. Thank you, Zack."

Zack sat down at the table. "Leila, I'm not immune to the turmoil you must feel because of the predicament you're in. I can either work on solving your problem or spend time answering questions. Wouldn't you rather I spend the time finding a solution? I'm sure, for example, that you want to know what's going to happen to you from here on. I don't know at this point. When I do, I'll tell you. There's no sense in wasting time talking about possibilities. Be aware, too, that I can't tell you everything I know. You've already deduced that I'm not an ordinary soldier or sailor. You're right; I'm not. Exactly what or who I am, I can't tell you."

"I've realized what a pain I must have been this morning before we got to the motel."

Zack grinned. "You were, but I'm over it. You've been cooperative since then. Now stand up and let me take a look at you." Zack eyed her up and down. "Now turn around slowly." When she finished a complete rotation, he said, "You sure look a lot different than the girl I met at Doc's."

"Having clothes that fit makes a big difference."

"So does the wig. It suits you. If I didn't know any different, I'd think it was your natural hair." Zack stood up. "I originally stopped by to ask you what kind of food you wanted for dinner. I've changed my mind. How would you like to go out to dinner?"

"What if the police recognize me?"

"They won't. I had to pause when I walked in the door, and I knew it was you. You're ready to be seen in public."

Chapter 32 Avoiding Detection

Miles mulled over the intel from his informant that the police planned to impound Anna's RV the next day for the CSI team to comb through it. He was positive they hoped to find fingerprints or DNA evidence such as hair fibers to identify the imposter. That wouldn't do at all. He knew the only fingerprints they'd find would be Anna's. He didn't know if Anna's fingerprints were in the system, but one set of fingerprints meant only one person had been living in the RV. There should be two sets: Anna's and the imposter's. The police would be confused by the results at first, but they'd open an investigation and start nosing around. Worse, their findings became a record. Miles didn't want either an investigation or an official record that hinted at the possibility that Leila and Anna were the same person. Eliminating Anna was the best solution. If they found her body, case closed. Unfortunately, he didn't know where she was.

On occasion, Miles needed to resort to unsavory methods to achieve a specific goal. He never dealt with criminal acts himself or left a trail that led to his doorstep. Long ago, he'd established contacts in the underworld to execute illicit acts, crime bosses who delegated the actual work to his underlings, another layer that insulated Miles. To avoid being traced, Miles used a code name and a burner phone when speaking to these individuals. He also paid handsomely to ensure their cooperation and his anonymity.

After locking the hall door and closing off the French doors to seal the library, he removed a burner phone from his safe and called a contact in Tucson. Miles explained that he needed an RV destroyed that same night, he didn't care how as long as it looked like an accident and gave the contact the address.

The crime boss balked at the short notice and the difficulty of the assignment. Destroying an RV didn't pose a problem; it was destroying it in the middle of an RV park near other vehicles that created the problem. Miles had suspected the boss might complain, so he'd quoted a price lower than what he expected to pay.

"Are you saying you can't handle the job?" Miles asked.

"No, but you left us little time to plan. With sufficient time to plan, it's a one-man job. I'm going to have to hire more guys to get this done tonight." He stressed the "tonight."

"Is that your way of asking for more money?"

They tossed figures back and forth and settled on an amount equal to Miles's original assessment of what the job cost. Miles smiled. Negotiation had always been one of his strengths.

Miles's last call of the night was to Henry to warn him not to worry when the news covered the RV accident. As expected, Henry argued, asking why it was necessary to make such a daring public move that risked exposure.

"It won't be traced back to me, Henry, just as your experiments haven't been traced back to you. No one suspects what we're doing. I have this end handled. I want you to stick to the science. We're ready to inject Adam; a team is already in place. I'm in the process of choosing the next baseline test subjects. I assume you want both men and women to gauge if sex affects the outcome?"

"You're pushing me, Miles. I'll be working with the results that come in about Adam. I can only do so much at a time."

"I'm getting tired of waiting. You know the compound works. You only need to determine the correct dosages and that's data analysis. Hire more assistants if you need help with that."

Chapter 33   Breakdown

Leila stretched leisurely in bed and greeted the morning with a smile. Zack had said she could open the blinds to let the daylight in or walk to the motel's coffee shop for breakfast, if she wore her wig. He didn't want her wandering too far yet. It wasn't a lot of freedom, but a world better than the nightmare of 24 hours ago.

The first item on her agenda was to call her attorney for an update when his office opened. She glanced at the small digital clock on the bedside table next to her and sat up abruptly. His office had opened an hour ago! She had slept in later than normal. That wasn't surprising after yesterday's sudden changes and emotional upheavals. Her body had needed the rest.

Leila automatically looked around for Hobie who was always there to greet her, waiting for her to get up and feed him. She had to stop thinking like that. She'd never stop missing him, but she knew Wendy was a wonderful substitute and would love him and take care of his needs.

She had to stop dwelling on what wasn't, what she couldn't control, and be more positive about her future, a future that depended a great deal on Mr. Bradshaw.

She pushed the bed linens aside, sat up, and picked up her phone.

Mr. Bradshaw had news, some of it good. The fingerprints taken at the Tucson lab matched those on file with the state. Of course, she knew they would. The good news was that the judge was ready to work on her new identification papers. The process was stalled until she provided her new name, date of birth, and a photo. Mr. Bradshaw also needed her to come to his office and sign the trust papers before he could file them.

Both those requests presented problems. The obvious one was getting to Mr. Bradshaw's office. The RV was off limits, so she needed transportation, and a photo caused a dilemma. She no longer had a smartphone to take a selfie. To go somewhere to have a photo taken, she had to wear her wig which squashed her natural hair, which would make her look awful, perhaps unrecognizable. She didn't plan on wearing the wig forever, so she didn't want her photo taken with the wig on. The new identification was useless if she didn't look like herself.

"You seem rather calm this morning despite the news about your RV," Mr. Bradshaw said. "I've been worried about you. I tried calling, but you didn't answer your phone."

"My old phone died." Leila grimaced remembering how it died. "Let me give you my new number."

After she did, she zeroed in on the first part of his

statement. "What do you mean about the news of my RV this morning?"

Mr. Bradshaw paused. "Weren't you staying in your RV?"

"No. I'm temporarily at a motel."

"And you didn't see the news this morning?"

"No. I woke up about 15 minutes ago. I had an exhausting day yesterday."

"I'm sorry to be the one to tell you this. Your RV was destroyed by fire last night."

Leila shot to her feet. "What?"

"A propane leak started the fire. Neighbors saw the flames and called the fire department. Fortunately, they contained the fire before it spread to other vehicles, but yours was a total loss. Pictures on the news showed only the sides were partially left standing. The roof had collapsed and the interior was nothing but burnt rubble."

As Mr. Bradshaw spoke, the volume of his voice weakened as though he was talking from a greater and greater distance. Leila's head spun. She sank to the bed and said nothing when the attorney stopped speaking.

"Leila, are you still there?"

She managed to squeak out a "Yes."

"I imagine this is quite a shock. Again, I'm sorry. Do you want me to call someone for you?"

Another squeak. "No."

"You're having trouble speaking. Take your time to

absorb the news and call me back when you feel better."

Leila didn't answer and Mr. Bradshaw disconnected.

The nightmare had returned. Piece by piece her life had been taken away from her until she was little more than a helpless waif in a personal war zone, a war she had little chance of winning. She'd woken up less than an hour ago determined to be positive. It didn't take long for that to be taken away from her either. Her phone rang. Her finger automatically switched it on.

"Leila?" she heard a voice from a distance. She looked around the room but saw no one. "Leila? Answer me." She recognized that commanding voice and looked down at the phone resting in her lap. Slowly, she raised it.

"What?" she said. "What's the point? It's too far to walk to Benson and I don't want my photo taken with the wig on."

Zack realized she was on the verge of going into shock or already had.

"Leila, get dressed and be ready to go. I'll be there soon to pick you up. Do you understand?"

"I'll never get my RV back now like I was supposed to."

"Leila, you agreed to play by my rules, remember?" Leila nodded, as though he could see her response. "You agreed to follow my commands. What did I just tell you to do?"

"Get dressed."

"You do that now and then wait in the room for me to get there. Repeat what I just said."

"Get dressed now. Wait for you."

"Wait for me in the room. Don't go outside."

"Wait for you inside."

"Good girl. Go now. Get dressed."

Zack hung up and rushed out of his room calling out to Doc.

"In the kitchen," Doc said. "Had she heard what happened to her RV?" Doc asked as Zack appeared in the doorway.

"Yes. She's lost it," Zack said. "Either in shock or 99% there."

Dr. Schwartz put down the knife he'd been using to cut an apple. "We need to get to her."

"That's exactly what I intend. I wanted you to know. I'll have to bring her back here."

"Of course, you will. Where else? I'm going with you. Let me get my medical bag from the office."

Within minutes, Zack and the doctor were in the car.

"Repeat what she said to you on the phone, Zack."

Zack did, almost verbatim. "It made no sense."

"It might. She was referring to issues that troubled her, only she wasn't giving you the context needed to understand them. That woman has been through too much in a very short time. A breakdown doesn't surprise me. News of the RV triggered it. I'll give her a sedative to calm her, then we'll bring her back here, so she isn't alone. Unless you have some objection, I'd like to let her stay with us. There's plenty of room in the house. I've been worried not only about how many problems she's faced but having to face them by herself in isolation. She's done an amazing job so far, but we all have our limits."

"No objection."

"Good. What about her possessions in the motel room? I'd prefer if she didn't go back there."

"I'll arrange for Sandra to pick them up and transport them if it's okay to give her your address."

"It's public record, so no, I don't object. I might suggest, however, that you disappear while Sandra is at the house. There's no need for her to connect the three of us. I assume you don't have to tell her why she's moving the clothes and other items."

"No. I give the orders, not the explanations. She's used to that."

"When we see Leila, use her name as often as possible to remind her who she is."

When Dr. Schwartz and Zack entered the motel room, they found Leila sitting on the end of the bed staring into space. The doctor hurried to her and put his medical bag down on the bed next to her.

"Leila?"

Leila looked up at him. "You're not Zack."

"That's right, Leila. Do you know who I am?"

Leila blinked. "You're Dr. Schwartz. Zack's gonna be mad again."

"I'm here, too, Leila." Zack stepped into her line of vision. "The Doc was worried about you, so I brought him along."

"I got dressed."

"I see that, Leila. You even remembered to put on your wig. Good job."

"How do you feel, Leila?" the doctor asked.

"Hollow, my insides are missing."

Dr. Schwartz opened his medical bag, pulled out a syringe, and filled it from a small bottle. "I'm going to give you a shot, Leila, to help you feel your insides again."

Leila leaned away from him. "Maybe no. No hurt when I'm hollow."

"How about this, Leila? You let me give you a shot and then Zack will take us back to my house, and we'll all have a good lunch."

"Breakfast first."

"I'll make you breakfast if you prefer."

Leila shrugged. "Okay, then."

The doctor injected her and put the syringe and bottle back into his medical bag and snapped it shut.

"Stand up now, Leila."

Leila wobbled to her feet.

"Hold her steady, Zack, while we get her to the car."

Chapter 34   Pearce

From his list of vetted possibilities, for their second test subject, Miles had chosen a man who lived in Pearce, a rural desert community 85 miles southeast of Tucson. The sparsely populated community was rarely featured in the Tucson news because of the distance from Tucson but close enough to dispatch a team with a drone. In its heyday in the late 1800s and early 1900s, Pearce had been a productive silver-mining town. Its current reputation as a ghost town attracts tourists. The team stayed comfortably at a local hotel posing as tourists while they monitored the subject. No one questioned their fictional forays into the desert to hike or visit the old mines.

The subject, christened Adam, lived alone in a small house on five acres of land outside of town. His favorite pastime was tending to his horse and a garden in the rear of the house, offering the perfect opportunity for the drone to spy on him. All did not go as planned, however, when they sent the drone in close to spray Adam with the inhaled anesthetic to put him to sleep.

"The surveillance team called me a few minutes ago. You're not going to like it, Miles," Henry said.

"The surveillance team has reported good results so far."

"So far. They haven't sent you the latest report. I told them to hold off because I was going to call you."

"They called you before me?" Miles asked with a note of incredulity in his voice.

"Your line was busy, and they wanted to get the news to us ASAP."

When Miles didn't respond, Henry continued. "Adam became aware of the drone. This morning when they sent the drone to his house, he saw it and tried to shoot it down."

Miles sat up straight. "Excuse me?"

"Pictures from the drone show Adam on his back patio with a shotgun leaning against a post. The team didn't react to that because it's common for anyone living in the desert to have a gun handy to kill snakes or other varmints. They'd seen the gun before in the surveillance photos. As the drone came lower than it had before, Adam picked up the shotgun and, in one smooth motion, aimed it at the drone and fired. It nicked the drone and spun it, but the team was able to regain control and get the drone out of there."

"Anna, and now Adam, have turned out to be wildcards."

"I think it was inevitable that complications were going to arise. Our subjects now are mentally healthy. They're aware and capable of reacting."

"Before we get to that, finish with Adam."

"Adam is a failure. Your team never had the opportunity to get the drone close enough to dose him. I suggest we forget him. For whatever reason, possibly the isolation of his home, he became aware of the drone, so he'll grab his rifle if he sees it again. He's a good shot; he may shoot it down the second time. Even if he didn't, he'd likely go to the police because he's smart enough to realize the drone isn't there by accident."

"Our new test subjects won't have the opportunity to go to the police or anyone else. I agree with you that we forget about Adam. Let him think the drone belonged to locals playing around or to tourists using the drone to locate old mines. Once the team snatches and puts a subject to sleep, the mobile unit will take them to the safe house in Tucson where we'll inject them. No more wildcards."

Chapter 35   Police Suspicious

Detective Forbes leaned back in his chair and rested his head in his clasped hands. "You buy that report on the RV fire last night being an accident?"

"Hell, no," Detective Morales said.

"Me neither. We should ask the fire inspector if he can determine exactly where the leak was."

"Already did. Said everything was too burnt to determine the location."

Forbes unclasped his hands and leaned forward. "What bothers you the most about the fire?"

Morales pushed aside the report he'd been working on and looked up at his partner. Their metal desks faced each other to facilitate conversation.

"The timing. Woman disappears one night and the next night the RV goes up in flames? Why return after she made a clean getaway? Why not start the fire as she leaves?"

"But you do agree it was a cover-up?"

"Definitely, but by someone else. Someone who didn't want us to go through the RV. It's a shame we didn't impound it when we found it."

Forbes sighed. "Paperwork. Always does slow us

down. By the way, how did she know about the raid that morning?"

"Not sure. Could have been a coincidence, but I doubt it. A better possibility is that someone leaked the information."

Forbes glanced around the detective room to check his colleagues' whereabouts before asking, "Someone in the department?"

"Hate to admit it, but yeah. That we found out where the RV was parked wasn't a secret, but the raid was."

"You want to keep investigating?"

Morales lowered his voice. "I do, but on the q.t. in case there's a leak in the department. The Missing Persons Report filed by her neighbor said Leila was in her 60s. Driver's license said 62. That's two confirmations of her age: one official and one from someone who knew her. Her neighbor in the Benson RV Park who called in after the news publicized Leila's disappearance said she was young: late twenties, early thirties, he guessed. At this point, we have two different women."

"The younger one took the place of the older one. We already suspected that."

"And if the younger one intended to impersonate Leila and steal the RV after she got rid of her, why go back to Benson? I can understand the younger one registering in an RV park instead of going to Leila's residence, but why not take off for parts unknown where no one's ever heard of Leila Petterson? It makes no sense to go to Benson unless she had a very good reason to."

Forbes nodded his head. "We need to find out what drew her back to Benson. Whatever it was, she must have finished her business and then moved to Tucson.

"Only to burn up the RV and vanish again? Ridiculous. That's why I think someone else torched it. Whatever began this chain of events happened after Leila left on her trip. We need to trace her movements back to her departure."

"How are we going to do that? The neighbors, and her friend Wendy, didn't have a clue where she went."

"We'll check her credit card for gas receipts. They may not tell us exactly where she went, but they'll give us a general area. Something's very off here. I want to find out what."

Chapter 36 Moving

Late in the afternoon on the same day that Leila had been moved from the motel, Zack found Dr. Schwartz in the living room sitting in an armchair with medical journals piled on the table beside him and on the floor. Leila slept peacefully on the couch with a brown and beige Afghan pulled up to her neck.

"How is she?" Zack asked quietly.

"She'll be fine. Her fragmented speech does make sense if we supply the context. She was delighted when I asked her if she'd like to stay here, rather than return to the motel. She said, 'No more alone.' I think we can both easily understand what she meant by that."

Zack nodded.

"You were correct in assuming she was in shock, but it wasn't severe, because her thought process was intact. With rest and in comfortable surroundings, she'll recover quickly."

"Did Sandra bring her clothes?"

"Yes. Thanks for telling Sandra to call when she was on her way. I prefered she didn't see Leila in her current condition. I took Leila to the back garden where she was content to stay while I answered the door. I didn't want to leave her alone for too long, so I asked Sandra to put the clothes in my study and let herself out when she was finished."

While the doctor was talking, Zack stepped over to the other armchair and sat down. He picked up a journal and flipped through the pages.

"And you, Doc? Why are you reading journals here instead of in your study?"

"When Leila wakes up, I want her to see me. It might startle her to wake up in an unfamiliar room. My presence will also assure her she's not alone."

Zack put the journal back on the pile. "With the number of journals you have piled around you, you must be catching up on a couple of years' worth of reading."

Dr. Schwartz laughed. "Not at all. I've already read them all. I'm doing some research for you. After our discussion the other day about the brain's involvement with age regression, I decided to skim through the Table of Contents in each journal. I don't recall reading an article about any research on age regression, but there's no harm in double-checking."

"With what these guys are doing, I doubt they're on the up and up or that they'd advertise their research in a journal."

"I agree. I did, however, set aside a few journals with articles about brain research. I'll reread them for any useful tidbits of information."

Leila stirred. She moved her head from side to side,

then slowly opened her eyes.

"Hi, Dr. Schwartz. Hi, Zack."

"Hi, Leila. Did you sleep well?" the doctor asked. "Yes, thank you." She looked around the room. "I'm not sure why I was sleeping ..." Her face brightened. "Yes, I do. You said I could stay here with you."

"You remember that?"

A cloud passed over Leila's face. "You meant it, didn't you?"

"I certainly did. Zack had your clothes brought here while you were napping."

The smile returned. "Thanks, Zack."

"I'll show you your room," the doctor said as he stood up. "If Zack will help you, you two can move your clothes out of my study and into your room. You might want to freshen up after that, Leila, and I'll go to the kitchen to start dinner."

Leila pushed aside the Afghan and swung her feet to the floor but hesitated before standing up.

"I remember waking up and I remember you telling me I could stay here, but the in-between part is fuzzy."

The doctor sat back down. "You had a shock. It's not unusual for the mind to temporally shut down after a shock. Do you remember hearing about your RV?"

"My RV? I ... Yes. Mr. Bradshaw said a fire had destroyed it. Is that true?" Leila looked from face to face.

"It's true," Zack said.

Leila slumped. "It's gone?"

"Yes. Who is Mr. Bradshaw?"

"He's my attorney." Leila closed her eyes.

Zack was about to ask another question when Dr. Schwartz put a restraining hand on his arm and shook his head.

The grandfather clock in the corner ticked away the minutes. "Is she out again?" Zack whispered to the doctor.

"No. I was thinking," Leila said and opened her eyes. "I called Mr. Bradshaw after I woke up this morning. That's when he told me."

"You told me on the phone that you'd never get your RV back like you were supposed to. What did you mean by that?"

"Don't rush this, Zack," Dr. Schwartz said. "Leila, let's go back to the beginning. Why did you go to an attorney?"

Leila summarized her need for new identification and her hope the attorney could help her. She took them through the developments, from the attorney setting up a trust naming her as the beneficiary to finding a judge who agreed to help with new ID.

"Very clever," the doctor said. "When you said you were supposed to get the RV back, you meant you'd inherit it."

"Yes."

"You also said on the phone something about it being too far to walk to Benson and not wanting a photo with your wig on," Zack said.

Leila explained the need to go to Benson to sign the trust papers, the lack of transportation, and the judge's request for a new name, date of birth, and a photo which she had no idea how to obtain.

"Ah," said Zack. "You didn't want a photo with your wig on because it didn't look like the real you."

"Yes."

"Those problems must have seemed insurmountable," the doctor said. "Then on top of that, the attorney told you about the fire."

Leila nodded her head. "After that, I don't remember too much."

"I must have called you shortly after you spoke to the attorney. You were in zombie land. The Doc and I came to get you."

Leila looked down at the floor. "I'm embarrassed."

"Don't be, my dear. You handled your problems extremely well before then. The stress simply became too much, and your mind needed a rest. Be aware that although we might not have understood your statements at the time, they were logical."

Leila offered a weak smile. "But the problems still exist, don't they?"

"Not anymore. We are here to help you."

"Call the attorney first thing tomorrow and set up an appointment," Zack said. "I'll drive you there myself."

"The photo?"

"We'll take some photos with my iPhone before you put the wig on."

Leila's smile widened.

The doctor stood up again. "Leila, let me show you to your room, then I'm off to the kitchen."

Zack tagged along as the doctor led Leila to her room. It was spacious enough to house a queen-sized bed with two side tables, a dresser opposite the bed with a TV hanging on the wall, and a reading chair in the corner by a large window. Dark furniture and greens, browns, and beiges in the bedspread, chair covers, and curtains screamed masculine décor. With a wave of his hand, the doctor indicated an ensuite bathroom, then excused himself and left. Between Zack and Leila, it only took one trip to transfer Leila's clothes and toiletries from the study to her new room, with Zack carrying the bulk of the bags. Zack dropped the bags on the bed; then he, too, left.

Although Leila preferred lighter colors, the masculine décor didn't bother her. The room was a hundred percent improvement over the motel room. It said 'home' rather than 'commercial.' She began opening bags and hung the clothes in a closet stocked with hangers. After she finished hanging the clothes, there were ten times more hangers left than she had used. Her underwear all fit into one drawer in the dresser. Lastly, she carried her toiletries to the bathroom. It may not meet HGTV's standards but suited

Leila just fine since she didn't have to share it. She pictured herself taking a long, relaxing bath in the tub or a quicker wash in the separate shower. The long countertop dwarfed the few products she put on it.

She lay back on the comfortable mattress and thought about the whirlwind of the last two days. She'd been so scared. Hopefully, being at the doctor's offered her the security she longed for.

Chapter 37   Police Track Imposter

Detectives Morales and Forbes started their day by re-interviewing Wendy Nelson. In answer to their questions, she said Leila had a doctor in Benson, a general practitioner, and an attorney who drew up her will. Unfortunately, she didn't recall their names.

The detectives then drove to Benson to interview Ted, Leila's neighbor at the Oasis RV Park, for the first time. They were aware of his phone call after the news story broke about Leila's disappearance but hadn't spoken to him themselves.

Ted proved to be the only interviewee in Benson eager to answer their questions. He confirmed his impression that Leila was in her late twenties, a pretty little thing. She was quiet and kept to herself. Ted thought she was sick because she'd taken the RV out late one night. The next day he'd driven her to the doctor's office, so he thought she'd been to the emergency room the night before. Then he took care of her cat for two days. Yes, she'd left the RV. Someone came to pick her up. He figured she'd had to go somewhere for tests or treatment. Shortly after, she'd left the park for good. He'd hoped she'd be fine, and then he saw the picture of her RV on the news, but the lady they showed was way too old to be Leila. Dang, that confused him.

The detectives let him ramble on because they picked up important information. Leila had left the park several times in secret. Most significantly, she'd been to a doctor. Ted didn't know the doctor's name but knew where the office was since he'd driven her there.

"Is there any chance she went someplace else after you dropped her off?" Forbes asked.

"No, Sir. I saw her walk into the office. Waited there, too, for her to come out. Couldn't leave that poor little thing to walk home, sick as she was. No, siree."

"How long was she in the office?"

"Didn't look at the clock or nothin', but I'd reckon close to an hour."

The detectives thanked Ted for his cooperation. Following his directions, they found the doctor's office easily enough. They stopped before entering to read his name on the plaque next to the door. In the waiting area, a receptionist sat behind a sliding glass window. She didn't hide her surprise when they introduced themselves and showed their badges.

"We're trying to locate Leila Petterson," Morales said. "Does Dr. Carter have a patient by that name?"

"I think so. Let me check." She turned to her computer and entered Leila's name. "Yes, here it is."

"When was the last time she was in?" Forbes asked.

The doctor entered the office to hand several files to

an office worker and heard Forbes' request.

"We don't give out information about our patients," Dr. Carter reminded the receptionist.

"But they're the police."

"It doesn't matter."

Morales and Forbes exchanged a glance imagining the reprimand awaiting the receptionist.

"Do you have a court order?" Dr. Carter asked the detectives.

"No. We're not going to ask for any medical information about her. We're only trying to trace her movements since she went missing in hopes of finding her."

"I'm sorry I can't be of help. Any information, including whether or not she was my patient or her appointment history or her records, is confidential."

"What do you think about his total lack of cooperation?" Forbes asked as they climbed back into the car. "Either he's strictly a by-the-book man or he's covering for her."

"He's covering for her. We already know the neighbor drove her here. He knows something we need to know."

"Do you think we can get a court order?"

"I doubt it. The judge will claim we're fishing," Morales said, "and he'd be right. Let's hold off on that until we find a good reason to ask for a court order."

"Where to next?"

"Attorneys' offices. There are only two in Benson. We'll have to check both."

The detectives entered Mr. Bradshaw's office first. They went through the same routine with the receptionist as they had at the doctor's office. This receptionist, however, was a bit smarter. "I can't answer that question. Let me check to see if Mr. Bradshaw has a moment to talk to you."

Mr. Bradshaw followed the receptionist back to the waiting area. The detectives introduced themselves and asked if Leila Petterson was his client.

"Yes. Miss Petterson is my client."

" 'Is' not 'was'?" Morales asked.

"I heard she was missing, but I haven't heard confirmation of her death, so yes, 'is' not 'was.' I'm sure you know that means attorney/client confidentiality is still in effect."

"Her friend Wendy Nelson told us you drew up her will," Forbes said. "Can you confirm that?"

"I cannot confirm or deny any of her business with me."

"Will you tell us if you've seen her recently?"

"No."

" 'No' you haven't seen her or 'no' you won't tell us."

" 'No' I won't tell you. I doubt I will be able to answer any more of your questions, so please excuse me."

"Well, that was a wasted trip."

"Maybe not. We've established that the doctor is

covering for her. My guess is the attorney is too. He was quick with the 'is/was' business, but I think his initial reply is the correct one. Leila is his client, not because her body hasn't been found, but because he's working for her now. It begs the question of why either one of them would help an imposter."

"What do we do next?"

"Wait for a copy of the credit card charges."

Chapter 38   Leila Becomes Sarah

Zack drove Leila to Benson to keep a 4:00 appointment with the attorney. After being cooped up in one place or another, Leila treasured the sight of the open desert vistas and the distant contours of the mountains and let the appreciation of their beauty empty her mind. A highway sign listing the distance to Benson as 8 miles pulled her back.

"Oh my gosh."

"What's wrong?"

"Money. I totally forgot about money. Mr. Bradshaw was very generous and said he'd wait until the trust settled for his fees. I'm thinking about all the hours I'll owe him for these extra visits."

"Don't worry about it; this is all part of setting up the trust."

"But I do worry about money, Zack. I'm floating in a land of make-believe. Motels, food, clothes, phone. I doubt you or Dr. Schwartz is footing the bill.

"You're correct there."

"Then who?"

"My boss."

"And you're not going to tell me who he is or why

he's supporting me."

"Right again."

Zack drove another mile in silence, aware that Leila was fuming beside him.

"Leila, I know now that you're not the airhead I thought you were the morning I extracted you from the RV. Let me talk to my boss about sharing some information, okay?"

"Okay."

"While we're at the attorney's, I'd like you to give him permission to deal with me directly."

Leila squirmed. "To keep more secrets from me?"

"No. I'll tell you about any interactions we have. The goal is to keep you safe. If you need to go to Benson again, to drop something off, for example, but don't need to do it personally, I'll do it for you. The less direct contact you have with past acquaintances, the better."

Mr. Bradshaw came to greet them in the reception area and stared at Leila for several seconds. "Leila, you look different every time I see you."

"Really different this time, I hope."

"Yes, I barely recognize you."

He locked the door behind them. "I scheduled you as my last appointment of the day and let my staff go home early to ensure our privacy. Would your friend like to wait here while we go into my office?"

"I'd like him to come with us." She introduced Zack. "He's the one who is keeping me safe. He rescued me when the police ..."

Mr. Bradshaw cut her off. "Don't tell me more than I need to know. If I was subpoenaed, I'd have to reveal information you'd prefer to keep secret."

As they walked down the hall to the office, Leila said. "I'm not sure exactly how to say this, but I want to give my permission for you to talk to Zack or answer his questions."

"In other words, I should consider him a surrogate acting on your behalf."

"Yes. Please."

After they settled into chairs around Mr. Bradshaw's desk, the attorney opened one of two three-ring binders. "Let's begin with your trust. All I need is your signature." He turned the binder around to face Leila and offered her a pen. "You sign here."

Leila did. "That was simple," she said as she laid down the pen.

"Not that simple. Now turn to each page earmarked with a yellow post-it. I will need either your signature or initials on those pages also."

"Why not the green ones?"

"Those are for me: the places where I will need to insert your new beneficiary's name."

Mr. Bradshaw guided her through the pages. When they finished, he picked up the binder and placed it on the credenza behind him then pushed the second binder toward her.

"Again?"

"No. That is your copy of the trust to take with you."

"I do have a question about the trust. What happens now that my RV's been destroyed?"

"Do you have insurance?"

"Yes."

"The answer to your question is a bit complicated. One of the papers you signed was a Power of Attorney, so I can act on your behalf to claim the insurance, and the reimbursement goes into your trust. To do that, I need your policy. Where is it?"

"In my house here in Benson."

"Can you get it?"

Leila glanced at Zack.

"I'd prefer she didn't," Zack said. "Her life is in jeopardy. The RV fire was no accident. Whoever was behind it has no idea where she is, and I intend to keep it that way. The smallest slip can lead to disastrous results. She no longer has keys since they were destroyed in the fire. All it takes is for a curious neighbor, seeing a stranger breaking into Leila's house, to call the police or to jot down my license plate number."

"Can you go to the house?" Leila asked Mr. Bradshaw.

"Not while you're still alive, so to speak," Mr. Bradshaw replied. "I'd need a court order to break into the house, and I can't get a court order without a death certificate. I've already given the need for a death certificate some thought in regard to the trust. I can't settle the trust without one. It can take years for a missing person to be declared legally dead without a physician's certification that the person has died or, in place of that, a court order. However, if there is circumstantial evidence that would lead a reasonable person to believe that the individual is deceased, jurisdictions may agree to issue death certificates without any such order. With the backing of Judge Hersey, I believe I will be successful in taking that route. It's less complex and time-consuming, although it will still take some time to settle the trust."

Leila sighed. "Everything is so complicated."

Mr. Bradshaw grinned. "Just think how complicated it is learning all the in's and out's of the law. Speaking of Judge Hersey, let's move on to the information he needs to complete your new identification. What name have you chosen?"

"Sarah Loughlin. Sarah with an 'h'."

The attorney spelled it out as he wrote it down. "Correct?"

"Yes."

"Out of curiosity, why that name?"

"I always liked the name Sarah. As to Loughlin, it was my grandmother's maiden name."

"I like that association. If anybody questions your similarity to Leila Petterson, it could be explained by reference to a different branch of the family."

"Age?"

"30. It's an easy number to calculate from."

"Birthday?"

"May 18, 1992."

"Photos?"

"I have several on my phone," Zack said as he pulled it out of his pocket.

They downloaded the photos to Mr. Bradshaw's computer, and the three of them picked the photo to send to the judge.

"I have all I needed," the attorney said, "unless you have any questions."

Leila shook her head. "Not that I can think of."

"I'll contact you when the new identification is ready and have you, or Zack, pick it up in person. It's safer than mailing it. I would like your phone number, Zack."

Zack complied.

"Before you go, I should tell you that two Tucson detectives visited me this morning."

Leila began to shake. "They came here? Why? How did they know you were my attorney?"

"They didn't; they asked if you were a client. They were fishing for information. I did admit you were a client because I am still working for you and will be settling the trust. I didn't intend to be caught in an outright lie. I didn't give them any other information."

"Do you know their names?"

Mr. Bradshaw opened a desk drawer and pulled out two business cards. "They each gave me a card when they introduced themselves." He handed them to Zack. "I don't need them."

"Thanks." Zack glimpsed at them before sticking them into a pocket. "One more thing. If Leila accrues any more bills, please send them to me." He handed the attorney his card.

"This one I'll keep."

As soon as Zack and Leila entered the house, Dr. Schwartz called out, "Dinner's ready; to the table, please."

When they entered the dining room, the doctor's back was to them while he set down a plate of potatoes on the table.

"Before we eat, I want to introduce you to Sarah Loughlin," Zack said.

The doctor swiveled around and smiled. "Doc, this is Sarah."

"Welcome, Sarah. Please join us for dinner."

Leila curtsied. "Thank you, Dr. Schwartz. I will."

"So, you have your new identification?"

"Not yet, but Sarah will be my new name. I'm hoping both of you will start using Sarah so I can get used to it."

Chapter 39   Hoover's Past

When Zack entered the house late one afternoon a week later, he paused to sniff the air. "Something smells good," Zack said aloud.

"It does, doesn't it?" came a voice from the office.

"Oh. Hey, Doc. You surprised me. Thought that was you in the kitchen whipping up a delectable treat."

"No, that's Leila, I mean Sarah. Do you have a minute?"

"Sure." Zack wandered into the office and flopped down into the chair.

Dr. Schwartz closed the journal he'd been reading and put it on the desk. "I have a possible lead for you. If you recall, I said I was going to reread several journal articles about brain research."

"I remember. You found something?"

"Not in the articles themselves, but two of them were written by Henry Hoover. He was a respected researcher working at Yale at the time the articles were written. The name triggered memory of a scandal. Hoover was fired quite suddenly. As far as I know, there was never a public statement issued by Yale as to why he was fired, but gossip attributed it to unorthodox experiments he'd been conducting."

"Whoa." Zack sat straight up and moved to the edge of his chair.

"Little was heard about him after that. I called several colleagues, by the way, this is gossip, too, who said Hoover couldn't find employment after that. He'd become untouchable by any reputable research lab."

"How long ago was that?"

"Several years. No one knows what became of him."

"I'll find out, Doc. He sounds like a prime candidate for the mad scientist behind these experiments."

"I thought so, too."

"I'll ask my CO to start a search on Henry Hoover. In the meantime, I'm off in the morning for a few days. There have been some developments I need to follow up on personally. The Department of Justice administers a database for missing persons called NamUS, but the database depends on either the police or families inputting the names of the missing and relevant information about them. That doesn't always happen. In addition to having his computer geeks keep track of NamUS, the CO has had them tracking local news stories about missing seniors anywhere in Arizona. They found three who matched the criteria we set: a man and two women. They were found, one each, in Phoenix, Flagstaff, and Prescott, all heavily populated cities compared to the isolated place where Sarah was attacked."

"You think they're changing their MO?"

"That's what I need to find out. I have a favor to ask before I leave. Sarah wants to know who is backing her financially."

"Sarah is a competent woman who has taken care of herself most of her life. Of course, it bothers her not knowing. It grates on her independence. Sarah is 62 going on 30; she's lived twice as long as you have, yet you treat her like a child by not telling her why you're helping her."

"My CO concurred. He's permitted me to tell her the basics, like how we came up with the theory of experiments on seniors and our wanting to find out who's behind them. She should also know that she is the only person we're aware of who has survived the injection and that we are protecting her because she is key to the solution. He doesn't want her to know exactly who we are or be involved in the investigation."

"And the favor is?"

"You know how to read people. I'd curtly plow through the story without paying attention to any adverse reactions. If she asks questions, I'd reply tersely, as usual, which irritates her. While I'm away, will you tell her for me?"

"Passing the buck?"

Zack grinned. "Sure am or trying to."

"Do you want me to identify you as government or military?"

"Whichever works. Does that mean you'll do it?"

"I will because I agree with you; I'm better suited for the job."

Chapter 40   Police Map Leila's Trip

Detective Forbes waved a piece of paper in the air as Detective Morales approached his desk in the detectives' room and hung his suit jacket over the back of his chair.

"A copy of the gas charges on Leila Petterson's credit card finally came in," Forbes said.

"We need to plot them on a map."

"I picked up a map of Arizona at AAA. The ones I tried downloading from the Internet were too small."

Morales glanced around the room. "Too many cops here. If we open a big map, which I agree we need, we'll attract too much attention. I want to prevent questions about what we're doing or why."

"Where do you want to go?"

The two detectives stared at each other.

"There's traffic in this room 24/7," Forbes said. "Forget doing it here. Wife's visiting her sister and took the kids with her, so my house is empty."

"You got beer in the fridge?"

"Yup."

Morales grinned. "I think your house is the perfect place. We'll get a couple of sandwiches and have lunch there."

Forbes picked up a pack of post-its off his desk and stuck them into his pocket. "Anything else we need? Map's in my jacket pocket."

"A marker. And the credit card report, of course."

The detectives spread the map on Forbes's kitchen table and marked the map with a large dot for each one of six Leila's stops.

"Either she has lousy gas mileage, or she fills up before the tank is empty," Forbes said.

"I vote for the latter. Look where she's traveling. Into the middle of nowhere. Wanted to make sure she wasn't stranded."

"She took the same route up and back."

"Up to where is the question."

Both detectives examined the map north of her last gas stop. Forbes indicated a spot with his finger. "That's got to be it."

"Yup. Alamo Lake State Park. Let's call the park to verify. You have the dates she was there?"

"In my notebook."

The state reservation system confirmed that Leila Petterson had had reservations for site B14 on the dates the detectives indicated. Since she hadn't canceled the reservation, they assumed she had been there. The ranger who answered the phone at the park explained that unless campers needed help, caused a commotion, or broke the park rules, the rangers had little contact with them. He checked a logbook but didn't find an entry for any problems with B14 on the dates of Leila's stay.

"So much for that," Forbes said. "No one saw her, or at least, no one remembers her. We don't know if the old Leila or the young Leila showed up there."

"Look up the park on your computer and see if they have a map of the park."

Forbes did, and they located site B14.

"Judging by the map, my guess is the old Leila arrived at the park. Gas stations are too populated for shenanigans without someone noticing something. There's plenty of opportunity at the park for someone to get to her. Easy, too, to dump the body anywhere along the road on the way back to civilization."

"And we know it was the young Leila who came back to Benson because she checked into an RV park instead of going to her residence."

"We now have a when and where of the real Leila's demise."

Chapter 41   Need New Analyst

"I'm still nervous about injecting three of them at the same time, Miles," Henry said.

"Why? Have you heard one word on the news that the police suspect the deaths are related?"

"No."

"Then stop worrying. I think you worry too much."

"And I think you worry too little."

Silence followed Henry's reply. "Miles?"

"You forget, Henry, that I am in charge of this operation. You are not to question my judgment again."

Henry mumbled some apology, keeping his anger to himself. Miles was making mistakes; Henry was sure of it. Miles thought of himself as a god capable of implementing any scheme he devised and his judgment above reproach. It wasn't. Science can't be rushed. Miles also forgot that it was he who developed the age regression compound. This whole project of theirs wouldn't exist without him or his science. Henry thought of himself as a partner; Miles treated him as a subordinate. If Miles wasn't going to take Henry's advice, it was time to begin secretly making his own plans.

"Do you have any results from the last experiments?"

"Not yet. One of my techs quit, and I was already shorthanded."

"Quit?" Henry sensed a note of alarm in Miles's voice.

"He moved back East to be with his family. His mother is quite sick, and he wanted to be closer to her. I think he's been homesick for a while, always grumbling about the heat out here. Nothing to worry about."

"I told you before if you were understaffed to hire another data analyst. Do I need to do that for you, too?"

Henry ignored the retort. "I've already notified personnel."

"Call them again and tell them to accelerate the search. We need to move on to the next phase."

Henry noticed Miles was back to "we."

Chapter 42   Zack's Boss

During Zack's absence, as promised, Dr. Schwartz called Sarah into his office. She sat down on the edge of her seat and wrung her hands. "Am I in trouble?" she asked.

"Not at all. It's been a pleasure having you here." The doctor smiled. "I especially appreciate your help in the kitchen. Although I like cooking, I enjoy a break from time to time. I don't like cleanup, and you've taken over that chore."

"It's the least I can do."

"I understand you've asked Zack who is financially supporting you."

"All the freebies I'm getting. I take that back. All the things I'm getting: the motel, the clothes, and a phone, to name a few. I'm accruing a debt to someone. I don't like 'owing' especially when I don't know to whom or how the person will expect the debt to be resolved."

"I don't blame you. Zack asked me to speak with you on his behalf to answer those questions."

Sarah relaxed and sat back in her chair.

"Let me begin with a disclaimer. Neither Zack nor I can tell you certain things because you don't have the necessary government security clearance to know them.

I think, however, that you'll be satisfied with what I can tell you."

The doctor explained the story began when notice was taken of the high number of missing seniors in the Tucson area. The government sent Zack to investigate. Since many of the missing had some form of dementia, the police attributed the incidents to seniors wandering off into the desert and getting lost. Zack didn't buy it. In some cases, it might be true, but the numbers had escalated too high for all the seniors and their deaths to be labeled as accidents. Hearing Sarah's story gave Zack the connection he needed. He believed that the missing seniors had also been injected, but the injection didn't work on them because the brain masterminded the age changes and didn't work on people whose brains had deteriorated.

"You mean we were like experiments? And the injection worked on me because I didn't have dementia?" Sarah asked.

"Yes. We think you were their first success. Zack is sure they, whoever they are, were tracking you to see how you reacted and what you did. If Zack's theory was correct, you were in danger of being terminated if your transformation became public."

Sarah began to shake. "You mean all those people were killed to hide their secret experiments?"

"Yes."

"What kind of monsters are they?"

"Psychopaths, people without a conscience."

"And I am the only one who survived?"

"As far as we know, yes. Zack's boss allocated the funds to protect you, so, in answer to your question, the government is paying for the things you need."

Sarah rested her elbows on the edge of the doctor's desk and rested her forehead in her clasped hands. Dr. Schwartz gave her the time she needed to process the information.

"I'm evidence," she said when she dropped her hands to the desk. "They're protecting me because I'm the one piece of evidence they have against these monsters."

"Sarah, I don't want you to think you're unimportant as an individual."

Sarah grinned. "It's okay if I'm evidence if it leads to the monsters and their capture." Sarah straightened her back. "I'll be all those poor people who died rolled into one. I'll speak for them."

"You continually amaze me, Sarah. I thought you'd be upset."

"I've been upset since this whole thing started. What upset me the most was not knowing. Thank you, Dr. Schwartz. I feel a lot better understanding my situation. I assume the part I'm not to know is what group in the government is protecting me and exactly who Zack is."

"Correct, or what their plans are."

"I'm curious, of course, but I can accept that."

"Any other questions?"

"Two. May I go out in the neighborhood? Like walking to the shopping center?"

"If you wear your wig, I don't see why not. You're not a prisoner here, Sarah."

"The second question is a bit delicate. I need some feminine products, but I don't have any money."

"I should have thought of that." The doctor reached into his pocket, pulled out his wallet, and handed Sarah five twenty-dollar bills.

"Thank you. I'll pay you back after my trust settles. It may take a while."

"No need to pay me back. I'll put it on the government tab, and they'll reimburse me. When you need more, tell me."

Chapter 43   More Missing Seniors

Phoenix, Arizona

Zack ran into the usual confrontation of Feds versus local authorities. The police were leery of disclosing information and getting nothing in return. If the Feds were interested, they knew something, and the police wanted to know what that something was.

Zack was prepared for the confrontation. He used his identification from the Agency for Healthcare Research and Quality, the same ID he had shown to the Tucson police and explained that the agency had noticed an alarming number of seniors had been reported missing in Arizona, especially in the Tucson area. He'd been sent to investigate.

The Tucson police categorized the deaths of the majority of those missing seniors as accidents, seniors suffering from some form of dementia who had wandered off and gotten lost.

While Phoenix wasn't part of his original assignment, their recent case had caught his attention, and he asked about their statistics on missing seniors, how many had been located, and if they'd been alive or deceased when found. Zack made no mention of his belief that the majority of the Tucson missing had been injected with a compound and left to die.

Mollified, the police cooperated. Zack controlled his normal impatience as the police reviewed their statistics with him. Because the numbers hadn't escalated from one year to the next, nothing they said warranted his full attention, until they brought up the one case that interested him.

Sally Duffy was an active 69-year-old living in an urban housing development. Every day she walked the half mile or so to a Starbucks to join her friends for coffee. When she didn't arrive one morning, they called her cell, but she didn't answer. Alarmed, the friends traced her normal route back to her house which was locked. They called the police.

"We broke into Duffy's house in case of an accident, but she wasn't there. Nothing was disturbed or out of place. We knocked on every door between her house and Starbucks. Nothing. No one remembered seeing her or anything unusual."

"There was that one woman who saw a white van."

"Forgot about that."

"What white van?" Zack asked.

"A neighbor reported seeing an unfamiliar white van driving down the street: no make or model, no markings and, of course, she didn't write down the license plate number. A van driving down a residential street? There are a million reasons for that. How do you trace a vehicle with the only description being 'a white van'? The neighbor didn't see Duffy anywhere near the van, so we dismissed it as unimportant."

Zack commiserated with them. "Can't blame you," he said. Inside, however, Zack sensed the white van was a vital clue.

"You suspect foul play?" Zack asked.

"We have nothing to indicate that, but Duffy's friends insist she wouldn't just take off. By all accounts, she was happy and well-liked."

"No mental or physical problems?"

"None that we're aware of."

Flagstaff, Arizona

Zack's routine at the Flagstaff police station mimicked the one in Phoenix: suspicion, explanation, mollification, acceptance, review of statistics, and finally a discussion of the one case which interested him.

The victim, John McDonald, was a healthy 71-year-old man who lived in an apartment complex with his dog Rufus. He walked the dog twice a day in a nearby park. The man was reported missing when an irate neighbor called the park manager complaining about the dog's barking outside her door, which was adjacent to McDonald's.

Knowing McDonald kept good control of the dog, the manager responded immediately and found Rufus barking frantically and pawing on the door. The manager knocked on the door. When McDonald didn't answer, he used his passkey to let himself in. The dog rushed past the manager when the door opened and ran desperately from room to room looking for his master. The manager called the police.

According to the manager, McDonald was quiet but friendly. The only person who complained about him was his next-door neighbor. But she complained about everyone, not just McDonald: someone parking too close to the line in the parking lot so she had trouble getting out of her car, the noisy kids who played on the lawns, the dog walker who didn't clean up his dog's poop.

"Do you think the disappearance involved foul play?" Zack asked the detectives.

"We do. Because of the dog. The first odd thing was finding the dog outside the apartment. Neighbors swore McDonald never let the dog outside on his own," one detective said.

"And the dog's behavior," his partner added. "It knew something was wrong. When Animal Control came to pick him up, they had a hard time corralling him. When the officer picked him up to put in a cage, the dog whined when the officer touched his side. A vet examined the dog and found a large bruise. The vet believes someone kicked him. A CSI then examined the dog for trace and recovered tiny paint chips in the fur near his paw nails."

"That didn't surprise us at first because the dog had been pawing on the apartment door when the manager found him. What did surprise us was that the paint chips were two colors: green, the color of the door, and white."

"Any idea where the white came from?"

"Only a theory. We think McDonald had taken the dog on his usual walk to the park where someone abducted him. While they were forcing McDonald into a vehicle, the dog intervened, and the abductor kicked him away. Before they took off, the dog pawed on the vehicle door. When they drove off, the poor mutt ran home."

"Any motive?" Zack asked.

"None whatsoever."

Prescott, Arizona

After the usual dance, Zack learned the details of the third victim, a 73-year-old female named Delores Menendez. She was a retired social worker who donated her time two mornings a week at a local daycare center. Parents dropped their children off at the center from 8:00 to 8:30 a.m. depending on their work schedules. Delores was outside during that hectic period to help parents unload or to shepherd the kids into the center.

On the morning of her abduction, Delores was outside as usual. Many parents and kids reported seeing her as she walked from car to car and greeted them. Absorbed with their own needs, neither parent nor child paid attention to what became of Delores, except for one four-year-old boy who said a big car ate her. The police initially dismissed his statement as the imagination of a child, but a teacher paid more attention.

Since the boy's verbal skills were limited, the teacher asked the boy to draw a picture of what he'd seen. Using a black marker, the boy drew a large, square-shaped box with two circles to represent tires and a rectangular opening in the middle of the box. The stick figure representing Delores was bent in the middle with the bend pointing toward the inside of the box. The boy used colored crayons to add a sun and a tree. When the teacher asked him to color in the box, the boy rummaged through the crayon box. Not finding the color he wanted, he pushed the crayon box away. The boy had pointed to the paper, white paper, and said, "No crayon." When asked if he'd been scared because the car ate her, the boy shook his head. Delores had been waving to him, so he waved back and followed his mother into the center.

After the boy left, the police and the teacher interpreted the drawing. The boy's perspective had been a side view of the vehicle. Judging by the large, square shape, they believed the vehicle was a van, and the opening in the middle, the van's sliding side door. The kid had seen Delores being pulled into the van with one arm wrapped around her waist and, most likely, the hand of the other arm covering her mouth. Delores hadn't been waving in a friendly manner. Either she was gesturing for help, or her arms were flailing naturally from the jerking of her body as it was pulled into the van.

Without a definite answer as to the color of the van, Zack speculated. It may have been an odd color that didn't match any of the crayon colors, or the boy didn't find the color he wanted in the crayon box because a white crayon wasn't there. Zack opted to believe the latter.

"At first, we couldn't believe the audacity of abducting someone in such a crowded place," one cop said.

"Sometimes it's the safest place for a crime," Zack said. "A person's view is limited to a small area. The more crowded it is, the smaller the area. I'm sure the parents focused on their kids to make sure they didn't wander off, especially in the path of an oncoming car. Lack of sightlines, lack of interest in anything outside the business at hand."

"Yeah. We came to the same conclusion. They didn't know who was standing three feet away from them."

"Do you know approximately where the van was parked?"

"No. Because of what we just said. The parents wanted to drop their kids off quickly and get out of there. Most of them had to get to work."

Back to Tucson

On the four-hour drive back to Tucson, Zack reviewed the cases of the three missing seniors. The jurisdictions had not connected the cases. There was little reason for them to do so, because on the surface, other than the ages of the victims, they had insufficient information to tie them together.

All three seniors had disappeared on the same day in the morning. If the police had considered connecting the cases, they'd dismiss the possibility as geographically impossible because of the distance between the cities. It told Zack there was more than one team involved. The police had no inkling of the scope of the operation or the motive behind it. Lack of motive stymied them.

All the cases involved white vehicles, a trivial detail to the police because it was too generic. The abductors only made one clean getaway. They hadn't in McDonald's case because of the dog. Sloppy preparation as far as Zack was concerned because the dog had provided evidence. Zack doubted the abduction teams were professional. In the Menendez case, a young boy had witnessed the abduction. Other than his drawing suggesting that a van had been used, and the iffy identification of it as white, the boy wasn't able to provide the police with any clues. It did, however, help Zack to connect the cases.

The police didn't know what Zack did. While each jurisdiction treated its case as a singular occurrence, Zack added the three to his list. Whoever was behind the experiments was broadening the base of operations and accelerating the time between experiments.

Chapter 44   IDing Hoover

"Henry Hoover's your neighbor, Doc," Zack said the next afternoon.

Dr. Schwartz put down the coffee pot on the kitchen counter. "Excuse me? He lives in Tucson?"

"Better than that. He lives in North Tucson, a couple of blocks from here. I drove past his house this morning. Nice place."

"I assume your CO found him."

"Compliments of the IRS."

"What else was in the report?"

"Not until you get that coffee poured."

The doctor poured two cups and pushed one in Zack's direction.

"Now talk."

"Hoover has worked at Underwood Labs, a pharmaceutics company, for years. He lists his occupation as a scientist for which he receives a modest income. The income doesn't fit with Henry's lifestyle in North Tucson. We suspect he's got money coming in from an unreported source."

"Perhaps he's supplementing his income from savings or investments?"

"He'd still have to report income from investments which he doesn't unless he's investing under an alias or has offshore accounts. As for savings, after he was fired, he didn't report any income for the next year. Bet he used up his savings during that time. Suddenly, he has a modest paying job and moves to upscale North Tucson."

The doctor took a sip of coffee and leaned against the counter. "Who owns Underwood Labs?"

"Still working on that. It's one of those companies owned by another company, etc."

"You mentioned pharmaceutics. Do you know more precisely which pharmaceutics?"

"It appears the lab works on testing for other companies as an independent third-party verification rather than on products they're developing. Good news is that in searching for information about the company, the CO cast a wide net. One of the techs found a help-wanted ad for a data analyst. The CO wants to send in an undercover man. We have a great candidate who is a whiz at data analysis. He also has a science background although they left that off the phony resumé they created. The ad mentioned 'needed immediately,' so our man is flying out today to be in place if Underwood contacts him for an interview."

Zack stopped talking when he saw Sarah in the doorway.

"How long have you been standing there?" Zack asked.

"Only a few seconds. I smelled the coffee and wanted a cup. All I heard was something about an undercover man." Sarah held her hands. "You're talking about something I shouldn't know. I'll leave."

Sarah turned to leave, but Dr. Schwartz stopped her.

"Since you're already here, Sarah, let me pour you a cup to take with you."

Chapter 45   Fate of Missing Seniors

Anxious to hear the progress on the latest subjects, Miles picked up his phone and called Henry. "Any results yet on the latest subjects?" Miles asked.

"The compound is working; they're regressing. I've made several trips to the safe house. It's rather exciting seeing the changes in person. We'll monitor them for another couple of days until we're sure the compound has worn off."

"Any conjecture on the number of years they've regressed?"

"As you know, I injected the compound in varying dosages. I don't know yet whether Anna's extreme reaction was because of a too-high dosage for her small size or another factor. I'll know soon."

"Are you keeping track of their reactions?" Miles asked.

"Of course. The compound starts to take effect almost immediately. Most notably the body twitches. Betty's twitching has stopped; she received the lowest dosage. I believe that means the compound has dissipated, and she's regressed as far back as she will go. I won't know for sure until I get the results from the others and can compare them. What do you plan to do with them after I have all the results I need?" Henry asked.

"They'll be disposed of in a place where their bodies can't be found. You agreed to disposal in the beginning. Subjects suffering from dementia were confused and fearful. What way is that to live? We did them a favor by ending their misery."

"But Betty, Carol, and Bob are healthy. You let Anna and Adam live."

"Think, Henry. Adam hasn't been a problem; we never injected him. He's still living quietly on his ranch and keeping to himself. He may think the drone was nothing but local kids pestering him. But Anna? She's been a wildcard, and we've lost track of her."

"She's staying under the radar."

"Don't develop a conscience now, Henry. Remember your experiments at Yale; you caused the deaths of two people then."

"Those were accidents. I've come a long way since then."

"Yes, you have, Henry. Thanks to me, I might add. My decisions have protected you and your science since I hired you. Think of all your test subjects as lab animals, like the mice and monkeys you occasionally used. In that sense, the last three don't have any more value than your previous subjects. Would you prefer to let Betty, Carol, and Bob live? They're all publicly active. People will notice they look younger. The age regression will draw attention, especially after they recount their abductions, which they will since we didn't dose them and render them unconscious before contact with them. We kept them sedated after that, so any memories will be fuzzy and fragmented, but the initial contact will be clear. If Anna hears about them, she might decide to go public. No one has a hint about what we're doing, and I plan to keep it that way. Would you prefer we raise questions and invite scrutiny?"

"No, of course not."

"Then we go forward. Any other news?"

"The lab hired a new analyst, Michael Tucker, who has a topnotch resumé."

"Did you vet him properly before he was hired?"

"Yes. He checked out. Currently, he's working in a lab upstairs where he's proven to be fast and accurate and even proposed an improvement on the format for reports on legal experiments. He keeps to himself, doesn't engage in conversations with other employees in the locker room or breakroom, is polite but standoffish, and doesn't ask questions about the work he's been assigned."

"Give him a try."

"I plan to."

Chapter 46   Undercover Analyst

Recognizing the phone number his CO had given him, Zack said, "I've been waiting for you to call," when he answered the call. "How'd the interview go ... Umm."

"Michael Tucker. Hired me on the spot."

"Michael?"

"Figured it was easiest to keep my real first name since I'm used to responding to it. It's a common name so I didn't see it as a problem."

Zack sat down on the recliner in his bedroom and rested his feet on the ottoman.

"When do you start?"

"Already did. They wanted me to start the day after the interview."

"They didn't vet you?"

"They vetted me before the interview. CO says they called him. He told them his company was merging and how he hated losing me, etc."

"What's all that noise I hear?"

"I'm walking around a mall. I don't trust them. They can't interfere with the burner phone, but they can eavesdrop with a listening device. Lots of noise will drown out my voice."

"I assume you keep the burner phone in a safe place?"

"Behind a vent in the long-term hotel suite I rented. I carry the sanitized iPhone with me. I don't think they'll look for a burner phone, but in case they do, it's safe."

"Learn anything yet?"

"The building is your standard oblong box. The lab I was assigned to is toward the end of the second-floor corridor. I noticed an elevator at the end of the corridor and casually walked by. An employee caught me. I said I was a new hire and wondered if the elevator went to the ground floor instead of my having to walk to the bank of elevators in the center of the building. He told me the elevator was off-limits and warned me to stick to what I was told to do, like using the central elevators, if I wanted to keep my job. Makes me think that elevator goes to a special place in the building, like a secret lab."

"Sounds like a friendly place to work," Zack said.

Michael laughed. "They're big on secrets around here. The first day started with my signing a non-disclosure agreement. After that, some pretty little thing took me on a tour of the places I was allowed to go in the building. Those and no others. She blamed the restrictions on the confidential testing they do."

Zack heard a "humph" and a distant female voice say, "I'm sorry, mister." From the ensuing short conversation, Zack pictured the woman's kid running into Michael. He graciously accepted the woman's apology and headed toward a food court where most of the tables were empty and chose a table safely out of earshot.

"Did you see or hear any mention of Henry Hoover?" Zack asked.

"None. They don't have a directory near the central elevators like most buildings do. Anyone going past the lobby needs an ID badge. I doubt few of those are visitor badges."

"None of your coworkers mentioned him?"

"No. Work isn't mentioned in breakroom conversations, other than a general complaint or two about heavy workloads, long hours, or such. Nothing specific about the labs where they work or what they do. If I asked a direct question about Hoover, I'd have the Gestapo on me. Best I can do is keep my ears open. If they like secrecy, I want to stand out as not being inquisitive."

"I assume you haven't seen anything of interest to us."

"Nothing I'm working on hints at your experiments. It's all standard data entry. I'm not in a high-level security lab. Figured my best bet is to impress them by showing off my skills and hope they move me to another lab."

Chapter 47   Sarah's New ID

Sarah received the phone call she'd been waiting for. Judge Hersey had completed her new ID and it was ready for Sarah to pick it up at Mr. Bradshaw's office. With Zack in and out or sequestered in his room most of the time, she was hesitant to ask him to take timeout to drive her to Benson. The roundtrip drive and time in the attorney's office amounted to a minimum of three hours.

Sarah broached the subject at breakfast. She and Dr. Schwartz sat leisurely at the breakfast table while Zack stood at the counter downing his coffee.

"My new ID documents are ready," Sarah said.

Zack lowered his coffee cup to the countertop. "Drat. I forgot about them."

"What's the problem?" the doctor asked.

"I have to pick them up in person in Benson at my attorney's office."

"I'm sorry," Zack said. "I can't take you there today. Maybe tomorrow."

Dr. Schwartz glanced out the window. "What a beautiful, sunny day. I was thinking about taking a drive."

Zack laughed. "Sure you were, Doc."

"How about I drive you to Benson, Sarah?"

Sarah's face brightened. "You will?"

"I'd appreciate it, Doc," Zack said.

"I think we'd both prefer you spent your time chasing down our psychopaths, right, Sarah?"

"Absolutely."

Once more, Sarah enjoyed the desert vistas during the drive to Benson. When they arrived at the attorney's office, Dr. Schwartz opted to wait in the car while Sarah went inside. Mr. Bradshaw gave Sarah a packet containing an Arizona birth certificate, an Arizona identification card, an Arizona driver's license, a certificate of citizenship, a death certificate for Leila, and an application for a Social Security card. The judge had not been able to get her a Social Security card or a passport because they are Federal documents. She'd apply for those using the Arizona documents the judge had supplied. Mr. Bradshaw suggested she apply for a Social Security card immediately.

Sarah hugged the documents to her chest. "Thank you so much, Mr. Bradshaw."

"You're welcome. I've begun the process of settling your trust. I'm waiting now for permission to break into your house so I can get your RV insurance policy to file a claim. Where are your personal papers?"

"In a portable file storage box in the back of my bedroom closet."

"I'll take the box and bring it here to safeguard it which also allows me access to all your papers should I need them. Are you still planning on selling the house?"

"Yes."

"Furnished?"

"That's the easiest."

"As soon as I have access to the house, I plan to send in a crew to pack up your personal items in preparation for the sale. I'll put those in a storage facility. After the estate settles, you can go through the locker and keep what you want or dispose of it all."

When Sarah climbed back into the car, Dr. Schwartz asked, "Are you now official, Miss Sarah Loughlin?"

Sarah grinned. "I am. You have no idea what a relief it is to know I can function normally again."

"Oh, I might."

"May I ask for some advice?"

"Certainly."

"Mr. Bradshaw will be taking all my personal items out of my house before it goes on sale and put them in a storage facility. He said I could keep them or toss them. Which should I do?"

"That depends on whether you want to make a clean break from Leila Petterson's life. Do you want nostalgic possessions around to remind you of your old life, or do you want to start fresh and begin a new one?"

Sarah wondered what other people would do.

Chapter 48   Undercover Man in Lab

Michael Tucker's second call to Zack sounded more promising. Michael reported that he had been stopped that morning in the lobby where a guard accompanied him to the locker room and told him to store all his personal items in his locker, including his phone. Michael did as he was told. After Michael emptied his pockets and put on his lab coat, the guard frisked him.

Michael debated between complaining about the personal intrusion and keeping his mouth shut. It seemed unnatural not to say anything about the unusual procedure, so he settled for a tactful question.

"Have I done something wrong?" Michael asked.

"No," the guard answered. "I'm taking you to another lab."

Michael wished the guard had been a bit more eloquent with his explanation, particularly about their destination, but decided not to probe any further. There was a good chance the guard didn't know, and asking questions was contrary to the unwritten company policy. Having to empty his pockets of all personal items and the frisking was enough to tell Michael that he was going to a high-level security lab.

After the frisking, the guard attached a badge to his lab coat with a warning not to lose it and to be sure he always wore it while in the building. The badge had a large metallic silver dot in the middle, but nothing written on it to identify its purpose. The guard wore the same badge. Michael deduced the dot encoded his name and tracked his movements around the building.

As soon as they approached the "off-limits" elevator, Michael smiled to himself. The guard was escorting him to a secret lab. Inside the elevator, the control panel showed two buttons: one for the first floor, one for the second. "Watch," the guard said and pressed both buttons at the same time. They descended to the unmarked basement level.

As he and the guard walked down the hallway, Michael noticed a series of unidentified doors, each requiring a finger scan to unlock the door. The guard stopped in front of the third door on the right.

"Third door," the guard said in case Michael had not counted.

The guard knocked on the door. It registered that the guard had access to the floor but not to the labs. A sliding panel in the door opened revealing a set of eyes. The guard identified himself and Michael. "Right," a voice said. The guard turned and left before the door opened.

When it opened and Michael stepped inside, an involuntary "Wow" escaped his lips. He was looking at state-of-the-art equipment in a computer room with four workstations.

"Yeah, we like it, too." A tall, thin man with a head of bushy brown hair and brown eyes introduced himself as Wayne Oatsdale. "I'll be your supervisor." The word "supervisor" suggested a hierarchy; Oatsdale wasn't the "boss" or top man and Oatsdale didn't name the person who was.

Oatsdale pointed out a door leading to a bathroom and explained they didn't leave the room except for lunch in a dining room down the hall. "A catered lunch," he added, "since we are not allowed to bring any personal items down here. A cart comes by mid-morning and mid-afternoon if you want a snack."

"We are currently understaffed," Oatsdale said as he led Michael to a workstation. "For the time being, there'll only be the two of us. It means more work for us, and you're expected to work overtime if needed. However, if the boss is satisfied with you, you'll find a generous raise in your salary as compensation for the strict rules we follow and any necessary overtime."

Michael noted that he'd never been asked if he wanted this change in status or agreed to the new working conditions. He did, of course, because the extreme precautions signified he was closer to his real goal.

"I assume the guard frisked you before bringing you down here?" Oatsdale asked.

"Yes."

"You'll be frisked again on your way out before leaving the floor. You'll leave your lab coat and badge with the receptionist in the lobby before exiting the building and pick up a clean lap coat and your badge in the morning. The badge allows you access to our private elevator."

"I assume I go to the locker room first to retrieve my stuff before checking out in the lobby."

"Yes. Before we get to work, I'm taking you to be fingerprinted. When you come in tomorrow, your right index finger will open the lab door."

Michael hoped the CO had remembered to switch his fingerprints to his phony name and records.

Chapter 49   Another Missing Senior

The Sierra Vista, Arizona, local news headlined a story about a missing 65-year-old man. According to his wife, Sam Wiley had gone to Home Depot to buy a couple of chisels he needed for a rocking horse he was making for their grandchild. She became worried when he didn't come home and didn't answer his cell; she called the police. The police found his car in the Home Depot parking lot with the driver's door slightly ajar and tracked the GPS signal from his cell to the vacant land which borders Highway 90 on either side of the road. Police immediately suspected foul play.

The north end of Highway 90 ends at Interstate 10 which runs east toward New Mexico or west toward Tucson, roughly 50 miles away. Because there was a 50-50 chance the abductors were headed for Tucson, Channel 13 News picked up the story and included it in their 5:00 evening news.

When Zack saw the news, he immediately headed to the Home Depot in Sierra Vista where he easily found the abduction site because it was surrounded by police cruisers and crime scene tape. Using his Agency for Healthcare Research and Quality ID, he introduced himself to the detectives at the scene. He wasn't exactly welcomed because they were busy, but they gave their permission for him to walk around the site if he didn't touch anything.

The scene reminded him of the Menendez abduction in Flagstaff: busy area, no witnesses. Zack pictured the abduction team backing their van into the parking space next to Wiley's car, thus placing the van's sliding side door a couple of feet from the driver's door and limiting action to the narrow strip between the two vehicles. The vehicles effectively blocked a view of the abduction, unless a shopper happened to pass by the space between the vehicles at the same moment they grabbed Wiley and happened to look in that direction. Zack believed the team was poised for action as soon as Wiley entered the narrow space. When he stopped to unlock the car door, it only required a minute to grab an unsuspecting Wiley and get the surprised man into the van, as it had with Delores Menendez. Backing into the space also allowed the driver to make a quick getaway.

Zack asked the detectives one question before he left the scene. Had they found a shopping bag with Wiley's purchases? No, they had not. Zack hoped the bag was overlooked when they removed Wiley from the van, leaving behind a piece of evidence.

Detectives Morales and Forbes from the Tucson Police Department also heard the story about Wiley's disappearance which reminded them of Leila

Petterson's unresolved case. The cases were quite different, but Morales's honed senses told him there might be a connection.

The detectives didn't visit Sierra Vista; they didn't have to. Morales simply picked up the phone the next day and called the Sierra Vista police and asked to speak to the detective in charge of the Sam Wiley case.

Detective Garcia was baffled by the total lack of clues: no motive, no witnesses, the victim's good reputation and lack of enemies. He didn't know if it was a crime of opportunity or if the victim had been targeted. The victim was too poor for it to be a ransom kidnapping and wasn't involved with any crime organizations for it to be retribution. On the other hand, while robbery was the most obvious motive for a crime of opportunity, kidnapping the victim didn't make sense. "One strange thing happened at the scene. Hold on a minute." Garcia searched through his pockets to find the business card Zack had given him. "Ever hear of a Phillip Johnson from the Agency for Healthcare Research and Quality?"

"Yeah. He contacted us a while back. Said he was investigating the high rate of missing seniors in the Tucson area."

"Why's he interested in Sierra Vista?"

"Good question. I might call him to ask. Do you have his phone number handy, so I don't have to dig around in my desk looking for his business card?"

Garcia gave Morales the phone number, and the two

agreed to keep in touch.

Morales's call surprised Zack who wanted to seem cooperative but had to guard his information to prevent leaks. A leak might warn the ring he was after, especially if the press got ahold of the story. Zack reiterated that his primary investigation had centered in the Tucson area but was not limited to it. He offered Morales a gem.

"I learned of an abduction case in Prescott while I was checking their stats. A woman was kidnapped under circumstances very similar to Wiley's in Sierra Vista." Zack summarized the case without adding any of his personal insight. "I was struck by the coincidence and wanted to check it out."

"I don't believe in coincidences," Morales said.

"That's why I'm telling you. My job is a fact-finding mission, not to solve crimes. You might want to call Prescott PD to delve more deeply into both cases."

"Thanks for the tip," Morales said. "We've learned the when and where of Leila Petterson's kidnapping but hit a wall after that."

"Care to share the when and where?"

Zack was impressed by the detective's intuition and persistence in working Leila's case. Morales was the type of man he liked to work with: a diligent man who wasn't afraid to break protocol if necessary. Although Morales never mentioned his belief there was a leak in the police department, Zack surmised as much by the detective's methods.

Chapter 50   Tucker Meets Hoover

"I'm in the right place," Michael said to Zack. "Yesterday, I began work on a chart, changing variables to see how the changes affected the outcome. None of the variables were labeled, but I recognized some fields as age, height, weight, and sex."

"Any idea what the purpose of the chart was?"

"I'd hazard a guess that it was for dosages. I think they're setting the perimeters for how much or how little of a dosage is effective within certain perimeters, the 'outcome' being the age regression. The computer does the calculations."

"That was fast, giving you a top priority project."

"They're shorthanded. Four workstations and only Oatsdale when I arrived."

"Any chance of getting a copy of the charts?"

"Not if you ever want to see me again. I'm being closely watched and tested. Oatsdale placed me at a workstation where my monitor is within his sightline, and any printouts go to the printer next to his desk. As to being tested, last night I was sitting at an outside café enjoying the mild night air after being cooped up all day in that claustrophobic lab. A co-worker I recognized from the dining room happened to walk by and joined me. 'Happened' according to him. I believe he followed me there. As we conversed, with him doing most of the talking, he'd slip in questions about the lab. I sidestepped most of them, but when he blatantly asked me which lab I was working in, I told him I spent enough hours at work and preferred to leave the job there. Afterhours were for relaxing."

"What was his reaction?" Zack asked.

"He shrugged and said he was only making small talk. No problem if I didn't want to answer. I was sure he'd been testing me when I got to the lab today. During the late afternoon, the hallway door opened. Whoever opened it had clearance to unlock it. Oatsdale turned in surprise and stood up to greet the newcomer with a 'Good afternoon, Dr. Hoover' and introduced me."

"Doctor?" Zack said. "A bit of self-promotion."

"Hoover's a little gnome of a man. Guess he figured the 'doctor' elevated his status. He wanted a printout of the results I had to date and demanded I stay until I finished the report. A bit anxious and pressed for time, I'd say."

"His latest victim went missing yesterday. I'm thinking he might want to change the dosage and needs the results of your work to determine how much to give him."

223

Chapter 51   Falling-out

"You jumped the gun, Miles. I'm not ready for another subject," Henry said. "I have the data but not the complete analysis for Betty, Carol, and Bob."

"Back up a minute, Henry. What did the analysis show for them?"

"They all regressed, but the number of years varied depending on the amount of compound injected. It does seem the women regressed further back than the man."

"Doesn't that give you a baseline?"

"It's not that simple, Miles."

Miles tapped his fingers on his desk impatiently while Henry blabbered on about the importance of accuracy which demanded more than a simple observation of change in appearance or how the women regressed further back than the man.

"If you want to quote an age regression of so many years to your clients, male versus female, we need to establish reliable perimeters," Henry said. "Three subjects are not enough to set the perimeters. Betty and Carol both regressed, but I have yet to establish the ratio of years versus the amount of compound used."

"And how long is that going to take?"

"Please remember that I have been short-handed. Data entry was slow because of it. The new hire is fast which will speed things up on that end. However, I still need time to review the figures the computer gives me. I also don't have any comparison for Bob."

"You have another male now for a comparison, don't you?

"Yes. I've named him Carl, by the way, and I wasn't expecting him. You dispatched a team without my knowing."

"I have the teams surveilling vetted subjects to ascertain the most advantageous times to pick them up. I told them to act if a perfect situation arose."

"And what am I supposed to do with Carl before I determine the amount of compound to use?"

Miles rolled his eyes. "You have two choices, Henry. Keep Carl sedated while you play around with your data or give him the same dosage you used on Bob and see what happens. I suggest the latter."

The conversation ended with both men on edge and annoyed with the other.

Chapter 52 Zack Enlists Morales

Under his alias as Phillip Johnson, Zack called Detective Morales and invited him for a drink at the 19th Hole after work.

"Why?"

"I want to talk to you about Leila Petterson."

"Why can't you stop at the station?"

"I think you know the answer to that."

Morales mulled that over. How did Johnson know, or suspect, there was a leak at the station?

"Why the 19th Hole?"

"It's quiet that time of the day. Most of the golfers are long gone; it's still early for the dinner crowd. I'd like our conversation to be private. If you prefer another bar, name it, if it's not packed with an after-work crowd."

"The 19th Hole is fine. Does this invitation include my partner?"

"Just you for the moment. After listening to what I have to say, I'll leave it to you to decide if you want to include him."

"5:30?"

"Thanks, Morales. See you then."

Zack arrived at the rendezvous early to choose a

private table. Most customers sat on the patio or in the informal dining room where customers gathered to drink as well as eat. The bar area, an alcove off the dining room, only had three small two-seaters and no standup service at the bar. Zack picked the corner table and the chair against the wall with a full view of the dining room and ordered a beer while he waited for Morales.

After spotting Zack, Morales passed a waitress on his way to the table. "I'll have a beer," he told her. Morales scooted his chair so his back, too, was against a wall, because cops don't like exposing their backs or not being able to see who's approaching.

"So, you want a clandestine meeting out of the station," Morales said after he sat down. "I doubt it's about statistics. Makes me think you're not Phillip Johnson from the ..." Morales pulled a business card out of his pocket and read, "... Agency for Healthcare Research and Quality." He set the card on the table.

Both men stopped talking while the waitress brought the beer. "Do you gentlemen want menus?"

"No, thanks," Zack said. The waitress smiled and left.

Morales took a long swig of his beer. "Ah, that tastes good."

"I'm associated with several Federal agencies," Zack said. "I did misrepresent myself when I said my job is a fact-finding mission, not to solve crimes. You're aware of the high number of seniors who go missing in the

Tucson area?"

"Of course."

"That's what originally brought me here. I was truthful about that. But I didn't want only the stats; I want to find out why. Those seniors are being murdered."

Morales was taking a swig of his beer and sputtered. He used a napkin to clean himself off. "You have proof of that?"

"I'd been working on it. Then I met Leila Petterson. She's the key to the answer."

"And now she's disappeared, presumed dead."

"She's not dead."

Morales plunked his beer down on the table instead of taking another sip. "How the hell do you know that?"

"Because I have Leila in protective custody. If you want to help unravel the mystery behind her disappearance and the seniors' deaths, I'm asking you to work with me. They're being used as experiments. I want to take down the whole operation."

"And who are you? Your real name's not Phillip Johnson."

"No, but since I'm known around the station with that name, it's best to stick with it."

"What is it you want me to do?"

"Follow someone to and from work."

"You can't do that?"

"I want them followed in an official police cruiser,

so, no, I can't do it."

"And have them stopped, harassed?"

"No. Only followed. I want the person to know he's being followed; the idea is to make him nervous enough to crack."

Zack saw the waitress approaching and held up two fingers to order beers. She nodded and spun around.

"So, all you're asking me to do is have some guy followed?"

"Initially, yes. If my plan works and the guy you follow breaks, it will expose the operation. It's our door in."

"You mean the Feds."

"Or the Feds and Tucson PD if you want to be a part of it and get credit."

Again, the two men remained silent when the waitress returned and put down the two beers and picked up the empties. "Enjoy," she said and left.

The hiatus gave Morales time to contemplate Zack's proposal.

"If I follow this guy for you, for how long?"

"Might only take a day or two. He's already nervous; you're just the icing on the cake to push him over the edge."

"When do you want to have him followed?"

"A few days from now. Once I know you're in, I'll finalize my plans and call you."

"I need something more concrete than a

conversation in a bar. I want to meet Leila."

Zack paused to drink his beer. He knew at some point he and Morales had to trust each other.

"I can arrange a meeting, but you'll need to give me a little leeway. I'll pick you up and take you to her."

"Me and my partner. If we agree we want in after meeting her, we bring in my lieutenant. I may bend the rules at times, but I'm not a cowboy."

"Was I correct in assuming you think there's a leak in the station?"

Morales stared at Zack for a moment. It was his turn to trust.

"Yes," Morales said. "On the Petterson case, yes, because of the delay getting the paperwork through to impound the RV and then it being torched before we could get it."

"Is it possible the lieutenant was the leak?"

"No. He'd been off duty when all that went down. Besides, I've worked with him in enough tricky situations to know I can trust him."

Morales picked up Zack's business card off the table, slipped it back in his pocket, and stood. "I'll call my partner tonight and let you know what we decide. Thanks for the beers."

Chapter 53   Detectives Meet Leila

Zack pulled into a parking space in front of number 16 at a nondescript motel. He turned off the motor and turned sideways to talk to Morales in the passenger seat and Forbes in the back seat.

"She's nervous about meeting you. I had to convince her to talk to you, so go easy on her, okay?"

"Why is she nervous?"

"She's been on the run trying to keep a low profile. Police don't fit with that agenda. You'll understand better when you hear her story."

Zack pulled his phone out of his pocket. After hitting several buttons, he paused, then said, "We're outside, coming in now."

The three men exited the vehicle. Zack unlocked the motel door. By the time the detectives' eyes adjusted to the darkness inside the room from the bright outdoors, Zack had closed and relocked the door.

"Hey, what the hell is this?" Morales said after he spotted Sarah. "You said Leila Petterson was here, not the imposter."

"They're both here," Zack said.

Morales spun on his heel and glanced around the

231

room looking for another person.

"I'm Leila Petterson," Sarah said.

"Leila Petterson is 62 years old," Morales said. "You're what? 30?"

"I was 62, now I'm 30. I'm Leila and the imposter. I'm one and the same, or both, however you want to say it."

"Unbelievable, isn't it?" Zack said.

"Unbelievable is right," Morales said. "What kind of scam is this?"

"You mentioned during one of our conversations that you were suspicious of the destruction of her RV before CSI had a chance to inspect it. My guess? You expected to find two sets of fingerprints: Leila's and the imposter's. You would have found only one set because Leila and the imposter are the same person. The fire was arson, not an accident. They wanted you to keep believing there were two different women. You came to listen to her story. Give her a chance to tell it," Zack said.

Morales took two steps toward the door.

"We're here, Morales. We might as well listen," Forbes said.

"Fine." Morales folded his arms across his chest. "Talk."

Sarah began her long story from the day she'd been driving to Alamo Lake State Park. One or the other detective often interrupted the story with questions. As the story progressed, both detectives were so fascinated that their tones sounded more inquisitive and less like a grilling. By prior agreement with Zack, she never mentioned Dr. Schwartz, only that she had gone to a psychiatrist which was where she met Zack. At that point, Zack took over.

"I took her into protective custody prior to your raid. We have fingerprint confirmation, by the way, that she is Leila Petterson. She was the clue I needed to figure out what caused the deaths of the other seniors. They were all experiments. The others died, either from the injection itself or they were killed because the injection didn't work. I believe the latter. Their mistake had been injecting seniors with dementia. Leila's brain was healthy."

"Why did they let her live?" Forbes asked.

"We think she was their first success, and they wanted to see how she reacted. She was being tracked until I stepped in. I can guarantee that if they found her now, she'd be terminated."

"We keep saying 'they' and 'their.' Do you know who 'they' is?" Morales asked.

"Yes. But until I know you're 'in,' I can't divulge that information. I don't want or need a separate investigation interfering with mine."

"You said in the restaurant that you want us to follow a guy to make him so nervous he'd break and expose the operation. Is he one of the heads of the operation?"

"Yes. Timing is critical. If the guy does break, we need to follow up immediately. It will be a huge undertaking. I'd welcome Tucson PD's help."

"We definitely have to take this to the lieutenant," Morales said. Forbes nodded. "I want you there, Johnson. What about Leila coming, too?"

"No. I will not expose her; it's too dangerous."

Chapter 54   Zack Needs Sarah's Help

"It took time for the forensic accountants to follow the trail, but they succeeded," Zack said to Dr. Schwartz. "Miles Grayson owns Underwood Labs."

"Never heard of him."

The two men sat comfortably in the doctor's living room enjoying a pre-dinner glass of wine. In the background, they heard music from the kitchen and the occasional banging of a pan or cupboard door as Sarah prepared dinner.

"He's a multi-millionaire who owns a lot of businesses that he hides under parent companies. He could easily afford to build and hide Hoover's lab."

"Can you connect the two directly?"

"Not yet. Grayson lives in LA. Phone records show he receives and makes calls to Underwood Labs, which is natural since he owns it. Calls both ways go through an internal switchboard, so there's no way of tracing a line to a specific person or office or lab. My guess is Grayson and Hoover communicate through Hoover's lab phones to keep their communiques undetected. We have to trap Hoover into making a call from his home to Grayson."

"You're sure Grayson is involved?"

"He has to be: his lab, his money. Hoover certainly didn't have the money to establish and run his own lab or rent one. Besides, Hoover lists his job as an employee of Underwood on his tax forms. It's not a direct connection but works as a circumstantial one." Zack swirled the wine in his glass. "I have a meeting scheduled with Morales, Forbes, and their lieutenant to explain my plan for the takedown. The detectives are on board, and they implied the lieutenant was leaning in that direction. The key to launching the plan is shaking up Hoover to get him to contact Grayson outside the lab."

"How?"

"It involves Sarah. Do you think she's strong enough to help set a trap?"

"A qualified 'yes.' She's strong enough if she feels safe. She helped you by letting Morales and Forbes interview her, didn't she?"

"Only after I promised the meeting would be secret, and the police wouldn't take her into custody, and I'd be by her side the whole time. What I have in mind is entirely different. She'd be center stage by herself."

"And in danger?" Dr. Schwartz asked.

"I don't think so. She'll be wearing a wire, and I'll be close by. I'd jump in immediately if I thought the situation was going sideways."

"Ask her, but don't ask her to do something blindly:

cue her in the same as you would any operative. Tell her who she'll be meeting, describe the physical environment, and what she's to do or say. Explain where you'll be and what you'll do if you think she's in any danger."

Dr. Schwartz reached for the decanter of wine to pour himself another glass but withdrew his hand.

"Why not invite her to join us for a glass of wine? If I suspect she's reticent to cooperate, I'll let you know."

Zack went to the kitchen. "Sarah, do you have time to take a break and join the Doc and me for a glass of wine?"

"Oh, I'd like that. Let me get these potatoes in the oven first. Would you open the oven door for me?"

"Sure."

Once the potatoes were in the oven and Sarah had set the timer, she and Zack walked together into the living room. Dr. Schwartz filled all their glasses and nodded to Zack to begin. Sarah raised her glass to take a sip when Zack said, "How would you like to meet the man responsible for injecting you?"

Sarah's hand shook and wine spilled over the edge of the glass. The doctor jumped up and took the glass from her and put it on the side table.

"Don't move, Sarah. Let me get a towel."

Sarah patted her clothes with the towel, but the dark red splotches refused to vanish. "Looks like you owe me some new clothes, Zack," she said. "I doubt these stains will come out."

"Zack, you and I must talk about your brusqueness," the doctor said as he sat back down. "You need to learn to be a little more diplomatic."

"Sorry, Sarah. I didn't mean to scare you."

"You didn't scare me. You startled me. Is it safe to pick up my wine glass again?"

"Start at the beginning, Zack. Explain the situation and what you're trying to achieve. Once Sarah understands, introduce the part you'd like her to play."

Chapter 55   Plan to Raid Lab

Zack, Morales, and Forbes met in Lieutenant Jensen's office at the station. Like many police stations, the Lieutenant's office was at one end of the detectives' room with a plate glass window overlooking the room. Morales and Forbes had already briefed the Lieutenant, or chief of detectives, who was interested in participating but wanted to learn more before committing himself. For their conference, the Lieutenant had lowered the blinds on the window and the adjacent glass door to ensure their privacy.

"The lab we're interested in is in the basement of Underwood Labs, owned by Miles Grayson and operated by Henry Hoover. He likes to call himself a doctor, but he's not," Zack said. "Grayson lives and works in LA which is out of your jurisdiction, so we'll take care of him. Our joint goal is to stop activity in Tucson since it is the hub of the operation."

Zack put a rough diagram on the Lieutenant's desk, and the men gathered around it.

"It's a high-security lab in the basement, accessed by a private elevator. Here," Zack said pointing to the diagram. "Employees have a badge to access the elevator, and it tracks them anywhere they go in the building. They are not allowed to bring anything into the lab or take anything out."

Zack slid his finger across the diagram. "The individual sectors of the operation are in small rooms along this corridor. Doors are opened by fingerprint identification, so only the employees working in the sector have access to it." Zack tapped his finger on the space at the end of the corridor. We believe the lab itself is located here."

"How many sectors are there and how many employees?" Lieutenant Jensen asked.

"Not including the main lab, we believe there are seven sectors with anywhere from two to four employees per sector. The employees are segregated from each other so it's difficult to get an accurate count." Zack pointed. "Notice on the left side of the corridor, one room is double the size of the others. That's the employee dining room with monitors in each corner to discourage exchanges of information about the lab or the function of each sector. Employees go to the dining room in shifts where they're served lunch since they can't bring food into the lab with them. Because they keep the employees separated, we doubt any of them have a full picture of the lab's overall operation and purpose. That works in our favor. When they're rounded up, most are innocent and will agree to give us testimony when they discover what trouble they may be in."

"If it's a high-security lab, how do you know so much about it?"

"I have an undercover in the lab; the information comes from him."

"And your undercover will get us downstairs."

"Yes."

"What about access to the individual sectors?"

"Each door has a slat that opens. We'll flash a Federal warrant. I doubt they'll refuse to cooperate. If they do, there are more forceful options. We'll take them one sector at a time, handcuff whoever exits, and gather them in the dining room under armed guard. As I said, most of them are innocents doing one specified job. I don't expect much trouble."

"I'm missing something," Lieutenant Jensen said. "This is sounding too easy."

"That's only the lab. We'll have simultaneous raids on other locations. The nasty work is being done outside the lab. They have teams that operate drones and vehicles which surveil subjects and capture them, bring them to the lab or some other secret location and then dispose of the bodies in the desert. Those guys are dangerous because they'll be prosecuted and know it. We'll have SWAT teams bring them in."

"Which part are you asking us to do?" Morales said.

"I'd like you to handle the lab since it's in your jurisdiction. Their victims have not been restricted to Tucson. Leila Petterson is an example. Morales, I told you about the case in Prescott that was like Wiley's in Sierra Vista."

Morales nodded.

"There was also one each in Phoenix and Flagstaff that I know of. We don't want jurisdictions to be a problem, so Federal agents will take care of the traveling teams."

"You know who they are?"

"We have the storage unit where the vans are kept under surveillance. If we don't catch the teams there, when we raid the lab, we'll also serve a subpoena for Underwood's list of employees. The head of the lab is listed as a paid employee. They will be, too, under some innocuous title like 'driver.' Might take a little longer to round them up, but we will."

"I'm in," the Lieutenant said. "I will, however, have to bring in the brass to commit those kinds of resources."

Zack turned to look at Morales and Forbes. "Tell him," Zack said.

Morales hesitated. "We think there's a leak in the station," he finally said.

"In this station?"

"Yes, Sir." Morales went on to explain the problems with impounding Leila Petterson's RV and how the delay cost them evidence.

"If we do have a leak, Lieutenant, it could blow the whole operation," Zack said.

"And you're sure it's in this station?" the Lieutenant asked Morales.

"Yes."

"You, Forbes?"

"I agree with Morales."

"But you have no proof?"

Morales and Forbes both said "No" at the same time.

Lieutenant Jensen sat down behind his desk and looked from Morales to Forbes to Zack.

"I don't like hearing this, but you're right, Johnson. A leak could blow the takedown, and I certainly don't want these people to continue operating in my city, or any other, for that matter. I'll tell you what I'll do. First of all, Morales and Forbes, I'll arrange to have a cruiser assigned to you for Johnson's plan to follow the suspect. That needn't go further than this office. Secondly, I'll ignore the chain of command and go directly to the brass downtown about both the takedown operation and the leak. If we do have a leak, I'd like it to be handled in-house. You have any objection to that, Johnson?"

"None."

"Speaking of leaks, I have a question," Morales said to Zack. "You whisked Leila away before the raid when we planned to arrest her, or the person we thought was impersonating her. How did you know about the raid? Do we have another leak?"

"No. The information did not come from anyone in

the station. If you think about it, you needed an arrest warrant. To get one is a process outside the station. I can't say more than that."

"You don't need to," Lieutenant Jensen said. "If I know it wasn't a leak from us, I'm satisfied. How about you, Morales?"

"As I see it now, arresting her would have served no purpose." Morales laughed. "Probably would have led to you Feds breathing down our necks, and that always gets messy."

Chapter 56   Sarah Meets Hoover

Sarah hesitated before knocking on Henry Hoover's front door. She disliked the bright turquoise color so often used as a decorative desert color. Personally, she didn't see any association between the color and the desert except for the few turquoise rocks she'd seen here and there. She ignored her distaste and knocked.

"Hi, Mr. Hoover," Sarah said when Henry answered the door.

A fleeting look of surprise passed across Henry's face. "I don't deal with solicitations or door-to-door salesmen," he said and began to close the door.

"I'm Leila Petterson. Don't you recognize me?"

"I don't know any Leila Petterson." His shaking hand belied his remark.

"How can you forget me? I was your first success, wasn't I?"

"I don't know what you're talking about."

"Don't be upset, Mr. Hoover. I only came to thank you for giving me back my youth."

"You're talking nonsense."

"I'm sure you know perfectly well I'm referring to the injection, Mr. Hoover, but I can understand why you're keeping it a secret." Sarah smiled. "Thank you, again; that's all I wanted to say."

Henry closed the door in her face and ran to the living room window. He watched Leila stroll casually down the brick walkway and turn right when she reached the sidewalk. She disappeared after she passed the high hedge that separated his yard from his neighbor's.

Henry ran outside to the sidewalk to see where Leila went. She was gone, totally gone. There wasn't a trace of her: not on the sidewalk, not on the street, not in her neighbor's yard. The only person he saw was a man walking his dog. There was no one in the cars parked on the street, and he hadn't heard a car start and drive away. Henry shook his head as though to rid himself of a hallucination. Impossible, he told himself; he wasn't given to flights of fancy.

Henry paced in circles around his living room until he smelled his dinner burning. Smoke swirled around the kitchen. He turned off the burners and grabbed potholders to move the pans away from the heat. The smoke and the unrecognizable black mess in the pans stunk. He threw up his hands in frustration.

Despite his agreement with Miles that he'd only call from the lab, Henry picked up the phone. This was an emergency.

"How did she know who I am or where I live?" Henry yelled.

"Henry, calm down and tell me what you're talking about."

In between pauses to catch his breath, Henry recounted Leila's or Anna's visit.

"That's impossible, Henry. Listen to yourself. Anna appears at your door all by herself and then, poof, she disappears into thin air?"

"You think I was imagining it?"

"I think you've been working too hard. When was the last time you took time off to relax?"

"With you pushing me all the time to hurry? When do I have time to relax?"

For the first time, Miles questioned Henry's stability. "I'll look into it."

"You told me no one suspected our project yet I've been exposed. My ass is on the line and you're going to 'look into it.' Your concern is so touching. I expect more than that." Henry slammed down the phone.

Outside, the man walking the dog stopped at a car parked in front of Henry's neighbor's house and popped open the truck.

"You okay?" Zack asked as he reached out a hand to help Sarah climb out of the trunk.

"I am now," Sarah said as she gulped in fresh air. "How did I do?"

"Excellent. Get in the passenger seat and slide down out of sight."

While Sarah did and pulled her wig on, Zack closed

the trunk, opened a back door for the dog to jump in and closed it, and slid into the driver's seat.

"Did Hoover make that phone call you wanted him to make?"

Zack pulled out into the street. "Won't know until I check with the guys. I need to get you and the dog home first."

"Will you tell me if he does? If our little ruse worked?"

Zack glanced over at Sarah. "That's all?"

"I'd love to know more, but I doubt you'll tell me. I'll be satisfied knowing I played a small part in catching these monsters."

"That wasn't a small part. If all goes well, you may have broken the case wide open and have these guys running scared."

Sarah clapped her hands. "Good. I ran scared for long enough; now it's their turn."

During their conversation, Zack had driven the couple of blocks to Dr. Schwartz's house. The dog began barking when he recognized the street and pawed at the window. Zack stopped the car in front of his owner's house and let him out. The dog ran to the front door with his leash trailing behind him. The owner, Evan, heard the barking and opened the door long before Zack had a chance to ring the doorbell. The dog turned in circles, then put his paws on Evan's leg and licked his hand.

Evan squatted down to rub the dog's head. "Good

heavens, Zion, calm down." He looked up at Zack and laughed. "You'd think he's been gone for weeks instead of an hour."

"I appreciate your lending him to me, Evan."

"No problem." Evan stood up to shake Zack's hand. "The Doc's helped us out from time to time. Glad to return the favor. Say 'Hi' to him for us."

"Will do."

Chapter 57   Police Follow Hoover

Henry never ate dinner after Anna's appearance on his doorstep. He did clean up his mess in the kitchen because his fastidiousness forced him to; it didn't take long. He opened a window to let out the smoke and picked up the pans with the unrecognizable charred messes in the bottoms and walked them outside to throw them in the garbage. It was more expedient to buy new pans than try to scrub the old ones clean. Cooking another meal was out of the question; he was upset, not hungry.

Instead of eating, Henry sat, paced, and stared out the window while focusing on two questions: how had Anna known who he was and how had she found him? The only conceivable answer was that someone had betrayed him. Someone in the lab? He shook his head. He and Miles had been so careful while setting up the lab to make sure none of the employees understood the real purpose behind their work. Employees were told they were working on testing products, like the labs upstairs, except theirs were the highest priority, the most top-secret products. Each sector had its own projects and did not confer with other sectors. If a problem arose, they came to him to solve it. Henry thought briefly of the new data analyst but dismissed the idea he might be involved. He knew less than any of the others. His work was mathematical computations; he didn't know what the fields he manipulated represented. The outside teams were more aware of the operation, but those thugs had too much to lose if captured. They were, quite simply, criminals who faced a lifetime in prison, or worse, by betraying either Henry or Miles.

That left Miles. Henry was angry with Miles for his lack of concern when he reported Anna's appearance, but what would Miles gain by betraying him? Miles still needed him to perfect the formula. The questions and possible answers rolled around in Henry's head until they exhausted him, and he finally fell asleep.

The next morning, the questions still bothered him, but the sun shining in his window uplifted his spirits. A new day, a fresh attempt to find answers. He made himself a hardy breakfast, more than his usual, to make up for missing dinner the night before. Cooking breakfast was a little tricky because he'd thrown out the pans he usually used. He made a note to himself to stop at a store on the way home and buy new ones.

As Henry backed out of his driveway, he noticed a police cruiser parked two houses down from his. He dismissed their presence as unimportant until he approached the first stop sign on his route. The police car was now two lengths behind him. How annoying.

Getting a ticket was not on his agenda, so he played the part of a conscientious driver, came to a full stop, and looked both ways. As he drove through the intersection, he hoped the police would turn and get off his tail. They didn't. They followed him block by block, turn by turn, unnerving him. Henry wiped sweat from his forehead.

When Henry turned into the Underwood Labs parking lot, he slowed down and watched in his rearview mirror as the cruiser drove by. Henry breathed a sigh of relief as he pulled into his assigned parking space and took several minutes to compose himself before opening the car door. The police had no reason to follow him. After all, they hadn't flashed their lights or pulled him over. Henry reviewed the route he took from home to the lab. The drive was along streets that anyone might take to leave his neighborhood to get to major arteries. It was all a coincidence.

Once in his lab, Henry's work absorbed him, and he forgot about his unpleasant morning drive. Using the latest data analysis, he decided on the dosage he'd use to inject Carl, the latest subject from Sierra Vista. They'd kept Carl sedated in their off-campus test center, an older house surrounded by a high privacy fence two blocks away from the lab. A man and woman team living as a couple occupied the house and kept a normal routine like other residents on the block.

The basement, however, had been converted into a soundproofed, locked mini clinic without windows where the team took care of the subjects brought there. Henry realized "jail" was a more appropriate term than "clinic," but his sensibilities didn't allow him to use the word. The mobile units drove down the secluded driveway and used the rear door to transfer the subjects into the house. Henry had visited the house several times when Betty, Bob, and Carol were confined there to witness their transformations firsthand. Tomorrow he'd visit Carl to inject him. Henry hoped the chemicals used to keep Carl sedated wouldn't interfere with the effect of the injection.

When Henry drove out of the parking lot into the flow of traffic, he noticed nothing unusual. Having to turn left at the next light, he often glimpsed into his side view mirror watching for a break in the traffic to change lanes. He almost missed his opportunity when he spotted a police car several cars behind him. Not again! At the last minute, he changed lanes and then pulled into the turn lane. A green light and a break in traffic allowed him to make the turn immediately. He slowed down and kept one eye on the rearview mirror. Nobody followed him.

Two blocks later, there was the police car again. Henry's hands shook. Was this another coincidence or were they really following him? Of course, it didn't have to be the same police car. He didn't know how to tell one from another. He'd almost reached his street with the police on his tail when the red light on top of the car flashed and the siren wailed. Henry pulled over to the side of the road. What had he done? A little fancy driving when he'd turned off the main road but nothing illegal. He rested a hand over his rapidly beating heart.

The police did not pull up behind him. Lights still flashing and siren wailing, the police car zoomed by him. Henry sat quietly for five minutes to let his heart calm down before he put the car in gear and drove the last half block home.

As soon as Henry entered the house, he remembered the pans he'd planned to buy on the way home. He debated whether or not to go back out or improvise as he had for breakfast. Improvise won. After dinner, another thought plagued him. Should he call Miles and report the situation with the police? Why bother? If Miles was behind the betrayal, he'd silently gloat. If he wasn't, he'd blame it again on Henry's overactive imagination. The police hadn't stopped him or given any other indication they were following him. They'd driven right by the lab this morning and, tonight, they'd whizzed by before he turned on his street. Henry turned on the television hoping an interesting program on the History Channel might divert his attention from the endless round of questions.

The next morning was a replay of the one before. A police car waited on his street and pulled out behind him. This was not a coincidence. Henry wanted to jump out of his car at the stop sign and demand to know why they were following him. He didn't have the nerve. By the time Henry turned into the parking lot, his hands shook on the steering wheel, and sweat dripped down on his face. Once again, the police car ignored him and drove past.

The receptionist in the lobby noticed the pallor on Henry's face. He dropped his briefcase case and his hands shook as she handed him his lab coat and badge.

"Are you all right, Dr. Hoover?"

"Yes, yes, thank you. I had a fright driving to work. A car missed hitting me by inches. A shock, yes, but I'll be fine."

"Do you want me to call someone?"

"No, no. I'll relax once I get to the lab."

Except he didn't.

Chapter 58   Hoover Cracks

"It's working," Zack announced as he walked into the kitchen. "Thanks again, Sarah. Your performance got the ball rolling."

"Good morning to you, too, Zack. Why don't you pour yourself some coffee and join us," Dr. Schwartz said.

"I can't help it," Zack said as he took a cup from the cupboard. "I get straight to the point."

"No harm there if the people you're addressing know the context."

Coffee in hand, Zack joined the doctor and Sarah at the table.

"Got a call from Morales. They followed Hoover to and from work yesterday and again this morning. Judging by his driving, he became more nervous each time they followed him. Morales said his driving was downright erratic this morning. It was lucky he didn't cause an accident."

"That's something to consider, Zack. You don't want innocent people hurt."

"Yeah. I told them to back off a little so they weren't right on top of him. At this point, seeing the cruiser part of the way should be enough. Now I'm curious to know what he'll do about it. Wish Tucker, he's the undercover in the lab, saw him during the day, but those employees are locked up in their cubicles all day."

"Why does anyone want to work in those conditions?" Sarah asked as she stood up to get the coffee pot.

"They're paid very well. Tucker said he's paid double what he'd expect in a similar job elsewhere."

Zack sprawled back in his chair while Sarah refilled their cups.

"We won't know what he's doing in the lab, but I asked Morales to sit on the lab in an unmarked car in case he leaves during the day. I'm curious whether he'll go somewhere, and if so, where."

Chapter 59 Visit to Safe House

Henry made a beeline to his office at one end of the lab and unlocked the door. The small room, containing a desk, one chair, a computer, and several filing cabinets, was his personal workspace. When the door was open, he had a view of the lab. When closed, he had the privacy needed for confidential phone calls.

Before he closed the door, he spotted Ramon wiping down a lab table. Ramon had strict instructions not to tinker with anything in the lab unless he'd been specifically assigned to do so. Henry realized it would look odd if he left Ramon without a task.

"Ramon, I have some calls to make. While I'm busy, take an inventory of the chemicals. Mark down any chemical that is less than a quarter of a bottle full."

"Yes, Doctor."

Henry closed the door, dropped his briefcase case on the desk, and while still standing, dialed Miles' phone number. He tapped his fingers impatiently on his forehead until Miles answered.

"The police are following me," Henry said with preamble. "And don't tell me it's just my imagination."

Miles rolled his eyes: first Anna, now this.

"Slow down, Henry. Give me a detailed account of when and where they're following you."

"It started yesterday morning ..." Henry continued with a thorough description of his unnerving encounters.

"They didn't pull you over or follow you into the parking lot?"

"I just told you they didn't. I've never seen a cop car on my street before. And two mornings in a row, they're waiting practically outside my door?"

"I agree, Henry, it is very odd. How did you react?"

"I was nervous; how else would I be? But I drove calmly as though I didn't know they were there."

"That's good, Henry."

Miles wasn't sure he believed the police were following Henry, but he had an easy way to check. If they were, he'd find out why. If they weren't, Henry was becoming a liability, and that wasn't acceptable.

"I'm going to call one of my sources, Henry, to find out why they're following you. It may take some time, but I should have an answer for you by the end of the day."

Henry's grip on the phone relaxed. "Thank you, Miles."

"In the meantime, how are you coming along with Carl?"

"I plan to review my notes one more time, then go over to the safe house to inject him."

Miles wanted to scream when Henry said, "... review my notes one more time." The man needed a fire under his butt to move forward; he'd check and recheck *ad nauseam*. This was not the time, however, to upset him further.

"Good," Miles said. "I'll look into this police business and talk to you later."

Henry did try to review the data but had difficulty concentrating. He was no longer sweating, and his hands were steady, but his mind jumped back and forth between the data and the police. Maybe Miles was right; he did overdo the review process. For once, maybe it was time to jump in and inject Carl and not worry about reviewing his notes again. Henry had been worried that Carl might have been sedated for too long. No matter. If Carl began regressing, that was proof the compound worked regardless of what else might be in his system. If he didn't, Henry would hold that up to Miles as an example of why things can't be rushed.

Henry packed a vial and syringe into a traveling case to see for himself what condition Carl was in and called ahead to let the team in the safe house know he was coming. On his way out of the lab, he checked with Ramon.

"How's the inventory coming?" Henry asked.

"Almost done."

"I need to go out. When you're finished with the chemicals, go ahead and inventory the other supplies.

We might as well put in a complete order for everything we need."

"Yes, Doctor."

It wasn't until Henry reached the edge of the parking lot that he remembered the police. He reprimanded himself for not thinking clearly. If the police were following him, he certainly didn't want to lead them to the safe house. Henry spent several minutes looking up and down the street but didn't see a police car. Well, of course, he didn't. They'd assume he'd be in the lab all day. Nevertheless, he kept a close eye on both his rearview and side view mirrors. He made a right, then another right two blocks down, and drove by the house. Nothing. No sign of a police car. A couple of other cars, but that was just normal traffic in the city.

Henry circled the block and came back to his destination. He pulled over to the side of the street and waited. The car behind him passed by without paying any attention to him. The street was empty. Satisfied, Henry drove the car down the secluded driveway and parked.

Unbeknownst to him, the car that passed by circled the block again and drove slowly by the house where the driver had last seen Henry and spotted Henry's car at the end of the driveway. He noted the street address and parked further down the street waiting for Henry to leave.

When the team, Paula and Nick, escorted Henry to

the basement, he was horrified by Carl's condition. Carl leaned sideways in his chair with his head drooping down on his chest. Henry suspected the arms on the chair kept Charles from keeling over.

"Is he always like this?" Henry asked.

"For the last few days, yes. We have to spoon-feed him and he's wearing diapers."

"He's over-sedated. Why did you let him fall into this state?"

"Why didn't someone check on him sooner?" Nick answered testily. "We were following orders. It's not our fault if you guys screwed up."

Henry had no intention of tangling with a 6', 190 lb. thug. "I suppose it is our fault. Your new order is to stop sedating him until further notice. Open the door to his cell. I'm going to give him an injection."

"Fine."

Afterward, Henry hurried out of the house to get back to the safety of his lab. He never noticed the car that pulled out behind him.

The rest of the workday was wasted. Ramon finished the inventory, and Henry sent him upstairs to Purchasing to turn in the order and go home after that.

"Thanks, Doctor." Ramon said. Getting home early was a rarity.

"We'll be busy tomorrow. Be sure you're on time and ready to work."

The phone in his office rang in the late afternoon.

"Henry, I'm sorry it took so long to get back to you, but I have good news. The police are not following you. There have been home burglaries in your neighborhood recently, and the police have increased the presence of patrol cars."

"Do they think I'm a suspect?" asked Henry incredulously.

"No. It was only a coincidence. If they suspected you, they would have stopped you."

Henry didn't believe the explanation. If the police were patrolling the neighborhood, they'd drive up and down the neighborhood streets, not follow him all the way from home to work and vice versa.

Henry had an idea. He checked out of the lab as usual, but instead of driving straight home, he drove to a nearby Macy's to buy replacement pots and pans. If he spotted the police during the drive, he'd know they were following him, not randomly cruising around his neighborhood. Sure enough, he spotted a police car after parking at Macy's. It wasn't on his tail; it parked two aisles over. After making his purchases, Henry opened the trunk to store the packages and, without being obvious, check for the police car. It was still there.

Henry took a slightly different route home and saw the police car along the way. Miles had lied to him.

Chapter 60   Leak in Police Dept.

"Want to buy me another beer?" Morales asked Zack on the phone. "Same place, same time?"

"Sure."

Zack grinned when he hung up. Another meeting meant Morales had intel for him that he didn't want to discuss at the station or on the phone. Zack showed up early, as he had before, to discover all the tables in the bar area were full. He chose a table in the dining room as far away from occupied tables as possible and ordered two beers.

"Bit busy tonight and rather noisy," Morales said after he sat down and picked up his beer.

"Better than busy and quiet. The noise will help drown our conversation."

"Ah," said Morales, "Nothing tastes better than that first sip of beer. Good news." He took a piece of paper out of his pocket and slid it across the table.

"What's this?"

"An address to add to your warrants. Good call having a plainclothes man tail Hoover today."

"I figured he was nervous enough to do something stupid."

"He did. Drove to that address and stayed about 20 minutes. Thought he was being clever and drove around the block first looking for a cop car."

"Any idea who lives there?"

"It's owned by another one of Grayson's companies. Don't know who's staying there or why Hoover went there."

Zack folded the paper and slipped it into his pocket. "Thanks."

"More good news. Lieutenant got a call today from Lieutenant Atwater. He's the night watch commander. Let me stress that. Night watch. He was on duty when we planned the raid on Leila's RV and made plans to tow it."

"Your leak."

"Looks like it. He called my lieutenant and wanted to know if we were running surveillance on anyone in Hoover's neighborhood. Of course, he didn't use Hoover's name; he defined the area by street names. Said he was following up on a complaint."

"Uh-huh."

"Lieutenant wants to know if he should add the new location to our side of the takedown."

"I'd like him to. Does he have enough men?"

"Yeah. Downtown brass wants him to use the SWAT team to tackle the lab, so we only need a couple of us from the station. How many Feds will accompany us to serve the warrants?"

"Four should be plenty unless the Lieutenant wants more: two to go down to the lab and two to serve subpoenas in the offices. I'll assign another two to join you at the new location."

"When?"

"We're still searching for property owned by Grayson capable of storing and maintaining the vans they use: a garage, a warehouse, something of that nature. When we do, it's a go. If they're not within your jurisdiction, we'll cover those locations."

Chapter 61 Hoover Disappears

After his last conversation with Miles, when Miles had lied to him, Henry spent a fretful night pacing around his house questioning Miles' motives. Why didn't Miles believe him when he'd reported Anna's visit and the police cars following him? Instead of Miles worrying about a security breach, he'd treated the incidents as though they hadn't happened. Why? Add to that, Miles' reticence to allow him the time he needed to complete the experiments. Did Miles think he'd found a working compound and the rest was unnecessary? Did Miles think he didn't need Henry anymore because the compound was ready to market? Those thoughts stopped Henry's pacing. That was it. "Ah," Henry said aloud, "Miles thinks I'm expendable like our test subjects! Well, I'm not."

If Miles believed he could lie and insulate himself from the project and still benefit from it, he was wrong. Henry planned to inject himself with the compound and begin anew, leaving Miles empty-handed: without the compound and without the formula. Henry sifted through the papers he had at home pertaining to the formula, burned them in the kitchen sink, and washed the residue down the drain.

During the night, he packed any relevant information he needed, such as his offshore account number and the cash in his home safe into his briefcase. After the horrible year following Yale's firing him when he was nearly starving, Henry had developed a habit of stockpiling cash. He liked to open the safe from time to time and count the money. Feeling the money in his hands satisfied his need to feel secure.

The cash offered security once again as he counted it out before dividing it into envelopes to put in the briefcase. He had almost $11,000 in $100 bills: enough to pay for what he needed until he left Tucson for good and settled in a different city, or a different country, where he'd go into business for himself. He put $500 in his wallet to pay for 'traveling' expenses to eliminate the need of opening the briefcase in public. It amused him the money fit easily into his briefcase. Of course, the money wasn't enough to open his business; he'd get that from his offshore account. He didn't need another fancy research lab. All he had to do was purchase the chemicals and a few pieces of equipment to go into production. Miles wasn't going to hang him out to dry while he sat comfortably in his LA mansion five hundred miles away.

The next day at the lab, Henry prepared more of the compound because he had used the last vial on Carl. He gave his assistant Ramon a list of the ingredients he needed and added several that he didn't to camouflage the genuine contents. Anyone trying to duplicate Henry's formula using all the ingredients on the list would fail.

As Ramon prepared Henry's worktable with the ingredients, empty vials, and other paraphernalia, Henry retreated to his office to remove papers related to mixing the compound and shredded them. He busied himself until Ramon's lunch hour in order to mix the compound when he was alone in the lab. When completed, he filled one vial with the compound and wrapped it and a syringe in a protective sleeve. He added the sleeve to his briefcase and then returned to his worktable to fill six vials with another substance.

After lunch, Henry asked Ramon to transfer the six vials on the worktable to foam- protected slots in a case while he opened the safe hidden behind a swinging door in a cabinet containing ordinary lab supplies. "When you're done, Ramon," Henry said, "please close the safe and make sure it locked automatically. Then clean up the worktable and go upstairs to check my box in the mail room for any messages."

In his office, Henry rechecked his file cabinet, then sat down at the desk to recheck the computer to assure himself that he hadn't left any pertinent records about the chemicals he used for the compound or the formula itself. He was sorting through a pile of miscellaneous papers and pretended not to notice as Ramon approached his desk.

"Uh. Excuse me. Dr. Hoover," Ramon said.

"What is it, Ramon?" Henry asked without looking up.

"There weren't any messages for you. It's 5:00. Was there anything else you need before I leave?"

Henry acted surprised and lowered the paper in his hand.

"5:00 already? You go ahead. I'm going to catch up on this paperwork, then I'll be leaving myself. Have a good evening."

"Thank you. You, too."

Henry lowered his eyes and shuffled through some papers while listening to Ramon's footsteps crossing the lab and opening the hallway door. When it shut, Henry continued to sit at his desk to make sure it didn't reopen. Satisfied, Henry walked to the hall door and peered out the slot in the door to watch Ramon enter the elevator. Henry then sprang into action.

Before he left, Henry took a nostalgic look around his state-of-the-art lab. He hated to leave it. If only Miles wasn't so greedy and had let the project evolve in the time required, he wouldn't have to. Miles was so confident, overconfident, that he'd kept the project secret. In the end, he hadn't, had he? He'd pushed and made mistakes. How else could Anna have appeared on his doorstep?

Henry locked the briefcase by rotating the sequence

of numbers on the combination lock. He was one of the few allowed to bring or take items in or out of the lab. He'd check out of the lab as he normally did as though he planned to return the next day. The receptionist didn't blink an eye when she saw Henry's familiar briefcase. She collected his lab coat and badge as usual and wished him a pleasant evening.

While she was busy checking out other employees, Henry slipped around the corner to the central bank of elevators instead of exiting out the front door. He smiled. Without the badge on, no one was tracking his movements. He took the elevator down. It took him to a small foyer with a door to the loading docks. The door in the foyer was locked from the outside, not from the inside. It prevented unauthorized personnel from entering the main building but not from exiting it. He cautiously opened the door and scanned the loading platform for activity. Several employees were busy unloading a truck in the far bay and paid no attention to him. He walked to the open bay door in front of him and went outside. The air smelled sweeter that evening.

Henry moved into a grove of five Palo Verde trees that obscured him and called a taxi, giving specific directions to his whereabouts. When he saw the taxi enter the parking lot, he stepped out of the grove and waved, so the taxi driver easily saw him. The taxi dropped him off at a Best Western hotel near the airport.

A bellboy saw Henry exit a taxi lugging a briefcase

with him. From the difficulty he was having, the bellboy assumed the briefcase was heavy. He stepped up to Henry and held out his hand.

"May I help you with that, sir?"

Henry turned his side to the bellboy, putting his body between the briefcase and the bellboy. "No. I've got it."

The bellboy hid his surprise at the protective motion as though he'd threatened to pull the briefcase out of the man's hand. "As you wish."

Another taxi pulled up, and the bellboy pushed his cart to it as the taxi driver unloaded suitcases from the trunk and a man helped his wife out of the cab. Once the suitcases had been transferred to his cart, the bellboy followed the couple to the reception desk. The funny little man was still there, awkwardly filling out forms with one hand and clutching the briefcase in the other. When it was time to pay, the man had to put the briefcase down. Although he tried, there was no way to get out his wallet and take money from it with one hand. He put the briefcase down on the floor between his legs and squeezed his legs tightly to the sides. The man finished his business and left. The bellboy decided two things: one, there was something very valuable in that briefcase, and two, he had a great story to tell in the employee's lounge.

The couple he was helping had pre-registered and paid in advance. There was little for them to do except sign a couple of forms and pick up their keys. As the bellboy pushed his cart down the third-floor corridor to their room, he noticed the odd little man. He was having trouble with his key card. The bellboy was prepared to stop and help when the door swung open. It had closed again before the bellboy passed by, but he noted the number of the room, 309. He'd add that to his story in case his coworkers wanted to catch a glimpse of the peculiar guest.

Henry locked the hotel door behind him. He'd made it. He had rented the hotel room for a week under an alias, given phony information on the registration forms, and paid in cash. All untraceable. The busy staff would take little notice of an individual occupant, or one that registered as an older man and left as a younger one.

After treating himself to room service for dinner, Henry prepared an injection for dessert.

Chapter 62   Lab Misses Hoover

Ramon didn't know what to do when Dr. Hoover didn't show up for work. He was always on time. Ramon fidgeted for half an hour before deciding he had to call someone and picked up the lab phone to notify security.

Security responded immediately. They banged loudly on the lab door since they couldn't open it. The sound reverberated down the hallway alerting employees in their cubicles that something was amiss. Several doors opened. When Ramon opened the lab door, several workers witnessed security entering the lab.

The security guards walked through the pristine lab; there were no signs of a struggle. Ramon insisted everything had been normal when he'd left the lab the night before. Dr. Hoover had been in his office doing paperwork. A guard pointed toward the office door.

"Open it."

"I don't have a key; only Dr. Hoover has."

One officer suggested they break it down; another said they should check elsewhere in the building first before violating the doctor's inner sanctum.

The receptionist in the lobby confirmed that Dr.

Hoover had not picked up his lab coat and badge that morning. The last time she had seen him was the evening before when he checked out.

"Did you see him exit the building?"

"No, I was busy with other people who were checking out. I wasn't watching him."

After the guards found Henry's car in its assigned parking space, they returned to their office to review the lobby security tapes from the night before. They saw Henry handing his lab coat and badge to the receptionist. In the corner of the tape, a group of employees entered the lobby from the direction of the elevators and blocked their view of the diminutive doctor. He didn't appear on the tape again. The officers switched to the security camera that focused on the entrance. They didn't see Henry on the tape, but he might have been hidden by the taller exiting crowd. Since Henry no longer wore his tracking badge, the security officers were going to have to identify every employee on the tape at the time they lost sight of Henry and interview them. Before beginning the tedious task, they notified James Hargrove, President of Underwood Labs, of Henry's disappearance.

Hargrove immediately called Miles and outlined the measures they were taking to find Henry.

"Should I call in the Tucson police?" Hargrove asked.

"Not yet. We don't want to send out an alarm and

embarrass the doctor if there is a simple explanation. I am concerned, however, about the safety of the research he was doing; he would want that protected if something happened to him. I want you to carefully pack the contents of his safe. The lab assistant knows its location. If he doesn't know the combination, break the safe open. I will fly out immediately: should be there within two hours. I want you to meet me at the airport with the contents. I'll call you en route and tell you the time my pilot expects to land and where to meet us."

Miles called his pilot and told him to prepare the jet for immediate takeoff to Tucson.

"Henry, what have you done?" Miles asked aloud in his empty study.

While Miles contemplated possible explanations for Henry's absence, the employees in his lab did the same thing. Despite the security measures, word had traveled from cubicle to cubicle after Ramon informed them the doctor was missing. Doors normally kept locked opened and whispered words traveled up and down the corridor.

Michael Tucker, Zack's undercover, focused on how he might inform Zack. He decided bold was the only answer. He told Oatsdale, his supervisor, he was developing a migraine and if he didn't take the medicine stored in his locker, he'd soon be useless. After hearing of Henry's absence, Oatsdale concentrated on implementing security measures to encode their data.

He simply told Tucker to go.

Tucker grabbed his phone from his locker and called Zack. "Now. Hoover's missing and the whole lab knows it."

"Where are you?"

"Upstairs in the locker room."

"Stay upstairs. We need you for access to the elevator."

Tucker thought he'd been alone in the locker room, but he heard the pneumatic puff of air as someone closed the door quietly. He ran to the door, but whoever had been there had vanished.

While Zack called Morales (who called the Lieutenant who called brass who called SWAT) and his FBI unit to deploy teams to various pre-assigned locations, Miles met James Hargrove at the airport. The company president turned over the booty from Henry's safe. Within 15 minutes, Miles was back in the air and tore open the package. He sighed with relief with he saw the vials carefully packed in a container marked with yesterday's date. Three times, he rummaged through the papers in the box but didn't find a copy of the formula. He wanted both, but the compound was good enough. He'd hire another scientist, one less erratic than Henry, to break down the compound and duplicate the formula.

Chapter 63 Sarah Depressed

As Zack walked through the centrally located kitchen, he ended one call; the phone immediately rang again.

"Yeah, I'm on my way. SWAT there yet?" He listened. "10 minutes."

Seeing Dr. Schwartz and Sarah sitting at the table, Zack said, "It's going down," without breaking his stride, and he was gone.

"What's going down?" Sarah asked.

"I believe he means they're raiding the lab this morning."

"And they'll get all those people?"

"I doubt that. They'll shut down the lab, but there are several peripheral locations. I doubt they'll be able to get to all of them at one time. We may not see Zack for days."

"But I'll be free? I won't have to worry about someone coming after me?"

The doctor paused to pour more coffee.

"Not yet, Sarah. Don't celebrate yet. Not until Zack gives the word. You may now be in more danger than ever. I'd prefer you stay in the house until we hear from Zack."

Sarah's eyes misted. "But why?"

"You are the star witness to prove the allegations against Hoover and Grayson. Without you, the case against them falls apart. If there's ever a time when they'd like to get rid of you, it's now."

"First, I was an experiment, now I'm evidence. Will I ever be plain old me again?"

The doctor rested his hand on top of hers.

"Your life has forever changed, Sarah."

Sarah withdrew her hand and stared down at the table.

"And it keeps getting worse. I had hoped when Zack caught these monsters, I'd be free."

Dr. Schwartz put his hand under her chin and gently lifted her head until they established eye contact.

"Did you believe it would be that simple, Sarah?"

Sarah squirmed and said with a half-smile, "I said 'hoped.' I'm so tired of hiding."

"There'll come a time when you won't have to. We've spoken before about where you might like to live. Let's concentrate on the future and starting over and generate some enthusiasm for that."

Sarah shrugged. "As you've said before, once this story comes out, I'll be a celebrity, especially if I stay in the Tucson area. I don't want to live in the spotlight. I have a new name but no past. Even if I go into Witness Protection like Zack suggested, I go someplace new where no one knows me. I'll have no friends and only be eligible for entry-level jobs where an employer doesn't care about past experience. And I'll always have my memories haunting me."

"Remember, too, that I said the past is only important if you make it so. People generally won't pry unless you give them a reason to. Witness Protection will give you a generalized past and find you a job. If it's not to your liking, go back to school. You have your youth again. Take advantage of it. As to your memories, you also have good ones. Think of those. You're strong, Sarah, or you wouldn't have made it this far. Call on that strength to get you through this last part of 'Leila's' life. You'll feel differently when you're out on your own again."

"Maybe. Please excuse me." Sarah stood up and wandered off in the direction of her room.

Dr. Schwartz watched her go. Sarah always cleaned up the dishes after a meal; she considered that her contribution for staying at the house. The doctor didn't mind tidying up after breakfast, but in addition to their conversation, her walking away and forgetting the dishes was symptomatic of depression. She had a lot to face yet that could drain and damage her if she remained depressed. He poured himself more coffee and let his mind roam. How could he help her?

Chapter 64   Lab Raided

SWAT parked in front of the entrance to Underwood Labs and police cruisers parked helter-skelter around their vehicle. Together they swarmed the lobby. Everyone in the lobby froze except for Zack and Michael Tucker.

"This way," Tucker said and headed down the corridor to the elevator. Part of the SWAT team jammed into the elevator and began evacuating the cubicles on the ground floor while Tucker rode the elevator back up to get the remainder of the team not assigned to other duties: guarding the front entrance and the door to the loading docks.

A team member knocked on the first door. When an employee opened the slot, he faced the end of a rifle barrel. "We're serving a Federal warrant. Open the door." The employee did and the two workers in the cubicle meekly followed an armed escort to the dining room. An officer checked the room in case someone was hiding and then jammed the door open. They crossed the hall to the next door to keep movement in front of them as they worked their way down the corridor.

The elevator arrived with the second half of the team

who positioned themselves around the dining room to keep order as the room filled up. All went smoothly until they reached the third door on the right. No one responded to their knock.

"I've got this," Tucker said and opened the door with his fingerprint.

Oatsdale turned from his computer in surprise. An officer pointed his gun. "Hands off the computer."

Oatsdale held up his hands. "It doesn't matter; I'm finished."

Tucker pushed his way into the room. "Finished what?"

"You, Tucker. You're cooperating with them?"

"Finished what?"

"I've encrypted the files," Oatsdale said smugly. "They won't do you any good."

"You're good, Oatsdale, but I'm an expert. I'll simply decode them."

Oatsdale waved his hand in dismissal. "You don't even know what you were working on."

"You mean how changing the variables affected Hoover's formula?"

Oatsdale blanched.

"I'd keep this guy separate from the others. Until I talk to Zack, let's keep this room locked since I can get into it."

"Any idea where to keep him?"

"There's a small kitchen off the dining room. I'll go

upstairs and talk to Zack now." Tucker said to Oatsdale, "Take off your lab coat."

"No."

"Take it off," said an officer, "or we'll take it off for you."

Oatsdale raised his hand toward his badge.

"Grab his hand."

The officer not only did but handcuffed him and held him still while Tucker removed his badge.

"These give you access to the elevator," Tucker said. "Have all the employees remove their lab coats, or at least the badges. That will strand them down here, and you can pass them out to your team. Tell them to press the up and down buttons at the same time. The elevator automatically knows whether to go up or down. I'll take this one to Zack. Get another one to give to Lieutenant Jensen and tell him we've cleared most of the area and ask him to come down."

Tucker returned to an eerily deserted upstairs. Police officers patrolled the corridors keeping employees in their offices.

"Any problems?"

"Not really. We told them they weren't in trouble if they stayed in their offices or labs or whatever and didn't interfere. Several protested. They were arrested. It settled the rest of them down."

"Do you know where Lieutenant Jensen is?"

"Hold on." The officer turned his head and spoke

into the mic on his shoulder. A disembodied voice answered, "In the president's office. First-floor corridor on the right."

As Tucker entered the office, he heard James Hargrove say, "I'm telling you again, Dr. Hoover runs the lab downstairs. It's high security because he works with new curative medicines. That's all I know. His lab is separate from the rest of the building which I oversee."

"He's not a doctor."

"Excuse me?"

"Are you hard of hearing?" Zack asked. "Henry Hoover is not a doctor."

"But Miles said ..."

"You know Miles Grayson?"

"Of course, I do. He owns Underwood, including Hoover's lab."

"When was the last time you saw him?"

"About an hour ago. I met him at the airport to deliver a package. Imagine my horror when I returned here and found police all over the building. I still don't understand why you're here."

"What was in the package?"

"The contents of Dr. Hoover's safe."

"Mr. Hoover."

Hargrove shrugged. "Whatever."

"Specifically what were the contents?"

"I don't know. After we discovered Hoover was

missing, I called Miles to inform him. He was worried about the security of Hoover's latest work and asked me to have Ramon, Hoover's lab assistant, pack up the contents of the safe. Miles flew to Tucson in his private jet to pick up the package. I never looked inside it."

"What did Miles do after you gave him the package?"

"Flew back to Los Angeles."

Damn, Zack thought. Miles has the compound. As soon as Zack had the operation at Underwood under control, he'd fly to LA and pick up Miles. In the meantime, he phoned the FBI office in LA and ordered them to put Miles under surveillance, to check where his plane was, and if it was in LA, to make sure it didn't leave.

"Tucker," Zack said. "How's it going downstairs?"

"Good. One minor problem." Tucker explained the run-in with Oatsdale.

"I want you to go back down and work on decoding the data. We need it."

"I'm supposed to bring Lieutenant Jensen down to oversee processing the employees."

Zack turned to one of the Tucson cops. "Call Jensen on your mic, will you, and ask him to meet us at the elevator."

"Who else besides Hoover's lab employees has access to the private elevator?" Zack asked Hargrove.

"The security guards."

"How many are on duty now?"

"Eight. They usually patrol the corridors unless they're called to a specific incident."

"Off duty?"

"Sixteen. We have three shifts, eight per shift."

"Where are their badges?"

"The receptionist in the lobby keeps all badges not checked out."

"Some security."

"She's ex-military. No one messes with her, not even the guys."

"I'll send up some of the SWAT guys," Zack said to the Tucson police officers. "I want the security guards found and their access badges taken as well as the ones stored in the lobby."

"I told SWAT to collect the badges downstairs," Tucker said.

"Good. Let's go, Tucker. The rest of you wait with Hargrove. Make sure he doesn't use the phone. You have a cell, Hargrove?"

Hargrove took it out of his pocket and placed it on the desk. "One of you hold on to that."

"Are you going to tell me what this is all about?" Hargrove asked.

"Mass murder."

Hargrove opened his mouth to speak, but he was so stunned, no words came out.

A compliant group of employees sat quietly in the

dining room because a ring of armed guards surrounded them. Lieutenant Jensen arrived and introduced himself and Phillip Johnson. Although the higher echelon now knew Zack's real name, he was still referred to by his alias.

"We will be interviewing each of you individually, specifically about your job in the lab. Your responses and cooperation will determine whether you go home to your families tonight or spend the night in jail."

A collective gasp erupted. One brave man said, "But we signed a non-disclosure agreement. We'll lose our jobs."

"You've already lost your jobs. This lab is closed. You may refuse to answer our questions, that's your right, but I should add that if you do and we arrest you, the charge is mass murder. If we do release you today and you try to skip town, you'll be considered a fugitive and hunted down. I also do not want you talking to the press. Simply refer to that non-disclosure agreement and keep your mouth shut. We will consider anyone who talks to the press in a highly unfavorable light."

While Jensen spoke, it was as if he had pushed a button to instantly drain the color from the employees' faces. Several started to cry.

"Which one of you is Ramon?" Zack asked.

Ramon raised his hand.

"Come with me."

Zack took Ramon to Hoover's lab and grilled him on

his job, then on the contents of the safe he had packed up. Zack sized him up as a man competent at his job but not a self-starter. He followed directions without question and showed no motivation to go beyond Hoover's specific instructions. Zack deduced he feared Hoover and losing his lucrative job if he varied from Hoover's rigid demands. He had packed the papers in the safe but never read them; Zack wondered if one of them contained the formula. Ramon confirmed that the vials of the latest version of the compound had been prepared the day before. As Zack feared, those vials were now in Miles's possession, and Miles could have the compound analyzed and recreated by a competent scientist. Zack needed to get his hands on those vials ASAP.

Chapter 65 Safe House Raided

"Thanks, man, I appreciate it."

Nick hung up the phone and turned to Paula. "Time to get out of here. Something's going on at the lab. There's a SWAT team there. Let's go."

"And leave all our stuff here?"

"We can replace the stuff if they don't catch us. Otherwise, we'll be wearing orange jumpsuits and won't need the stuff."

"What about that guy downstairs?"

"Forget him."

"If they don't know about this house, he'll die."

"He's three-quarters dead anyway. That mousy doctor will break easily. They'll find this place, and I'd rather not be here when they do."

"At least leave the keys so they can get to him. Let me grab my purse."

Nick backed their car out of the garage and was halfway down the driveway when a squad car with lights flashing pulled into the driveway.

"Shit!" Nick jumped out of the car which continued to roll. A bullet whizzed by his head.

"Stop where you are," a voice commanded. "That

was a warning shot. The next one won't miss."

Nick didn't stop, and the next bullet didn't miss. Nick grabbed his leg and fell to the ground cursing. The car, however, did stop when it crashed into the squad car. An officer pulled Paula from the car, Mirandized and handcuffed her.

By now, three other police cars blocked the street. Morales and Forbes led four other officers down the driveway. Morales stopped near Nick squirming on the ground.

Nick stopped swearing long enough to say, "I'm hurt. I need a doctor."

"I'll call Dr. Hoover and see if he's available," Morales said.

The reply was enough to shut Nick up.

"Call an ambulance," Morales said to one of the uniforms. "And stay with him."

The detectives searched through the house.

"Plenty of evidence here to establish they lived here," Forbes said.

"Yeah. But why would Hoover come here? We're missing something," Morales said as they walked back toward the rear door.

They stopped at the entrance to the kitchen.

"Look at this," a uniform said and pulled open a full-sized door between the cabinets. "I thought a door here was odd. Look what's behind it."

Behind the door was a locked solid metal door.

"Should we call a locksmith?"

Forbes spied a key ring on the kitchen counter and picked it up.

"Let's see if any of these keys fit."

One by one Forbes tried the keys. The fifth key slid easily into the lock and turned. Forbes pushed the door open revealing a staircase that led to a dark basement. He flipped a light switch on the wall, which illuminated both the staircase and the basement below. The five men walked in single file down the stairs. When they reached the bottom, they gathered in stunned silence.

The men stood in a mini-sized kitchen with a sink, cabinets, refrigerator, and a rectangular table with two chairs. At the other end of the basement was an open bathroom with a sink and an unenclosed shower. Between the kitchen and bathroom, six cells lined the walls, three on each side, constructed of see-through metal gratings functioning as walls and a matching grilled door. The men recognized them immediately for what they were: jail cells. Each cell contained a single bed and a toilet. The interior of the basement had been constructed to permit an unobstructed view of the entire basement.

A groan from one of the furthest cells snapped them back to action. They ran down the corridor between the cells and found a man lying on his bed in the last cell on the right. Forbes fumbled with the ring of keys to find the key to that cell. The unconscious man had a weak but steady pulse.

Morales briefly heard the distant wail of an ambulance siren and ran back upstairs. It surprised him to see the paramedics already attending to Nick until he realized that had they not left the kitchen and basement doors open, they might not have heard the ambulance at all. The basement was soundproof.

"Forget him," Morales said. "I have a man in serious distress inside." Morales turned to an officer standing by. "Call another ambulance for that piece of trash."

Nick grabbed hold of a paramedic's arm. "I was first."

The paramedic twisted his arm free.

"You'll need a hand gurney," Morales said to the paramedics. To the officer, he added, "Tell them there's no rush on the second ambulance."

"You can't do that," Nick said.

"I just did," Morales retorted.

"It's police brutality."

"You guys slay me. What you did to that man inside is brutality. You get hurt, and you cry foul."

The paramedics had returned with the hand gurney, and Morales led them to the basement. They, too, paused in stunned silence at the bottom of the stairs.

"Victim is down on the right," Morales said.

The paramedics switched into professional mode. Morales left them to tend to their patient and climbed the stairs out of the "dead zone" to call Zack.

"How's it going over there?" Morales asked.

"Chaotic but under control. The lab rats are frantic, worrying about what's going to happen to them. Jensen's processing them."

"Where are you?"

"In Underwood's business offices getting info from Personnel and Payroll on all their employees to track down the outside teams. I have to catch a plane to LA in three hours."

"Can you get away for a few minutes?"

"For?"

"You've got to see this house. If I tried to describe it, you wouldn't believe me. We got the team in charge of it. They must have been tipped off because we almost missed catching them. Also found another victim. Alive but in bad shape. Paramedics are with him now."

"Any idea who he is?"

"I have a hunch it's Sam Wiley from Sierra Vista."

"Another witness. Excellent. Let me put someone in charge of collecting the company records, and I'll stop by shortly. By the way, while I'm gone, I'd like to delegate you to head the group sifting through those records to identify the outside teams. Tucker's busy here decoding data, but he can help you if needed."

"The group? Is that Feds or TPD?"

"Both."

"I get to boss the Feds around?" Morales asked with a grin. "My dream job."

Chapter 66   Hoover Injects Himself

Henry stood in front of the bathroom mirror to take a long look at the "old" Henry. He picked up the vial of compound in one hand and a syringe in the other. He looked from one to the other, realizing he was about to do what he'd always warned Miles wasn't protocol for a reliable outcome. It bothered him. Henry mentally reviewed each component in the formula. None of them screamed danger. Henry was sure he'd regress as the others had; he could not, however, predict any unexpected side effects with so little data from so few experiments. Miles had forced him to this untenable point. Henry sighed and plunged the needle into his arm.

After injecting himself, Henry threw the vial and syringe into a wastepaper basket. Since he'd already prepared himself for sleep and hung out the "Do not disturb" sign, he climbed into bed. The twitching began soon after, mild at first but annoying. Henry settled down and turned on the TV as a distraction.

The late news featured a story about Underwood Labs. He'd been sure the lab would report him as missing and had laughed at the irony. The news had not mentioned him, but something was going on at the lab. It showed pictures of a SWAT van and multiple police cars outside. The spokesperson for the police department said only that it was an ongoing investigation, and they could not release any details.

Henry drifted off to sleep and awoke again several times during the night. Each time he did, the twitching seemed more severe, more like shaking. He'd also developed a headache that grew more intense each time he woke up. At daybreak, he finally found the nerve to get up and check himself in the mirror. Henry admired his younger self. His skin had smoothed, especially the crow's feet around his eyes. Speaking of his eyes, his eyesight had improved. The prescription in his glasses was now too strong. He saw better without his glasses than with them. By the time he finished regressing, maybe he wouldn't need glasses at all. His hair, too, was rejuvenating, less gray and thicker.

What bothered Henry was his headache. He wasn't prone to headaches, and what started as irksome now felt like a hammer hitting his head. He didn't recall any of his test subjects, especially those on the 20-year compound, complaining of headaches. Damn Miles. Once again he'd fallen victim to the pressure Miles exerted on him to act quickly rather than to observe, record, and analyze. Henry held his pounding head between his hands and climbed back into bed.

The morning news reported Henry's disappearance

and showed his picture which distressed him even more. The police were now searching for him. He'd thought his younger self would be safe in Tucson for a few days while he planned where to go next. Now he was stuck here and dared not go out to get help for his headaches. Why hadn't he skipped town before his disappearance was discovered? Before the police searched for him. Miles, Miles, Miles. Miles took care of the pre-planning and details. In Henry's usual one-step-at-a-time mode, planning a quick and safe disappearance from the lab had so overwhelmed him that he'd had little time to plan beyond it.

Henry saw himself as a good-intentioned scientist working on a compound to improve life. Anna had thanked him for his gift, hadn't she? Henry saw himself as a candidate for the Nobel Peace Prize, not as a scoundrel like Miles was. Miles was the dubious author of death who had chosen to get rid of their subjects rather than let them live.

But here he was, hiding in a hotel room, not exactly the appropriate place for a scientist of his status. At least no one at the hotel had paid any particular attention to him; he'd simply blended in as another guest.

Chapter 67   Jeff Reappears

Sarah relaxed in the armchair in her bedroom reading with her feet propped up on the ottoman. She'd chosen the mystery novel *Running from Myself* because the title sounded so much like her present situation. A knock on the door and Dr. Schwartz's voice asking, "May I come in?" sidetracked her.

"Yes, of course."

When the doctor opened the door, he wasn't alone. Sarah froze, believing she was hallucinating. Standing next to him was a dog that looked like Jethro.

"Jethro?"

That's all the dog needed. He bounded across the room, flew into her lap, and began licking her face. Sarah laughed and struggled under the dog's wiggling body to close the book. She gave up and hugged the dog. She turned her head from side to side trying to avoid the dog's tongue so she could speak.

"What is Jethro doing ..." She stopped when she saw, not the doctor, but Jeff leaning against the door frame.

"Jeff?"

"In the flesh."

"It can't be," Sarah said at the same time Jeff said, "Jethro, calm down."

The dog stopped his frantic licking but refused to leave Sarah and sprawled across her lap. Jeff leaned over and kissed Sarah's cheek. Despite Jethro's weight on her legs, Sarah inched them over on the ottoman so Jeff could sit down.

"How? Why?"

"The doctor called me and said you needed a friend, so here we are."

"But how did he know where to find you? I didn't."

"You'll have to ask him. All I know is that he did. I was bummed when we lost contact."

"So was I. My phone was destroyed."

"He said that. Some friend of his located me."

Sarah immediately thought of Zack.

"The doctor said you're going through a rough time and needed cheering up. Jethro insisted on coming, too."

"You have no idea how glad I am to see both of you."

"Hear that, Jethro?" Jeff rubbed the dog's head. "Leila's happy we're here."

Jethro responded by trying to lick Sarah's face.

Sarah laughed. "Don't get him roused up again." She lost her smile. "My name's not Leila anymore. It's Sarah."

Jeff took Sarah's hands in his. "Leila, Sarah, it's all the same. You're the same person. What did

Shakespeare say, 'A rose by any other name is still a rose'?"

Sarah laughed. "If you want to be technical, Shakespeare wrote 'A rose by any other name would smell as sweet.' That was re-interrupted later to 'A rose by any other name is still a rose'."

"Bah. Too technical for me." Jeff leaned over and tickled her. "You know what I mean, right? You're the same person regardless of your name. If you want to tell me why you changed your name or whatever else is going on, fine. I'm listening. If not, that's fine, too. Don't get me wrong. I'm curious, but most of all, I'm just happy to have found you."

"It's that simple?"

"Yup. I missed you. I have since you left the park."

Sarah burst into tears.

"Hey, none of that." Jeff leaned over to hug her, but Jethro was in the way. They settled for a group hug.

"How long will you be here?"

"That depends on you. The doctor said you need a break away from here. Jethro and I are hoping you'll come home with us."

Sarah's face drained. "Leave here? Go away?"

"Hey, don't look like that. You don't have to. It's not a commitment; it's a 'timeout' like we had at Alamo."

Sarah grabbed Jeff's arm. "Jeff, I'd love to go with you. I just can't believe I can go. I need to talk to Dr. Schwartz. Are you sure you want me to stay with you?"

Jeff grinned. "I'm sure. How about you, Jethro?" He tousled the dog's head. "You want Leila, I mean Sarah, to come home with us?"

The dog barked in agreement.

"It's settled," Jeff said. "Go talk to the doctor. I'll take Jethro for a walk."

Sarah found Dr. Schwartz in the kitchen making lunch. When she entered alone, he asked, "Where's your friend?"

"Walking the dog. I have so many questions, I don't know where to begin."

"Perhaps it's easier if I explain."

The doctor began with his concern about Sarah's depression and her need for a change of venue. He remembered her talking fondly about Jeff in her journal and their early sessions and talked to Zack.

From the beginning, Zack had suspected a plant in the state park to keep track of her and Jeff fit the bill, so Zack vetted Jeff and concluded the undercover had not been Jeff. In tracking Jeff down, Zack had all the information they needed to contact Jeff who had enthusiastically responded to the doctor's inquiry about helping Sarah.

"Jeff doesn't know your situation; I leave that part to you. How much or how little you want to tell him is up to you."

"Is it fair not to tell him?"

"Has he asked you?"

"No. He said he was curious but didn't need to know."

"There's your answer, Sarah. Some people are content to let the past stay in the past. For now, enjoy being with someone your age who you're fond of."

"He wants me to go home with him for a visit."

"How do you feel about that?"

"I'd love to get away from all this."

"Then go."

"What does Zack say about my leaving?"

"He thinks it's a good idea. Gets you out of the danger zone. He doubts our dubious friends know about Jeff. If you go, he'll call you with the name and number of a contact in Mesa where Jeff lives in case you need help. We both want to see you smiling again."

Sarah did something she'd never done before; she hugged Dr. Schwartz. "Thank you, thank you," she said.

"Seeing you happy again is thanks enough. Now let me finish making these sandwiches. We'll have lunch, and you can be on your way. I left a suitcase in my office assuming you'd want to go. Use that to pack your clothes."

The doorbell rang.

"They're back," Sarah said and took off toward the door.

"Whoa. You don't answer the door, remember?"

Sarah stopped. "But it's Jeff."

The doctor caught up to her and put his hands on

her shoulders. "You assume it's Jeff, and it probably is. You must still be cautious, Sarah, wherever you are. The danger isn't over until Zack says it is. Stay here."

When the doctor answered the door, Jethro brushed past him and ran inside until his taut leash stopped him.

"Sorry about that," Jeff said.

"Let him go."

Jeff dropped the leash, and Jethro took off. Enthusiastic barking told them he'd found Sarah.

"There's a suitcase there for Sarah to use," said Dr. Schwartz pointing into his office.

Jeff grinned. "She's coming with us."

"Please be gentle with her, Jeff. She needs a friend, but she also needs a calm environment."

"Something really bad happened to her, didn't it?"

"Yes."

Their conversation ended when Sarah appeared around the corner with Jethro at her side. Jeff stepped into the office and picked up the suitcase.

"I'm so glad you're coming with us."

"Me, too."

"You go get packed up," Dr. Schwartz said, "and I'll get lunch on the table." He looked down at Jethro. "I don't have any dog food."

"No problem. He doesn't eat in the middle of the day. He'll be content if Sarah's in sight."

The doctor went to the kitchen while Jeff, Sarah, and Jethro headed for her bedroom. Jeff deposited the suitcase on the bed then gathered Sarah into his arms. Jethro lay down on the carpet near them.

"I'm really, really glad you're coming with us."

Sarah melted into his embrace. Jeff felt rather than heard a sob.

"I'm still having trouble believing you and Jethro are here. You're like my Prince Charming coming to rescue me."

Jeff laughed. "I've never been called Prince Charming before. However, if I'm going to whisk you away to my kingdom, we'd better get that suitcase packed."

Sarah opened the suitcase.

"That's pretty small," he said. "I guess you're not taking a lot with you."

Sarah eyed the interior of the suitcase. "It's plenty big. It'll hold all my clothes."

Jeff walked to the closet to grab a handful of clothes and was amazed to discover one handful emptied the closet.

"Would you go to the kitchen and ask Dr. Schwartz for some Ziploc bags for the bathroom stuff?" Sarah asked.

"Sure, if you tell me where it is."

"Straight down the hallway past the front door and through the living room."

Jethro picked up his head as his master walked to the bedroom door.

"You stay here with Sarah," Jeff said.

Jethro contently lowered his head again. By the time Jeff returned, Sarah had packed the contents of the dresser drawers and was folding the clothes from the hangers into the suitcase. She thanked him for the plastic bags, filled them with her toiletries, and added them to the suitcase.

"That's it," she said and closed the suitcase.

"That's all you have here?"

"That's all I own, period."

Jeff sank down on the bed next to the suitcase. "Period? Did something happen to the rest of your clothes? You had more than that at Alamo. What about your RV and Hobie?"

"Gone, all gone."

Sarah turned away from him so he wouldn't see the tears gathering in her eyes. Jeff grabbed her arm and pulled her down on the bed next to him. He put his arm around her shoulder and pulled her close. She turned and put her arms around his neck and sobbed into his shoulder. He rubbed his hand up and down her back.

"I'm sorry. I didn't mean to upset you."

Jethro came and rested his head on her knee.

The tableau continued for several minutes until Sarah lifted her head and wiped her eyes.

"It wasn't you; it was the memories that upset me. My RV was destroyed in a fire, a fire someone intentionally set. Fortunately, neither Hobie nor I was in it at the time. I couldn't take care of Hobie after that. He went to live with a friend. I came here."

A million questions popped into Jeff's mind. Topping the list was who would set her RV on fire. He remembered the doctor's warning to be gentle with her because she'd experienced something horrible. He left his questions unasked.

"Are you two ready for lunch?" a voice called.

"Be there in a few minutes," Sarah answered and disentangled herself from Jeff's arms.

"I can't say more right now," Sarah said to Jeff.

"You don't have to."

She leaned over and kissed his cheek. "Let me wash my face."

Despite the scrubbed face, Dr. Schwartz knew Sarah had been upset. He kept a close eye on Jeff, wondering if he'd made a mistake. They both seemed genuinely happy to be together, and he tabled his doubts. Sarah needed to spread her wings, and upsets were bound to occur as she did.

Before they left, the doctor reminded her about her wig out of Jeff's hearing. "Whenever you're in the Tucson area," he said. "Caution, remember? I want you to call me to let me know how you're doing, good or bad."

Sarah hugged the doctor and thanked him, then excused herself to go put on the wig. She'd hoped not to wear it in front of Jeff, but the doctor was right. Who knew who might see her on the way out of town?

Her reappearance with the wig startled Jeff momentarily. "Hey, that looks great. It suits you, but you look so different."

"My little disguise."

"It works. What'd you think, Jethro?"

Jethro barked and nudged Sarah's hand.

"I don't think I fooled him." They all laughed.

Dr. Schwartz dismissed his doubts about Jeff. The man must wonder why Sarah needed or wanted a disguise, but he took the unexpected in stride without questioning her. He and Zack had made the right decision.

Chapter 68   Grayson Stranded

Miles flew home to Bel Air and caught the story of the raid on Underwood Labs on the midday news. His initial reaction was smug. Sure, he'd miss the income if they shut Underwood down completely, but because of his quick reaction to the news of Henry's disappearance, he'd gotten ahold of the compound. He'd simply set up business elsewhere and watch profits soar. The news showed photos taken from the street of the SWAT and police vehicles parked in front of Underwood. The commentator said they had no information on the purpose of the raid but would keep the public informed as the police released details.

His first reaction quickly changed. What was the purpose of the raid? The number of vehicles was overdone if they were simply investigating Henry's absence. Had something else happened at Underwood, or had Henry been right all along? Miles had dismissed Henry's insistence that the police were following him and Anna's appearance at Henry's house as Henry's paranoia. He'd checked with the lieutenant, hadn't he? Had the police somehow gained insight into their operation? How? Perhaps Henry hadn't "disappeared;"

perhaps he'd been picked up by the police, and the raid was a consequence. Henry wasn't strong enough to withstand an interrogation. And just why, Miles asked himself, hadn't his well-paid informant warned him of their plans?

Miles fumed. He'd call his underworld contact in Tucson to eliminate the lieutenant. No sense leaving loose ends. Before he did that, however, he had other "housekeeping" chores to attend to. The Tucson police couldn't touch him in California, but Henry's paranoia had rubbed off on Miles. A vacation to another country without an extradition treaty with the U.S. sounded like a good idea. He'd keep track of the aftermath of the raid from afar and return to the U.S. when he knew he hadn't been implicated in Henry's activities. Oh, sure, as the owner of Underwood, the police would scrutinize a possible involvement, and if they found Henry or already had him in custody, Henry would name him as a co-conspirator, but they needed concrete proof and they didn't have it. He'd claim he believed Henry had been working on curative medicines, the same thing they told the employees, and had no idea Henry had branched out into other projects. All they would get from Henry or anyone else at the lab would be hearsay, and his lawyers would make mincemeat of those allegations.

Before Miles turned his attention to packing, he burnt the papers taken from Henry's safe. He'd read through them on the plane; they were charts and notes on the various experiments. While they might be handy in the future, Miles didn't consider them essential since the latest version of the compound served as a starting point for Henry's replacement. He didn't need notes on the failures.

Miles then carefully packed the vials into a leather duffle bag. The foam in the container already protected the vials, but Miles double-wrapped the container in a towel as additional protection from possible breakage. He put important documents he'd need, such as his passport and checkbook, in the breast pocket of his suit jacket, and added a stash of cash to his wallet. He wasn't trying to hide; he didn't have to. Besides, hiding implied guilt. He'd use his credit cards and personal checks as usual.

Before he packed a suitcase, he called the pilot to prepare the plane to be ready to go by the time he finished packing and drove to the airport. The phone rang and rang. Damn. He paid the man to be available 24/7. Where was he? The seeds of doubt bloomed.

Miles called his manservant, Ricardo, to the library and told him to take the Mercedes and go to their regular liquor store and buy a bottle of scotch. Miles read the befuddlement on Ricardo's face. Ricardo always kept the bar well-stocked and had never been asked to drive the Mercedes.

"Keep your eyes open," Miles said. "I want to know

if anyone follows you. Call me as soon as you park at the store."

"Yes, Sir."

Ricardo called 20 minutes later.

"I noticed a car behind me not long after I pulled out of the driveway, a black SUV," Ricardo said. "It followed me to the liquor store and parked a few spaces behind me on the street."

"An old or new SUV?"

"New."

"Go inside the store and waste time. Pick out a half dozen bottles of wine you like. Take your time picking them; ask the owner questions about various wines. Put them on my account, but they're a bonus for you. I won't be here when you get back. Carry on as usual during my absence."

"Yes, Sir. And the scotch?"

"Forget the scotch."

Miles grabbed a set of keys from his desk, disabled the GPS on his cell phone, picked up the duffle bag, and exited the back door of his house closest to the trees that separated his property from the neighbor's. He strode quickly across the open space until the trees engulfed him and paused there to watch for movement.

Ricardo had drawn surveillance away from the house unless there was more than one car. If so, he doubted they'd trespass on his property, meaning they were struck in a car on the street with a limited view. He bet they thought he was unaware of their presence. And who exactly was "they"? A new black SUV sounded more like Feds than the local PD. Bad news, very bad news. It might explain why his pilot hadn't responded to his call. Feds had the jurisdiction to ground his plane.

Miles cautiously made his way across the backs of several properties until he reached an adjoining street and walked down the street in the opposite direction from his house. Miles was furious at having to take evasive measures like some common criminal. He noticed one house with several newspapers stuck into the 'newspaper mailbox.' Assuming the house was empty, he walked up the driveway, hid behind a thick pillar of the portico near the front door, and called a taxi. When the taxi pulled into the driveway, Miles stepped into view as though he was emerging from the front door. He gave the driver an address in Malibu.

Miles owned the beachfront house in Malibu under an alias. It was a haven for him when he wanted to forget business for a few days and leisurely enjoy the sun and surf in private. He didn't know his neighbors, and they didn't know him. The closet was filled with casual beachwear, and he'd order food delivered from a local supermarket. Staying at the beach house shielded him from the police, the Feds, or whoever had him under surveillance.

After changing his suit for tan slacks and a lightweight navy sweater, Miles called for a grocery delivery, then poured himself a drink and went outside to the porch to breathe in the revitalizing salt air. He listened to the waves breaking on the beach and relaxed after his harrowing day. After the groceries arrived, he unpacked them and turned on the TV to watch the news while he cooked and ate dinner. There was nothing on the news about Underwood or the raid or the missing Henry. After dinner, he went back outside with another drink. Tomorrow was soon enough to worry about what came next.

The next morning, Miles began to plan. Staying in his Malibu hideaway was safe in the short term, but he needed to get far away from the LA area. Fortunately, when he'd bought the house, he'd also obtained forged ID under the alias in case anyone approached him thinking he was Miles. He'd claim mistaken identity and show them the forged documents. He tried calling his pilot one more time, but again, the man didn't answer. Miles cringed at the idea of taking a public plane or train or bus and mixing with the general population, so he called one of his underworld resources.

When the man answered his phone, he said, "Hold on a minute." Miles heard the raucous background noise diminish and a door close.

"Okay," the man said.

"I need you to arrange to get me out of town," Miles said.

"No can do," the man said. "Haven't you seen the

news? Your picture is plastered all over it. Big reward offered for information on your whereabouts. I wouldn't trust anyone not to turn you in."

"And you personally?"

"You know I never get personally involved. Too dangerous for me. Sorry."

Miles wasn't about to beg. He hung up and mentally crossed the man off his list of resources. No more lucrative deals for him. Miles was concerned about the reference to the news and turned on the TV. He flipped through channels until he found a news station currently on the air. Sure enough, there he was. He liked the headshot they used. It was one he'd had professionally taken for press releases.

The story that accompanied it was pure fiction. According to the report, Miles Grayson had been reported missing by a company he owned, Underwood Labs in Arizona, when he had not shown up for a scheduled business conference. The police found his car on the side of Stone Canyon Road. Because of the body damage to the car, they believe it was involved in an accident and that he might have sustained head injuries, causing him to be dazed and confused. The company was offering a $5,000 reward for information leading to his safe return. Viewers were told to call a special hotline number which was posted on the screen.

Miles wondered why whoever planted the story mentioned Underwood. Was it a subtle message to him that they had connected him to Henry's lab? Why warn him except to throw him off center so he'd make a mistake? Or had they used Underwood because the lab was on lockdown? Whatever the reason, the reward for finding him made him extremely vulnerable; a city of millions of eyes was searching for him.

Miles called another underworld boss and received the same answer. The third, Salvador, said, "You're much too recognizable now. Lie low for a while then get back to me when the furor dies down."

"Too recognizable?" If his picture was everywhere, Miles had to avoid public transportation, not only because of his distaste for it, but out of necessity. His thoughts drifted to the compound in his duffle bag. If he looked younger and stuck with his beach boy attire, he might convince Salvador to help him.

Chapter 69   Search for Grayson

"Having fun bossing the Feds around?" Zack asked Morales on the phone.

"You bet."

"How's it going with identifying the outside teams?"

"Underwood handed us realms of paperwork. I figured it was going to take us weeks to go through it. Then that genius of yours, Tucker, showed up. Using the names of those two we caught at the house, he figured out the codes the offices used for outside employees. He sat down at their computers and within ten minutes printed out the list we wanted. I offered him a job with Tucson PD, but he turned us down."

Zack laughed. "And now that you have the list?"

"We're breaking into combined teams of Feds and us to go after them. We still don't have any leads on the vans they used. Tucker suggested we go through Purchasing invoices for new vans, maintenance, computers and/or drones, modifications, cash dispersals, that sort of thing. The warrants didn't cover that, but Hargrove is cooperating and gave us permission."

"Any ID on the victim at the safe house?"

"It's Sam Wiley. He'd been heavily sedated. Doctors at the hospital are flushing it out of his system. He'll recover. What's up on your end?"

"Not much good. By the time my plane landed, we'd lost Grayson. His Mercedes left his mansion, and the surveillance car followed it only to discover the driver was his butler, not Grayson. By the time they got back to the mansion, Grayson had split so he's in the wind right now. If you're finished with Tucker, I want him out here to break into Grayson's computers."

"I'll get him on a plane. No good news at all?"

"We grounded his plane; he can't leave LA that way. We planted a story in the news which will have the entire population of LA looking for him. $5k to anyone who finds him."

Morales whistled. "That should keep him holed up somewhere while you look."

"I fear he'll inject himself with the compound to disguise himself. I'm having a sketch artist draw a version of Grayson as a younger man."

Zack and Morales wished each other luck and disconnected.

Chapter 70   Hoover Dies

The maid working on the third floor at the Best Western pushed her cart past the door of room 309 and stopped. Once again, the Do Not Disturb sign hung on the doorknob. She put her hands on her hips and frowned. This was the third day in a row. She couldn't imagine a guest not wanting fresh towels. Sometimes, guests hung the sign and forgot about it. While she was hesitant to disturb the guest, she also didn't want to be fired for not tending to her duties if the guest complained. She knocked on the door and announced, "Housekeeping." No one responded, nor did she hear any noise from the interior of the room. After knocking a second time and not receiving a response, her dilemma deepened. She wanted to check the room, but she also didn't want to walk into something unexpected. She resolved the problem by calling management.

After explaining the problem, management told her to wait by the room and sent up a security guard. He also tried knocking and identifying himself with no result. Finally, he used his key to open the door and called out "Security" as he entered. The maid waited outside.

The guard found the guest lying in bed. He looked

like he was sleeping peacefully, but the greyish-blue color of his face suggested otherwise. The guard backed out of the room and told the maid the guest had died and to go about her business. She pushed her cart to the next room, grateful she had not entered 309 by herself.

Management called the police who sent Detectives Mulroney and White who arrived at the hotel with an ambulance and coroner in tow. The scene puzzled them all. The body showed no sign of trauma or obvious cause of death.

"Any ideas?" Mulroney asked the coroner.

"Not until I autopsy him." The coroner waved to the paramedics standing in the hallway to remove the body.

The detectives moved into the bathroom to get out of their way.

"Nothing personal here," Mulroney said as he examined the countertop. "It's all standard hotel issue."

"Well, well, well, what's this?" White said. He was bending over the wastebasket and moving the contents with his pen.

Mulroney joined him and bent down to look.

"I pushed some tissues aside and uncovered this." White pointed to an empty vial and a syringe.

"Doesn't look like the usual drug paraphernalia. We better call CSI," Mulroney said and stuck his head out the door. "Hey, Doc, you might want to see this."

The coroner joined them. "See what?"

The detectives showed him the syringe and vial in

the wastebasket.

"Good find," the doctor said. "I'll look for an injection site."

After the body had been removed, the detectives walked around the bedroom without touching anything while they waited for the CSI team.

"Notice anything odd?" White asked.

"Yeah, there's nothing personal except one suit hanging in the closet and a locked briefcase. It's a combination lock. We'll have to pry it open to see what's inside."

"Better hold off on that until we get official permission to destroy his property. I haven't seen a wallet or cash or any other personal items a man generally carries with him."

"Me either. Might be in the briefcase. When CSI gets here and we turn the scene over to them, we'll check at the registration desk."

"I also don't like that we found only one vial and syringe. Whether the guy was on drugs or taking some kind of medication, you'd think he'd have backup supplies. If he can afford a room in this hotel, he's got money for a stash."

The detectives learned their mysterious hotel guest had used a phony name and address when registering and had paid in cash. No one at the desk remembered the man.

"Great," White said. "We have no idea who this guy

is. I'll call the morgue and ask Doc to fingerprint him." He also directed the CSIs to impound the briefcase, the vial and syringe, and check them into the police evidence locker.

Mulroney and White learned the next day that the fingerprints identified their body as Henry Hoover, a resident of Tucson, and an employee of Underwood Labs.

"Underwood Labs sounds familiar," Mulroney said. "Isn't that the place SWAT raided?"

"Yup. Morales and Forbes were in on that, weren't they?"

"I'll call Morales."

Morales and Forbes rushed to the morgue. Neither one of them had ever met Hoover in person, but he looked like a younger version of the guy on the security tape from Underwood and fingerprints don't lie. The coroner had not been able to determine a cause of death although he did find an injection site on Hoover's upper arm.

Morales called Zack with the news about Hoover's death and the odd circumstances in the hotel room.

"All we know for sure is that he's dead," Morales said.

"Did you find any drug paraphernalia, especially vials or syringes?"

"Only one vial and syringe in a wastepaper basket and an injection site on his arm."

"Have your CSIs tear that room apart. Hoover would have hidden the vials; we've got to find them. What did your lab say about the contents of the vial? Were they able to analyze it?"

"There was only a degraded trace amount left which made analysis impossible."

"Stay where you are. I need to make a quick call, and I'll call you back."

Zack called Dr. Schwartz. "I have a quick question, Doc." Zack explained the problem of identifying Hoover's cause of death. "Since we found a vial and syringe, we know he'd injected, or been injected, with something. The lab can't identify the residue in the vial. Any ideas?"

Dr. Schwartz thought back to his first encounters with Leila.

"Tell them to check for lithium in Hoover's blood. If it's present, I'd conjecture he was injected with his compound."

"Why lithium?"

"It's a mood stabilizer. It would help the person taking the compound from reacting too strongly. I suspected Leila, or Sarah, had been dosed with something similar. She was upset about her blackout and the physical changes, but she remained rational and calm under the circumstances. Lithium would help calm her. Does Hoover look any younger?"

"No one knows him well enough to tell. I'll tell

Morales to have his lab assistant, Ramon, do a facial ID. Thanks, Doc."

Zack called Morales back and passed on the doctor's instructions.

Chapter 71   Grayson Injects Himself

At the beach house, Miles prepared to inject himself with the compound and tried to recall what Henry had said about the side effects within the first few hours. Admittedly, he hadn't paid much attention; all he remembered was twitching and difficulty sleeping. Since Henry wouldn't be around to explain the side effects to potential clients, Miles decided to write down his reactions. Of course, he'd need to perform other experiments once his new scientist duplicated the original compound, but since he was going through the process, he wanted his own record.

After the injection, Miles tuned the stereo to a classical music station and sat down on a living room recliner. The music and the hypnotic effect of watching the waves break on the shore lulled him to sleep. He awoke early the next morning.

The music still played, and the waves continued their unrelenting drumming on the shore. It took him several seconds to remember why he was in the living room and not in his bed. The injection! So much for the expected side effects. He hadn't had difficulty sleeping. He held his arms and hands out in front of him. They were steady as usual: not one tremor or twitch. Henry had said the compound began working within hours. He stood up and almost ran to the bathroom mirror to see the changes effected by the compound.

Miles stared in disbelief at the mirror. He looked the same as he always: gray still streaked his blonde hair and none of his wrinkles had disappeared. At age 57, his face wasn't a network of creases, but they'd been there and still were. The compound hadn't worked! Why hadn't the compound worked on him?

An unwelcome thought crept into his consciousness. What if the vials didn't contain the compound? Miles took another bottle from the case. Instead of plunging a needle through the stopper on the top of the vial, Miles carefully teased it off. He tipped the vial to wet his finger and tasted it; it tasted like water. Miles searched his memory about basic chemistry. He then poured a tiny bit of the "compound" into a spoon and added a few crystals of salt: a basic test for determining if a substance was water. If they dissolved, there was a good chance the liquid was water. The salt dissolved. Miles threw the vial across the room. Water!

Miles paced around the living room. How had he ended up with vials of water? He backtracked the history of those vials. Henry and Ramon had prepared the vials; then Henry had disappeared. Ramon had packed the vials with the other contents of the safe the next day, and Hargrove had delivered the package to him at the airport. One of those three had double-crossed him; only one of them had a reason to. Henry. Henry had disappeared on purpose taking the formula and the real vials with him. Miles was amazed Henry had the wits for such subterfuge.

This twist of fate called for a new resolution: find Henry, get the vials and the formula, and eliminate him. To do both, he needed cash, lots of it. Money wasn't a problem, getting his hands on it was since he didn't dare appear in public.

Miles picked up the phone and called Ricardo.

"Ricardo, I need you to go to the bank for me."

"Mr. Grayson is not home at the present time. May I take a message?"

"Is someone there?"

"Yes. He's out of town. I'm not expecting him back in the near future."

Ricardo was warning him to stay away.

"Can you get to the bank and withdraw funds for me?"

"I'm sorry, Sir, but that's not possible. I do not have access to his business affairs."

Miles picked up on Ricardo's slight emphasis on the word "access."

"Are you saying my accounts have been frozen?"

"That's correct. I'll tell him you called when I hear from him. Please call again if I can be of further assistance."

"Thank you, Ricardo."

Miles hung up in a daze. One by one, his options had been thwarted. Miles opened the patio door to breathe in the salt air: a scent so strong it dominated all others. Miles stood tall. He was dominant like that scent and refused to be defeated by lesser men. He had one option left; one he hadn't wanted to resort to.

From the beginning of the project, a wall of secrecy defined every step of the planning. Miles knew full well the price of being caught. The wall he thought was protecting him was tumbling down. The game had changed. Instead of playing the part of the master planner, he'd now have to assume the role of a bewildered pawn.

He phoned his attorney, Kurt Fairchild.

"Miles, I can't tell you how relieved I am to hear your voice," Fairchild said. "Are you okay? Where have you been? The police have been searching for you since the accident."

"There was no accident," Miles said. "The story was bogus. I don't think it's only the police who are looking for me; the Feds may be involved. They've searched my house and frozen my bank accounts."

"Excuse me?"

"Does that sound like they're looking for the innocent victim of an accident?"

"No, it certainly does not. Why are they looking for you?"

326

"I'm not sure. Tucson PD raided a company I own in Arizona, a biotech company. I own the company but have nothing to do with its day-to-day operation. The man running one of the more secure labs, Henry Hoover, disappeared."

Miles thought about his meeting with Hargrove and the need to explain it. "Before the raid, the president of the company called me to report Hoover's absence. I'm sure you realize our clients depend on us to protect the research Underwood Labs does for them. Not knowing the cause of Hoover's absence, I instructed the president to pack up the contents of Hoover's safe and flew to Tucson to pick it up for safekeeping. Next thing I know, I see this bogus story on TV about my being in an accident and the manhunt for me."

"And you think the Feds are involved because?"

"Tucson PD does not have the jurisdiction to secure a search warrant for my house or to freeze my assets."

"True. What do you want me to do?"

"First, call off the manhunt so every Tom, Dick, and Harry isn't looking for me."

"I'll do that indirectly in a press conference. I'll announce that I've spoken to you personally and you're not hurt. You're staying out of sight because you don't understand why the police claimed you were in an accident when you weren't," the lawyer said. "I thought it odd that the news coverage never included a shot of the abandoned car which they normally do in circumstances such as an accident."

"Secondly, I want you to help me get out of town. I can't get to the bottom of this subterfuge holed up without resources, and I obviously can't trust the police to help."

"I'll begin legal proceedings to uncover who secured the paperwork and why. Getting you out of town is tricky. I must avoid any hint of 'aiding and abetting.' Let me think about how I might help."

Chapter 72 Missing Vials

"Hey, Doc, you home?" Zack called out from the front door.

"In the living room." Dr. Schwartz closed the journal he'd been reading. "I wasn't expecting you."

"I decided at the last minute to catch a flight. Nothing to do in LA but twiddle my thumbs until we catch a break on Grayson. I left Tucker there going through his computers, hoping he'd find something useful. The action is here, tracking down the outside teams and their vans."

"Any word on the cause of death for Hoover?"

"No. As you suggested, they tested his blood and found lithium, indicating he had injected himself with his compound. No lithium in the vial, but that doesn't mean much. The trace was too degraded to do much with it. We don't know if his compound killed him or some other reason; the autopsy isn't complete. What bothers me more is where one empty vial came from."

"You're sure neither the lab assistant nor the president, Hargrove, didn't take them?"

"Morales grilled Ramon, that's the lab assistant, until he nearly had a nervous breakdown. He swears

Hoover prepared 6 vials which were locked in the safe. Hargrove swears he never opened the package. Then there's the problem of how either one of them got vials to Hoover. I don't think they're involved. Ramon said when he clocked out the last night he saw Hoover, he left the doctor working in his office."

"Leaving Hoover alone in the lab before he disappeared when he may have tampered with the vials."

"Exactly. Grayson should have them, but they weren't in his house. Of course, he could have taken them with him. If Hoover injected himself with his compound, where did that one vial come from? If Hoover took all 6 when he left the lab, where are the other 5 vials? CSI didn't find any hidden in the motel room. Hopefully, we'll find the vials in Hoover's briefcase when they break it open." Zack consulted his watch. "I'm meeting with Morales in an hour or so. Maybe he'll have an answer. I came back briefly because if TPD did find the vials, I want to take possession of them personally."

"How about some lunch before you go?"

"Love some, Doc."

Dr. Schwartz made sandwiches, and he and Zack sat down at the kitchen table to eat. Midway through their meal, Zack's phone rang.

"It's LA," Zack said. "Might as well turn on the speaker so I don't have to repeat everything they say."

"All hell's broken loose," Zack's contact said. "Grayson's attorney, Kurt Fairchild, held a press conference. Said Grayson was alive and well and that he'd never been in an accident and that Grayson has no idea why the police claimed he had been. Made Grayson sound like an innocent victim of a police conspiracy. The press is hounding the LA Chief of Police for answers."

"Guess I'll be heading back," Zack replied. "Tell the chief to hold off until I get there. I have a meeting here and will catch the next available plane after that."

"Eat," Dr. Schwartz said after Zack hung up. "You need the nourishment."

Zack picked up his sandwich and took a bite.

"I sure am getting tired of bouncing back and forth between Tucson and LA. Good thing it's a short flight. I wondered why Grayson didn't call his attorney earlier," Zack said.

"Want my input?"

"Of course."

"Realize I'm speculating. As a psychopath, which he is, he's also a narcissist. He believed he could handle his problems himself, in his own way. You cornered him, and he needed help: hence, the attorney. He may have convinced the attorney of his innocence; he's quite capable of doing that. Note that he didn't turn himself in to resolve the issue. He won't do that. He's still looking for a way out of LA, perhaps using the attorney as a pawn, so he can be in charge of his destiny again."

"And just how do we find him in a city of four million people? We can't cover all the possible escape routes."

"Narrow down the choices. He'll try to disguise himself; that's where his personality will work against him. It won't allow him to disguise himself as homeless, for example. He'd consider that too far below his dignity. Eliminate hitchhikers and common forms of transportation. He's more likely to hire a private plane or a boat."

"With what? We've frozen his bank accounts."

"I'm sure he has offshore accounts. Tell the banks to be on alert for a new customer transferring in a substantial sum of money."

"He could borrow the money from one of his rich friends."

"He could, but I doubt he has many friends. A business associate is more likely. To satisfy the LA press and keep his associates at bay, you're going to have to make some type of innuendo about his involvement with crime here in Tucson. Make him a piranha so others fear that they'll be bitten if they help him."

When he arrived back in LA, Zack, the police chief, and other high-ranking officials met and planned how to respond to the press. They decided to hold a press conference. Zack proposed that they say Grayson is wanted for questioning concerning the disappearance of one of the leading scientists at Underwood Labs, a Tucson, Arizona, business he owned. They would imply, rather than accuse, Grayson of possible involvement. To create more interest, they also decided to double the reward.

* * *

After Zack left, Dr. Schwartz cleaned up the kitchen and returned to the living room to continue his reading. He had no sooner picked up his journal when the telephone rang. He sighed and picked up the phone.

"Hi, Dr. Schwartz, it's Sarah."

"Sarah, I'm glad to hear from you." The doctor put his journal back on the table. "How are you doing?"

"I'm happy."

Sarah described how she'd settled into Jeff's two-bedroom house on the outskirts of Mesa, how she enjoyed walks through the neighborhood or to the local stores, and mostly how she liked not having to wear a wig. The attorney had sent her part of the settlement of her trust, so she felt independent once again.

"And Jeff?"

"I think he's a keeper. We have a good time together. Sometimes, parts of my story leak out, and that usually makes me cry. He consoles me, listens if I talk, or tells me to put it in a box and close the lid if I don't want to talk. His philosophy is that we should concentrate on building the future, not dwelling on the past."

"Wise man."

"I do get bored when he's at work. Thank goodness for Jethro; he keeps me company, so I don't rattle around this house all day by myself."

"I bet he's happy to have your company, too."

Sarah laughed. "He is. Anyway, Jeff suggested I apply to be a substitute teacher. That's when I explained that I had a new name and new identity but had to leave behind Leila's old life, including my diplomas and credentials. He suggested I go back to school and get new ones. We decided an online university might be easiest, so we're checking the schools and curriculums together."

"He definitely sounds like a keeper."

"There's one thing I'm afraid of."

"What's that, Sarah?"

"That it's all going to come crashing down when I have to go back to Tucson to testify about what happened to me."

"Why don't you put that in your box and close the lid for now? Things may develop differently than Zack originally thought. Do you get Tucson news up there?"

"Some."

"Henry Hoover is dead. The cause of death hasn't been determined, but it's one less trial for you to worry about."

"His partner?"

"Zack hasn't caught him yet."

"But if he does, I'll have to testify?"

"We don't know that. The government wants to keep the success of their research secret. If they can keep you out of it, they will. Concentrate on school and Jeff and stay happy."

Chapter 73   Grayson Gets Money

Miles paced around his living room waiting for Fairchild's office to open. Things went from bad to worse to desperate since he last spoke to Fairchild. A TV news brief had reported, "Police are still looking for Miles Grayson, owner of Underwood Labs, a business he owns in Tucson, Arizona, where one of the scientists died in a hotel room. According to police, Grayson had visited Tucson close to the scientist's approximate time of death. The $5,000 reward for information leading to locating him is now $10,000. If you see Mr. Grayson, do not approach him. Call the special hotline number listed on the screen." Of course, his photo stared back at him from the TV screen during the report. Since he was a prominent businessman, Miles bet all the TV stations, as well as the newspapers, were running a similar report.

Damn. The publicity reawakened interest in finding him. They upped the reward to $10k making it more profitable for someone to betray him. Even worse, they implied he was dangerous by warning people not to approach him. Although they didn't accuse him of having a hand in a scientist's death, they certainly implied it. Were they talking about Henry? How did he die? What about the vials? Henry made 6; he'd been given 6 phony vials. Had the Feds confiscated the real ones?

Miles phoned several numbers at the lab. Every one of them played the same prerecorded message. "We're sorry, but Underwood Labs is temporarily closed." Double damn. His surveillance and tracking teams which supplied him with intel had been cut off.

The attorney had promised to think about how he might help Miles get out of town with the necessary funding to do so. An anxious Miles hoped Fairchild had positive results to report.

"I see the news has victimized you again," Fairchild said when he finally called.

"I had nothing to do with the scientist's death. I didn't even know he died until I saw the news. I'm more anxious than ever to get out of town. I doubt I'd be treated fairly if they do find me."

"I agree; they've made you a target. I can't get you out of town, but I thought of a plan to get you some money. How much do you need?" Fairchild asked.

"100k."

"Doable. Let's say a couple of months ago you spoke to me about opening a business in a foreign country and authorized me to spend the necessary funds on research to check the viability of such a plan. I agreed and proceeded. You owed me money at that point, but I also asked for a retainer to set up a corporation for the new company when you wanted to go forward with the project. Total cost 100k."

"And you won't have any trouble from the police?"

"No. Confidentiality applies. If they come up with some obscure law and subpoena me, I can show them the research and costs. I did a research project for another client who decided not to implement the project for financial reasons. I'll scrub the document to make sure his name isn't mentioned and draw up a retainer agreement for setting up a new corporation for you. Since I already made a statement to the press about your phony accident and implied police subterfuge, they know I am in contact with you. This new business between us demonstrates that you plan to continue in business once the issue is resolved."

"What about the Feds?"

"At this point, we officially don't know if they're involved. It's not public knowledge that they searched your house or froze your assets."

"And the funds?"

"Have one of your offshore accounts wire me 100k." Fairchild gave Miles the routing and account numbers he needed to wire the money. "By the way, wiring money into my business account will validate my claim that I'm working on your behalf. In the meantime, while I'm waiting for the funds to arrive, I'll scrape together cash from numerous sources so there's no one-to-one relationship between money in and money out. I will keep some of the funds to cover my fees."

"Of course."

"You'll have to figure out how to retrieve the cash which I'll pack in a box about the size of a briefcase with your name written on the top of the box. I suggest you pick it up at the office. I can't send it by courier."

"Do I have to pick it up personally?"

"No. A representative will do, but you must let me know who is coming and when."

"I'll figure something out," Miles said.

After disconnecting the call, Miles faced this new hurdle. First things first. He phoned the bank with one of his offshore accounts and arranged for the wire transfer. Number two on the agenda required contemplating options: who could he send to pick up the money from Fairchild? He poured a cup of coffee and wandered out to the patio.

His first idea was to contact Salvador again. He was the only one of his underworld contacts who indicated he might help in the future. Salvador might agree to pick up the cash. No, not cash, a package, although Salvador was smart enough to guess its contents. The crime boss wouldn't go himself but send an underling which meant involving another person. The more people involved, the greater the possibility of exposure, especially with the reward offered for information about his whereabouts. And if Salvador did correctly deduce the contents of the package, Miles acknowledged the possibility he might never see it. Salvador was, after all, a crime boss. Ripping off a client to whom he owed no loyalty was well within his code of behavior. Even if Salvador didn't keep the package for himself, Miles had to arrange to get the package from Salvador. More people, more complications. Miles put the idea of using Salvador on the back burner.

Miles leaned back on his patio chair to let the sun warm his face. Who else? Who could he trust? Miles abruptly sat up. Ricardo. Ricardo, his faithful butler! Ricardo, who followed his instructions without ever questioning them. Quick-thinking Ricardo who warned him away from his Bel Air estate when the Feds had arrived. As for the Feds, did they now have a wiretap on his house phone? In case the Feds were monitoring the phone, Miles called Ricardo on his cell.

"I want you to get a plain cardboard box approximately the size of a briefcase, fill it with papers from your household account files, seal it securely, and write my name on the top. Put the package in the trunk of the Mercedes and cover it. Keep the garage door closed while you do that. I'll call you back with the time I want you to take the package to Kurt Fairchild."

"The attorney?"

"Yes." The less Ricardo knew about the why's, the better protected he was in case the police or the Feds questioned him.

"Are you okay, Sir?"

"I'll be okay when I can come home. Are the Feds keeping the house under surveillance?"

"I think so. I see a black SUV driving by from time to time. It turns up the hill across the street. The only time I remember seeing a black SUV like that in the neighborhood was when one followed me to the liquor store on the day you left."

Ricardo had come to the same conclusion Miles had. The Feds had found somewhere in the neighborhood to 'hole up' and observe the house without being obvious.

"How are you doing, Ricardo?"

"I'm fine. The rest of the staff is on vacation while you're gone."

"Even the cleaning crew?"

"Yes, Sir. Nothing much gets dirty. Any minor cleaning, like dusting, I do myself. I prefer that to being asked too many questions."

"You're a good man, Ricardo, and will be amply rewarded for your loyalty."

A couple of days later, Fairchild notified Miles that his package was ready for pickup, and they arranged a time for Ricardo to come to the law office.

"Fairchild will give you a package," said Miles. "I want you to put it in the trunk of the Mercedes. It doesn't matter if anyone sees you do it. Once it's in the trunk, however, I want you to remove the cover on the box you packed and cover the box Fairchild gives you instead. Do it quickly. When you get back to the house, leave the garage door open while you take the uncovered box out of the trunk, then close the trunk and the garage door."

"To be sure I understand. I'll be bringing the box I prepared back into the house and leaving the package Fairchild gives me in the trunk."

"Exactly. Put the box you prepared in my study then go back to the garage. Do not open the garage door this time. Transfer the Fairchild package to the trunk of your car." Next came the riskiest part of Miles' plan.

"Once that's done, you're going to take a few hours off to go to Zuma Beach. Park in the southernmost section of the parking lot as close to the beach as possible. Go to the beach for a couple of hours but leave the car unlocked while you're gone."

"May I assume the Fairchild package will be gone when I get back?"

"Yes."

While Ricardo prepared for his car trip to the beach, Miles prepared for his, only he'd be walking. He donned a pair of shorts and a T-shirt, the scruffiest in his beach attire collection. After adding an old Dodgers baseball cap, one that concealed a good portion of his face, and a pair of wrap-around sunglasses, he examined himself in the mirror. Satisfied that he looked like most of the beach walkers he saw from his patio, he took a beach towel from the linen closet and wrapped a pair of thongs in it. He'd walk barefoot down the beach like everyone else, but the asphalt in the parking lot got hot, and he wasn't about to burn the bottom of his feet on it. Miles grabbed the handle on the glass patio door to slide it open and begin a leisurely trek down the beach, carrying the rolled-up towel under his arm. He hoped to arrive about the same time as Ricardo. Leaving the car unlocked for too long with all the money in it was dangerous.

Miles froze when he saw a man standing on the beach looking up at his house. His house? A neighbor's? Hard to tell from a distance. He waited until the man lowered his head and began walking further up the beach in the same direction Miles needed to go. Then he stopped again and looked up at the houses. Was he trying to identify a particular house or was he simply a gawker, one of those vacationers who enjoyed looking at houses belonging to the rich or famous? When the man moved on and then stopped again, Miles decided he was the latter. As the saying goes, "It was now or never." He had to have that money!

Miles walked straight down to the water's edge where the surf breaking over his feet felt refreshing. Not only refreshing but safe. Malibu beachfront homeowners did not like people walking in front of their properties but had little to say about walking on the 'wet sand' portion of the beach as it was considered public property. By now, a respectable distance separated them. Good. Miles slowed down whenever the man stopped to maintain a healthy gap between them. When they reached the southern section of Zuma, the man continued north along the beach while Miles headed into the parking lot.

Miles located Ricardo's Toyota and walked up to it without hesitating, as though he were the owner. He opened the driver's door and reached in to pop the trunk. After wrapping Fairfield's package in the beach towel, he closed the trunk and began the return trip to his house. The package was heavier than he had anticipated but knowing what it contained made him smile all the way.

* * *

"Any news on Grayson?" the supervisor asked the undercover Federal agent watching Miles' house.

"Not on him, but his butler made an interesting trip this morning. "Took the Mercedes to Fairchild's law office and came out carrying a box which he placed in the trunk. He returned to Bel Air and took the box inside the house. An hour later, he loaded beach paraphernalia into his car, a Toyota, and my partner followed him to Zuma. He's still there, sunning himself on the sand under the watchful eye of my partner."

"No attempt from Grayson to contact him?"

"None. I stayed here watching the house, but Grayson never surfaced here either. I'd love to know what's in that box."

"Don't think we can touch it unless we enter the house illegally. We'd need another search warrant. I doubt a judge would sign off on it since we already searched and have no 'cause' for a second search. We also run into the problem of lawyer/client confidentiality. If we enter illegally, any evidence we might find would be thrown out in court. I'll check with my superiors, but for now, the package is off-limits."

Chapter 74   Poetic Justice

Morales and Forbes took Zack to Lieutenant Jensen's office for their meeting before Zack left for LA. Hoover's opened briefcase sat on a side table: not a vial in sight, only envelopes and a wallet.

Zack walked over to the table. "Tell me the vials were in it, but you moved them elsewhere for safekeeping."

"Sorry," the Lieutenant said. "What you see is what we found when we smashed the lock and opened the case. The envelopes contain money, almost $11,000 in $100 bills."

"His running away money," Zack said. "I would have thought if he was double-crossing Grayson, he'd take the vials with him. The compound is worth millions if it's marketed. Leave a potential fortune behind? I don't think so."

"We also searched Hoover's house. The vials weren't there," said Morales. "Maybe Hoover was only concerned about his personal safety."

"Certainly, his personal safety was part of the equation, He knew we were on to him, but I can't accept his leaving years of work to Grayson and walking away empty handed."

"The vials went from Hoover's safe to Grayson so he must have them," Forbes said.

"We didn't find them when we searched his Bel Air house so they're still missing. One more reason to locate Grayson. That brings us to the question of why Hoover died," Zack said. "Any results on the autopsy?"

"The coroner finished it but cannot identify a definitive cause. On the autopsy report, for lack of a better answer, he wrote down heart attack as the cause of death. Sure, the guy's heart stopped, but it bothers him because he has no idea what caused the heart attack. There were no indications Hoover had heart problems prior to his death."

"What about all the stress he was under because of the lab?" Morales said.

"Certainly, stress can cause a heart attack," Zack said, "but remember he was on the run, and we didn't know where he was. That alone could lessen the stress. After the injection, he'd emerge as a younger man adding a layer of difficulty to our finding him. While I can't rule out stress as a possibility, I have an idea I like better. We know his early experiments were on people who suffered from dementia or other mental problems, and those experiments failed. He needed people with normal, healthy brains."

"Are you saying he had dementia?" the Lieutenant asked.

"No, I'm saying he didn't have a normal, healthy brain. I consulted with a psychiatrist who identified Hoover as a psychopath. Their brains are wired differently than the normal brain. I can't explain the anatomical details; if you're interested, the info is easily accessed on the Internet."

"Then why would he inject himself?" the Lieutenant asked.

Zack laughed. "Oh, he'd never think of himself as having a malformed brain."

"And not consider he might be adversely affected like his earlier victims?"

"Exactly. Bit of poetic justice, isn't it?" Forbes said.

Chapter 75 Grayson Escapes

Miles stuffed the money into his safe and poured a scotch to celebrate. Plenty there to get out of town, but how? His private jet was grounded. He could rent a different jet under his alias but as soon as he showed up at the airport and they saw his face, the game was over. As he watched the sunset and sipped the scotch, he let his mind wander. He thought about Anna who had managed to stay undetected for the first several weeks in her RV. Not to him, of course. She had to have had help later showing up at Henry's house. And not a word from his police informant! Or were the police simply pawns of the Feds? If she'd managed to be elusive because of her RV, why couldn't he do the same? The police or the Feds or, hell, all of Los Angeles was looking for him on busses, planes, or trains: all common modes of transportation. An RV fell into the uncommon category.

Later that evening, research on the laptop confirmed his suspicions that buying an RV was out of the question. Too much official paperwork, even if he bought it under his alias. He'd discovered he could rent one, but that too required official paperwork. Both options created a paper trail. An RV was out. He pushed aside the laptop in disgust. What other unusual mode of transportation might a fugitive consider for a getaway? He let his mind wander and then pulled the laptop back to do a little more research. Satisfied, he picked up his phone and dialed a number.

"Good thing I recognize your voice," Salvador said. "Don't recognize the number."

"Are you willing to do a job for me now?"

"Depends on what it is."

"Do you know a rogue cab driver or Uber driver who will work off the books?"

"I can find one. Drive to where? Need to give the guy some idea where he's going."

"Bakersfield."

"Roundtrip is a full day of driving. It'll cost you."

"How much?"

"You're a wanted man, my friend. The driver will guess something's not kosher so I need to find someone who won't ask questions and will keep his mouth shut. With my cut, $3,000."

Normally, Miles negotiated prices. Not today. Salvador knew he didn't have a choice.

"When do you want to go?"

"Yesterday."

"I'll get back to you. Should I call this number?"

"Yes."

Miles sighed in relief. Now to pack and be ready at a

moment's notice. He unearthed a duffle bag from the garage. After separating Salvador's cut and traveling cash, he sorted the cash into small stacks and wrapped them first in saran wrap and then in plastic bags. Those went in the bottom of the bag. On top, he laid a change of clothes and the money for Salvador. Lastly, he emptied his wallet and replaced his real ID with that of his alias, George Withers, and added his traveling cash.

Salvador called back several hours later.

"Tomorrow morning. The driver, let's call him Joe, drives a dark blue Chrysler. He'll pick you up around 10:00. Where?"

"The Starbucks on Pacific Coast Highway near the main entrance to Zuma Beach."

"Good choice. Zuma and Starbucks are busy places. You'll blend in with the crowd. How will he recognize you?"

"I'll be wearing shorts and a T-shirt and a Dodgers cap and sunglasses. I'll also have a duffle bag with me. I'll stand in the parking lot near the exit."

"Your name is Pat. Put my cash in an envelope which you'll give to Joe when he picks you up. He'll count the money, then you're off if it's all there."

"Thanks, Salvador."

The next morning, Miles arrived early at Starbucks and bought a cup of coffee figuring it gave him a legitimate reason to be there. Out in the parking lot, he struck a leisurely pose near the exit. He'd learned decades ago how to hide any nervousness to appear confident and in control during business meetings. As he sipped the coffee, he surreptitiously glanced at the people coming and going. No one paid any obvious attention to him. Obvious. But what if someone was keeping track of him the same way he was keeping track of them? Finally, an unmarked dark blue Chrysler pulled up to him.

"You Pat?" the driver asked.

"Yes."

"I'm Joe. Get in."

Miles reached for the rear door handle.

"Up front," Joe said.

Miles complied.

"Looks too much like I'm chauffeuring you around if you sit in the back," Joe said as he exited the parking lot. He drove up the street until he found an empty parking space and pulled into it. "Money," he said holding out his hand.

Miles opened the duffle bag and handed him the envelope on top. Joe opened it, withdrew the bills, and carefully counted them.

"Ok," he said. "We're in business."

"Please drive carefully," Miles said when Joe pulled out into the traffic, "so we don't attract any attention."

"Don't know why you want me to drive you to Bakersfield, don't care. But I can say that Salvador will be mighty upset if I don't get you there without any trouble. What I do care about is upsetting Salvador, so don't worry."

Miles, however, did worry and often turned to look out the rear window or side view mirror to assure himself that a car, especially a police car, wasn't following them. "Don't worry about a tail," Joe said. "I'm keeping track. If I'm suspicious, I know how to lose 'em."

Neither spoke again until they reached the entrance ramp to Interstate 5 heading north. "I ain't much for talkin' unless it's necessary," Joe said after he maneuvered into the middle lane. "Turn on the radio if you want."

For Miles, the two hours to reach Bakersfield felt more like four.

"We're getting close," Joe said. "Where in Bakersfield do you want to go?"

"The airport. United terminal."

Joe smiled. When Salvador approached him about the job, he'd figured his passenger was 'a man on the run' who wanted out of LA without being recognized or leaving a trail. After all, a flight from LAX to Bakersfield takes less time and money than driving. Had to be a good reason not to go by air.

Pat sat only a few feet from him during the drive. Between the brim of the baseball cap pulled down low over his face and the wrap-around sunglasses, Joe never got a good look at his face. He doubted he'd recognize Pat if he saw him on the street. When Pat identified his destination as the airport, Joe metaphorically patted himself on the back. He'd been right. Outside of LA, Pat, or whatever his real name was, planned to catch a flight to his real destination.

Only Joe was wrong.

Chapter 76   Clue to Grayson's Escape

"Hey, Doc, that hotel of yours still open?"

Dr. Schwartz laughed. "Any time, Zack."

"Good, thanks. I'll be there in a few minutes."

The doctor sighed and put away the journal he'd picked up again after his conversation with Sarah had ended and went to the kitchen to start a pot of coffee. Zack had sounded tired; he needed a little caffeine to perk him up.

Zack let himself into the house. "I'm here, Doc," he called out.

"In the living room."

Zack plopped down in a chair and sprawled out, his head resting on the back of the chair.

"You stay here," Dr. Schwartz said. "I'm going to the kitchen to get you a cup of coffee."

The doctor half expected to find Zack sleeping when he returned, but Zack sat up and reached out a hand for the coffee. He took the cup and sipped. "Ah, good coffee. I sure am tired of the police station variety."

"Bad day?"

"Worse than bad. Guy came into the Malibu station to put in a claim for the 10k reward. Said he saw Miles at a Starbucks on the Pacific Coast Highway get into a dark blue Chrysler. He couldn't swear it was Miles and only caught a partial license plate number because as he said, 'It all happened so fast.' For that he wants 10k?"

"How did he know Miles?"

"Has a cousin who resembles Miles. Teased him about it when Miles' photo appeared on the news. Same height, same body type. Cousin also dresses like the guy at Starbucks as do a million other beach bums. Thought at first the guy was his cousin. Called out to him, but the guy didn't respond."

"So, he based the claim on body type and attire more than facial recognition."

"Yup. Useless."

"Was Miles driving?"

"No. The so-called Miles was standing in the parking lot when the Chrysler pulled up to him; he opened the door and got in. The only positive we picked out of the guy's story was the reference to Malibu; it fits Miles' lifestyle. We searched property records for the owners of beachfront houses. We doubted Miles would settle for anything else. Nothing. Just in case, we're also looking into owners of all Malibu houses in a five-mile radius. If it was Miles in the parking lot and he was on foot, he would likely walk there. I can't see him walking five miles, much less any farther."

"If it was Miles, you know he's not alone. He's found someone to help him."

Zack threw up his hands. "And that makes the story worse. If he got out of LA, he's in the wind. Who's helping him? Why would they after the latest TV broadcast implicating him in the death of Hoover?"

"Not for the reward money or trying to be an upstanding citizen, someone who Miles paid off. What about the partial license plate number? Any leads from that?"

"We're working on it. There's a multitude of blue Chryslers registered in the LA area. Add in the guy only saw two plate numbers, 3 and 7, when he momentarily glanced at it as the Chrysler pulled out of the lot. He admitted 3 could be an 8; 7 a 9. What a waste of time!"

"Maybe not. Wait for the results from DMV on the license plates before giving up. You're tired and disappointed. You need more than coffee to revive your energy. Go to bed and get a good night's sleep."

The next morning Zack wandered into the kitchen. "Coffee sure smells good," he said.

Dr. Schwartz poked his head into the refrigerator. "Pour yourself a cup."

"What'a you looking for?"

"Bacon. How do bacon and eggs sound?"

"Scrumptious."

As they finished eating, Zack's phone rang. "And it starts," Zack mumbled as he reached for the phone.

Zack listened more than spoke during the conversation. It ended with Zack saying, "I'll be there in about an hour."

"Good news or bad?"

"Both. We now have a shortlist of possible drivers of the dark blue Chrysler. The most promising is Paul Joseph Flynn. He's an Uber driver, does odd jobs as a handyman, and has a rap sheet for minor offenses. That's the good news. It's rumored that the odd jobs he does include working for Salvador."

"The crime boss?"

"Yup. That puts Flynn out of our reach. No one rats on Salvador. If they do, they end up in the morgue. If he did drive Miles somewhere, he'll keep his mouth shut."

"Any chance of Salvador turning Miles in for the 10k?"

"None. Salvador stays far away from the police. His admitting to helping a fugitive escape would be like the Pope admitting he's in league with the devil." Zack shrugged his shoulders. "Miles is gone and we still haven't located the missing vials. We're meeting this morning to brainstorm how to proceed."

Chapter 77   Grayson to Vegas

In the United terminal, Miles bypassed the ticket counters and stopped at a car rental booth. Using his alias George Withers, he chose a light gray Honda from the available options. He preferred a luxury car, but the Honda blended in better with the thousands of other similar cars on the road. Using the map the rental agent had given him, he found Highway 58 which intersected with I-15, a major route to Las Vegas. Ah, Vegas: a city of anonymity with international flights. He'd enjoy the ambiance of Vegas for a few days playing baccarat or entertaining a beautiful woman while he decided where to go. Oh! Before trolling for women, he better ditch the beach boy clothes and buy more suitable attire. Forget the tailor-made clothes he normally wore; they took too long to make. Quality off-the-rack clothes would suffice.

Roughly halfway through his four-hour trip, Miles switched to the I-15 going north. When he began the ascent over the mountains to Nevada, he laughed. He'd done it! He'd outwitted the police and the Feds. As far as he knew, the manhunt for him had been confined to the LA area. Sure, some of those thousands of tourists flocking to Vegas every day came from LA, but they were preoccupied with hopes of getting rich or moaning over losses.

Twists and turns in the highway increased as he drove over the mountain summit and began the descent back down to the desert floor. During one turn, he thought he saw an obstruction farther down the road. The road turned again, and he lost sight of it. Another turn and he caught sight of the obstruction again. Not an obstruction, a roadblock. Police were stopping cars. "It can't be!" he shouted and pounded a hand on the steering wheel. How had the police, or anybody, known his route? Had someone tailed him from Bakersfield and guessed where he was going after he turned north on the I-15? In LA, Joe had said he could spot a tail if someone followed them. What if it wasn't 'a' tail, but multiple tails: several undercover cars which took turns pursuing them?

So engrossed had Miles become in countless questions he wasn't paying close attention to the road or his increased downhill speed. As he entered one sharp curve, the car drifted to the right off the road. Like many mountain roads in the West, the road only extended a foot or two beyond the white line; there wasn't any wide shoulder. He realized his mistake, hit the brakes, and pulled the steering wheel sharply to the left.

* * *

Detective Jesse Dermonde of the Las Vegas Police Department (LVPD) called the Malibu police station to notify them of the death of George Withers and spoke to Officer Josh Little. "ID says he's from Malibu. We hoped you'd make an in-person death notification for us. We can't find a phone number for him or his family."

"What happened?"

"Traffic accident. Drivers behind him on the I-15 said he was speeding as he entered a curve on the descent down the mountain into Nevada. He lost control of the car, skidded off the highway, and plunged down the hillside. He might have survived that; the hill isn't too steep. What did him in was smashing head-on into a large boulder partway down the hill. Calls poured into Highway Patrol about an accident. They had a roadblock set up a mile or so down the road checking vehicles on a tip about an illegal cargo of drugs coming from California. They dispatched two officers from the roadblock who got to the scene rather quickly for it being in a remote area, but the driver was already deceased. Traffic backed up for miles while they removed the body and retrieved the car. Lotta unhappy tourists anxious to get going and lose their money at the tables."

"Why LVPD? Isn't that a distance from the Nevada border?"

"Not much between the border and us except empty desert. We're the closest big city. Here's the odd part.

361

CSIs found upwards of 80k in a duffle bag wedged in the car. If he was traveling away from Vegas, we'd guess he'd been a big winner. But he was headed to Vegas. Who carries that kind of cash to Vegas?"

"Strange. How was he dressed?"

"In shorts and a T-shirt. Certainly wasn't dressed the part of a wealthy guy. Maybe he was just a courier."

"Any other personal property?"

"Sunglasses and a Dodger's baseball cap."

Little's antennae went up. "Has the press gotten wind of the story?"

"Yeah, but only the crash and the traffic jam. We kept finding the money to ourselves. Didn't want to release that info until we notified the family."

"I'll do that for you. What's the address?"

When Dermonde read off the address, Little's antennae twitched.

"Can you fax me a copy of his driver's license?"

"Sure thing. Let me know what to do with the money."

"Will do."

Little stared at the phone after he hung up. The accident, the money: both unsettling but what got to him was the address Dermonde had given him for Withers. No such address existed in Malibu. The description of the dead guy's clothes sounded familiar, too. A Fed, Zack somebody or other, had been in hours earlier to interview a guy claiming to have seen the missing Miles

Grayson wearing shorts and a tee. Hundreds of guys in Malibu dressed the same way including sunglasses and baseball caps, but the coincidence and the timing and all that money ... Little decided to call Zack. If he made a fool of himself by reading too much into the coincidence, so be it. He shrugged. Better that than screwing up by not passing on pertinent info.

Chapter 78 Grayson Found

Zack was working late at police headquarters in LA reviewing the results of the Tucson roundup of Underwood Labs outside teams and vans when his phone rang. When he answered, an unfamiliar voice said, "This is Officer Josh Little with the Malibu police. You asked us to report any sightings or rumors about a beach boy type being driven around in a dark blue Chrysler. I hope I'm not wasting your time with this ..." Little paused.

"Go on." Zack rolled his eyes: another false lead.

"I took a report about an accident involving a Malibu resident driving a Honda. The vehicle doesn't fit, but the driver fits the description with beach boy clothes, complete with sunglasses and a Dodger's cap. Thing is, the resident's ID showed a phony name and address and LVPD found a large stash of cash in a duffle bag in the car."

Zack gave Little his full attention. "LVPD as in Las Vegas PD?"

"Yes. The accident happened on the Nevada side of the I-15 which goes to Vegas. It was the closest big city to the crash site."

"Let's start at the beginning. Tell me the events in order."

Little did. "That's it," Little said. "I wasn't sure you'd be interested, but I'm not a big believer in coincidences."

"Me either. I'm very interested in your story. You did the right thing to call me. I'd like you to fax me a copy of the phony driver's license," Zack said and gave Little the fax number. "I'd appreciate your calling again with any more information you come across."

"You think it's important?"

"I do." Zack's imagination soared. Is it possible they'd finally located Miles? Miles was clever enough to have an alias to hide his real identity and to use when it suited his needs. Getting out of LA was a high-priority need for him. Vegas with its anonymity was a perfect place to run to. The phony name, address, and cash fit the scenario of Miles on the run. He wrote down the name of the LVPD officer Little had spoken to as well as Little's number.

Zack immediately called records and asked to put a rush on finding Malibu property records listing George Withers as owner, the name Little had given him. Within the hour, the fax machine beeped the arrival of Withers' driver's license. The picture on the license was small, of course, and Zack took it down to the lab to have the tech wizards blow it up. The larger the picture became, the grainier it looked. The techs played with the photo to achieve the best balance between size and clarity. Zack held a photo of Miles he'd brought with him next to Withers' photo. The men looked alike, but the similarity was not distinct enough for a positive ID. Not good enough. Too wound up to sleep anyway, Zack booked a flight on a red-eye to Vegas. He'd be at the LVPD morgue for an in-person comparison as soon as the building opened.

In the airport lounge, Zack chose a seat away from other travelers: an advantage of a red-eye. Fewer people crowded the airport. While he waited before take-off, he called Morales in Tucson. The cell phone rang for a longer time than usual before Morales answered with a "This better be good."

"It's better than good. I think we got 'im," Zack said.

No reply. "Wake up, Morales."

"Zack? 'You think you got 'im.' Who do you think ..." Morales shot up to a seating position. "Grayson? You think you found Grayson? Where? I wanna be in on the bust."

"Yes, Grayson. Sorry, no bust. I'm at the airport waiting to board a plane to Vegas. If I'm right, he's on a slab in the morgue. I'm on my way to Vegas to ID the body."

"Okay, I'm fully awake now," said Morales. "Vegas? How ... ?"

Zack interrupted him. "It's a long story. Let me give you the highlights before they announce boarding. I'll call you back in the morning after I see the body and answer all your questions."

* * *

At the LVPD morgue, Zack introduced himself to the head coroner by showing his Homeland Security credentials.

"What can I do for you?" the doctor asked.

Zack showed him Miles' picture. "I'm looking for this man."

The doctor examined it closely. "I do believe he's in the freezer. Come with me and we'll take a look."

Zack followed the doctor through the doors to an inner room. "Came in after an accident," the doctor said as he pulled out a drawer in the morgue refrigerator. "Haven't run his fingerprints yet."

Both Zack and the doctor closely examined the face. "Face is a bit banged up from the accident, but they look like the same guy to me. Do you have any other points of reference? I found a couple of old scars on the body. If the guy you're looking for has the same scars, we'd have a positive confirmation."

"I don't. I want the body shipped to LA for confirmation. We'll run the fingerprints in LA, too. I'd also like a copy of your autopsy report."

"I'll give you a copy now," the doctor said as he pushed the drawer closed and walked toward his private office.

"His clothes and other personal property?"

"Those are in the evidence locker. Jesse Dermonde is handling the case. Let me call him."

Dermonde didn't have the authority to release the evidence. He and Zack went to the CO who began by verifying Zack's credentials then sent Dermonde down to the evidence locker to pick up a sealed evidence box. Zack wasn't interested in the clothes, only finding the missing vials and the money.

The lieutenant laid out the stacks of cash on his desk. "Most of the cash is in the wrapped bundles just the way we found them." The lieutenant picked up the only unwrapped bundle with a red band around the stack and the amount of money written on the label. "We opened this one to count. All the bundles are about the same size so we guessed that all bundles would have an equivalent amount. We estimated 80k from this one bundle. I had the box double-sealed because of the money."

"I expected to find a case containing medical vials. Is it possible someone tampered with the evidence? Has anyone asked to see it?"

"No to both questions. I sent a note to the officer in the evidence locker not to check out the box without clearance from me and to let us know if anyone asked." He then signed the release form to turn the money over to Zack who jammed it back into Miles' duffle bag. Too many people had handled the duffle bag: checking for fingerprints was futile. The unwrapped bundles would yield all the fingerprints necessary to show who had packed them. The duffle bag was also an inconspicuous way of carrying the money on the plane with him.

While arrangements were being made to ship the body, Zack called Morales who answered his phone on the first ring. "Is it him?"

"I'm 99% positive. The cadaver was banged up from the accident, including the face, but both the coroner and I believe it was Grayson. The coroner identified old scars on the body which I'm having shipped to LA. I'll fly back on the same flight. We'll run fingerprints and find someone who knew Grayson to validate he had the same scars for a 100% positive match."

"Who?"

"Best candidate is his Bel Air butler. I also heard back from Records. George Withers owned a beachfront house in Malibu. It's all adding up."

After the LA coroner received the body, Miles' butler Ricardo confirmed Miles had the scars the Vegas coroner had found: one on his lower left leg and another across his shoulder. The fingerprints also matched.

Chapter 79   Aftermath

As promised, Zack called Morales as soon as he had 100% confirmation the body was Miles. When Zack finished recapping a detailed account of his trip to Vegas, Morales said, "So it's over."

"Almost. The hunt for Grayson, yes. But we still don't have those vials. I'm getting a search warrant for his Malibu beach house. If Grayson was skipping town, I'd expect him to take the vials with him because I doubt he planned on returning to LA. But they weren't with him. The beach house is the only place left."

"Call me back after the search. Meanwhile, I'll bring Forbes and the lieutenant up to date."

"Will do."

Several hours later, Zack called Morales back. "We found the vials, but there's one more mystery."

"And that is?"

"I'm boarding a plane now. I'll come directly to the station. I want to discuss the mystery with you, Forbes, and the lieutenant. Gotta go or I'll miss the flight."

When Zack arrived at the police station, Morales, Forbes, and Zack met in Lieutenant Jensen's office for their meeting.

"We found six vials in the beach house kitchen," Zack said. "One smashed, one opened, and the other four still in the carrying case."

"So, what's the mystery?"

"They were filled with water, not the compound. I imagine the smashed one was Grayson's reaction when he discovered the vials were useless. Hoover filled six vials; Grayson had six vials. Where did the vial Hoover injected himself with come from?"

"How do we know he mixed 6 vials worth?" Lieutenant Jensen asked. "What if he mixed only one? His tech Ramon never saw him mix the compound or put it into vials. Since Ramon had prepared the worktable with everything Hoover needed, and 6 vials were filled when Ramon returned from lunch, he only assumed Hoover had filled those vials with the compound."

"Ramon said while we were interrogating him that the worktable was messy when he returned, as it usually was when Hoover mixed the compound, which, by the way, he did from memory," said Morales. "It never occurred to him that Hoover didn't mix the compound."

Forbes said, "Ramon knew that Henry always mixed enough for 6 vials because he used only miniscule amounts of two of the ingredients. The amount was too small for the formula to be broken down for only one vial."

Morales threw up his hands in defeat. "We've

exhausted our searches with Grayson and Hoover. Grayson discovered the vials he had were only water. That eliminates him from having the vials with the compound. As for Hoover, we searched his house after his death," Morales said. "They weren't there either. One of them should have had the vials with him. Neither one did."

"What if he stored them somewhere like a bus station or train locker?"

"I doubt that," Zack said. "Too public. Both men were in hiding. If Hoover had the missing vials, he would have taken the vials with him.

The four men stared glumly at each other.

"Where do we go from here?" Zack asked.

Forbes, who had been leaning against the wall, straightened up. "I have an idea. Let me tell you a story. Last weekend, I went to my daughter's house for a barbeque. We were all outside in the backyard. She had baked chocolate chip cookies for the occasion, my grandkids' favorite. The kids kept pestering her for a cookie because they didn't want to wait until after we ate. Finally, she gave in and sent my grandson into the house to get 2 cookies: one for him and one for his sister. They happily munched away, then went back to playing. I noticed, however, my grandson put his hand in his pocket several times, took something out, and put it in his mouth. I called him over and made him empty his pocket. He'd taken 3 cookies, not 2, from the house.

He'd put an extra cookie in his pocket and was breaking off pieces of it to eat when he thought no one was looking. Extra being the keyword."

"You're suggesting Hoover filled an extra vial?"

Zack's eyes spread wide. "2 cookies required but one sneaked out in the kid's pocket. 6 vials required, but one sneaked out of the lab in Hoover's briefcase."

"That fits," Morales said. "If he only put 5 in the safe, Ramon would know. He filled 6 vials with water and one extra with his compound. If he had to mix enough for 6, bet he poured the remainder of the compound down the drain to be sure no one found it."

The others shook their heads in agreement.

"That one vial he used at the hotel, meaning we don't have any missing vials," Forbes said. "What do you think, Zack?"

"I concur. If those 5 vials existed, we would have found them."

"We have no proof," The Lieutenant said, "but we never will with Hoover dead. It's a logical solution. I suggest we accept it."

The mood in the room changed to relief.

"Now it's over," Zack said, "except for the paperwork, of course."

"Don't remind me. You staying in Tucson?"

"Briefly. I have a few stray ends to take care of, then it's back to D.C."

Morales reached out his hand. "Guess I won't see

you again but let me say it's been a pleasure working with you."

"What's this?" Zack teased. "You're admitting you like a Fed?"

Morales laughed. "There's an exception to every rule."

Zack continued his farewells, shaking hands with Forbes, and Lieutenant Jensen.

All Zack thought about after he left was sleep. He drove to Dr. Schwartz's house and let himself in. "Doc," he called out.

"In the living room, Zack." When he saw Zack, he added, "You look like you're ready to fall asleep standing up."

"I am. It's been a rough two days with no sleep in between. It's over, Doc. We got Grayson. He's dead."

"I certainly want to hear the full story but sleep first. Go."

Zack didn't argue; he slept through the night. The smell of coffee and the sound of sizzling bacon woke him up the next morning. During their leisurely breakfast, Zack told the Doc in detail of all that transpired since they'd last spoken. One loose end taken care of.

After breakfast, rested and full, Zack called the Malibu police and asked to speak with Officer Josh Little. After reminding Little who he was, Zack said, "You broke the case with your call."

"I did?"

Zack summarized what had happened after Little's call. "Sometimes, it takes only one small detail to break a case, and you gave us one. Unfortunately, you can't collect the reward because you work for the police. The best reward I can offer is to write a letter of commendation to your CO about your good instincts and the part you played in locating Miles Grayson. That will go into your file."

"Thanks. A letter means a lot; I want to be a detective."

Zack then made one last call. "You're free, Sarah. No more wigs."

From the Author

Thank you for reading *Death by Injection*. I hope you enjoyed it. I'd really appreciate your rating the book. If you add a few sentences for a review, that would be great!

FICTION
My other fiction books are listed below. To easily view the covers and read a description of the books, visit my website at www.maryleetiernan.com.

Mahoney and Me Mystery Series:
>*Stopping in Lonely Places*
>*Mahoney and Me*
>*Caught in Lies*
>*Santa's Naughty List*
>*Broken Hearts, Broken Bodies*

Dreams Untangled:
>*Silent Ending*
>*Waking Up Crazy*

The Narcissist

Running from Myself
The Inconvenient Sister
Caught (a collection of short stories)

Novels with teenage protagonists:
A Date to Die For
Calico Kate
When the Squeaking Starts...

NON-FICTION
If you're a history buff interested in the settling of the West, you might enjoy my history books. These books are also on my website, www.maryleetiernan.com.

Arizona:
> *Benson's Bad Boys*
> *Benson's Ride Through History: 1800-1945*

California:
> *The Early History of Sunland, California*
This title is available as a compilation of all 8 volumes or as individual volumes.
> Vol 1: *Hotels for the Hopeful*
> Vol 2: *The Roscoe Robbers*
> Vol 3: *The Parson and His Cemetery*
> Vol 4: *From Crackers to Coal Oil*
> Vol 5: *He Never Came Home*
> Vol 6: *Lancasters Lake*

Vol 7: *Living in Big Tujunga Canyon*
Vol 8: *From Whence They Came*

147 only
161 See
229 4 beers for 2 cops?
310 Drink

Made in the USA
Las Vegas, NV
14 July 2023